CW00822441

Hidden Darkness

The Andovia Chronicles Book 3

TIFFANY SHAND

DEDICATION

For Mum

ACKNOWLEDGMENTS

Editing by Dark Raven Edits
Cover Design Kristina Romanovic

DARK DEEDS

CHAPTER 1

Nyx Ashwood shot up onto the tavern's roof, her wings curling around her as she landed and did a quick scan of the street below. Aside from the torches inside the tavern, there was no light from the surrounding wooden shacks. Nor was there anyone on the street. She didn't have to look to see if anyone was nearby, though. Their thoughts would have given them away. She breathed a sigh of relief. The constant buzz of thoughts from the surrounding houses made her grit her teeth. At least when she reached the woods, she wouldn't have to hear so many of them. Luckily, most of the villagers were asleep. The sound of their thoughts would have been even worse if they were awake.

She had already checked on her foster parents, Harland and Mama Habrid. Habrid was asleep and Harland was still down in the bar serving drinks. Neither of them would notice she was gone.

She flapped her wings and took off, careful to stay well above the rooflines so no one would see her. A cool breeze stung her face, and she breathed in the scent of pinecones and fresh leaves. Nyx would have been happy if she got to stay in the forest all the time. At least there would be no one subjecting her to the constant onslaught of their thoughts.

Nyx always feared someone might spot her. But one good thing about her curse was being able to hear people's thoughts and know when people were around. It was becoming harder for her to keep her curse secret around the rest of the villagers. Her tribe despised her enough already for being a fae foundling. The Shivani tribe didn't like people who were different or at least looked different from them.

With her large iridescent wings, pale skin and her long hair that frequently changed colour, she looked very unusual compared to them. Most of the tribe were tanned with dark hair and green eyes.

She glided over the rooftops. Soon trees spread out before her like dark gnarled beasts in the shadows. Her long dark pink hair blew over her face as she navigated her way over them. The night sky hung over her like a heavy blanket, with no moon or stars — which she was grateful for. Sometimes hunters ventured out into the woods, although it was rare so no one would spot her.

Nyx relished the feeling of freedom that she only got during flight. She had to be careful around Harland, the man who had taken her in as a child, for he never found out about her late-night excursions. He thought he had clipped her wings when she was young, so she couldn't run away. Nyx would never lose her wings. She couldn't imagine not being able to fly.

The cave finally came in sight and a faint orange glow emanated from inside. Good, that meant Traveller had returned here. It had been weeks since the merchant had come to her village. Her tribe despised Traveller and most people refused to even trade with her. Except for Nyx.

She landed a short distance away from the cave and folded her wings back. When she took a step forward, energy crackled against her skin. As if an invisible wall of energy blocked her way. Nyx reached out as more energy pulsed against her fingers. Odd, she had never encountered anything like this on her previous visits to see Traveller.

What had changed?

As a trader, Traveller always welcomed people. She didn't put up wards to keep them away or else she wouldn't make any profit.

Nyx pushed against the wall of energy. Gods, what would she do if she couldn't get to Traveller and get what she needed from her? Nyx knew Traveller had to be in there since she sensed her familiar energy inside. This was where she always stayed. Despite the unwelcome greeting she always got from the rest of the tribe, Traveller always came for a drink in the tavern. Nyx had seen her earlier that night. She stopped for a moment to listen.

Aside from the usual sounds of the forest and murmurs from the dryads who lived there, no thoughts buzzed through her mind. Nyx ignored their usual chatter since they weren't her intended quarry.

Traveller's thoughts were often harder to hear. That was one of the reasons why Nyx liked her. She didn't know why Traveller seemed to have an immunity to her curse nor did she care.

Nyx continued to push against the wall and sighed. Her curse wouldn't do her much good since there were no thoughts to read and no one around for her to use her influence on.

Why had Traveller put up some sort of barrier? Didn't she want anyone to come and visit her tonight? Or perhaps she had set up a private meeting with someone and wanted to keep everyone else away. Although Traveller must have known Nyx would come to see her, as she always did whenever Traveller passed through this part of the lower realm.

Nyx had noticed Traveller seemed on edge back at the tavern and had kept looking around as if searching for someone. Traders were always a wary bunch, but Nyx had never seen Traveller act like that before. Maybe she had had a disagreement with someone. Nyx hadn't been able to talk to Traveller earlier for fear Harland would notice their interaction.

She considered calling out for Traveller but decided against it. If Traveller was hiding from someone, Nyx didn't want to draw any unwanted attention.

Curse it. She needed to get through. Traveller never stayed near the village for more than a day or night at most. This was the last chance she had to get the drug she needed from Traveller.

Nyx pushed against the invisible barrier and her hands sparked with energy. She gasped and stumbled forward as the barrier finally gave way. She stared at her hands. Why had they glowed? Was this some kind of new manifestation of her curse?

She didn't ponder that thought for long and hurried towards the cave. For all, she knew the ward might spring back up and block her out again. She only hoped if it did so, it wouldn't trap her. Inside, the cave's walls dripped with dampness from the nearby river.

Traveller had lit a fire that cast dancing shadows around the rough stone walls. Moss grew in several places and insects were dotted around, yet they never seemed to bother Traveller.

Traveller looked up as Nyx came in. "I thought I'd be seeing you." Traveller had pointed ears, pale skin and long silvery hair. Nyx knew that was why her tribe mistrusted the trader. Strangers were never welcome here. "You shouldn't have come here tonight. I came here for a respite, not to trade."

Nyx's usually blonde hair often changed colour. Recently it turned dark pink. Her ears had once been pointed too before Harland had had them cut off to make her look more normal.

"Why couldn't I reach you?" Nyx asked. "A barrier blocked my way but—" She couldn't admit to Traveller about the strange light that emanated from her hands. She had no idea how she would explain what that even meant. Sometimes she wished she had someone to talk to, someone who could give her answers about her curse.

Nyx had used her curse to read people's minds and influence them when she had thought they might be able to help her. She had questioned them at length and then made them forget all about it. That way she wouldn't expose herself to anyone. Harland had always warned her never to reveal her curse to anyone and threatened to give her a damn good beating if she did so. But he wouldn't hurt her. He had always been too afraid of her to take his anger out on her. Her curse gave her power and he knew it.

"Because something dark is coming. You shouldn't have broken through my ward." Traveller ran a hand through her long hair. "That took me hours to construct. I don't have the energy now to create another one. You should go. I haven't got anything to trade with you now."

Ward? Nyx had heard of them, but such a thing was unheard of here in the lower realm. No one but Joriam had the power to create them. Wards took a lot of energy and someone would have to be a strong magic user to do so. Someone who was true Magickind.

"I — I'm sorry. I didn't have a choice."

"Dark things are wandering the night. You need to be more careful."

Nyx scoffed. "I don't fear the night." Night was her favourite time. The only time she could have true peace and freedom to be herself. And get away from Harland.

"You should fear the night. Dark spirits are roaming loose in this world and no one can hide from that." Traveller wrapped her arms around herself.

"Spirits can't hurt people." It wasn't unusual for Traveller to tell her about her adventures whenever Nyx went to visit her. But what had brought on the sudden warning about evil spirits? Most people in the lower realm didn't believe in such things.

"Don't be so sure of that." Traveller looked around, still on edge. Just as she had been at the tavern. "But I said, you should go. Now. I won't be held responsible if anything happens to you."

"I need some more Nilanda." Nyx tugged a coin pouch of her belt. "I have gold." It had taken her almost two weeks to get enough coin to buy the drug. It had been a risk, too, sneaking coins away from the different pouches she had stolen and then handed off to Harland. So how she had managed to steal a few more that Harland hadn't known about just so she could get enough money.

Traveller frowned. "You know how dangerous that substance is. It can lead to death or sap people of their magic if taken for too long. That's why they only use it in healing houses." She turned and rubbed her hands over the glowing fire.

Her eyes widened. Traveller liked money. Why had she decided to warn her about the drug? Nyx knew the laws around Nilanda. It was powerful but addictive. She had heard the warning more than once from the trader. It annoyed her more than it deterred her. "I know the risks, but I need it." Besides, she didn't have magic. Only an annoying curse that she needed to get under control.

"Why?"

Nyx hesitated. Traveller had never asked her that before. "That's not important."

"You can't suppress your gift forever. Do you want to lose your abilities?" Traveller wrapped a long cloak about her shoulders and shivered. "The drug can't help you all the time. Sooner or later its effects will leave you too damaged to do anything."

"My what?" She furrowed her brow. Nyx had no idea what the trader was talking about.

"Your magic, girl." Traveller gave her an incredulous look. "There's no point in trying to hide it anymore. I've always known about you."

"I don't have magic. Other than a small spark like all my tribe has." She sometimes used basic spells, but her abilities didn't extend beyond that. Hearing people's thoughts wasn't magical.

Traveller gave a harsh laugh. "I know you are a mind whisperer. You shouldn't stay in this realm. People will come looking for you."

Nyx gaped at her. "Why?" She couldn't imagine why the trader would even suggest such a thing. Traveller had never warned her about anything other than the Nilanda before. "Is something wrong? You seem on edge tonight. Is someone after you?"

Had someone seen her stealing? No, she was always careful. Even if she got caught, she could use her influence on them to make them forget they had seen anything. Nyx didn't know how her curse worked but when she touched people they fell under her control. She could make them do whatever she desired.

"I've always known what you are, Nyx. Your powers are so strong I'm sure your tribe can feel them too." Traveller took a step back. "Your energy has grown so much in the time I have known you. I am surprised anyone can be around you for long. The energy from a mind whisperer is not a pleasant thing unless you know how to control it."

"I — I don't have powers. I'm cursed." She couldn't believe Traveller would suggest such a thing. How could she have magic? "What's a mind whisperer?" The term sounded almost familiar to her, but she had no idea where she had heard it before.

"You are fae, girl. A rare kind too. You need to leave. Darkness will swallow this land soon and you are at the heart of it." She pulled her cloak tighter and settled down on a boulder. "A mind whisperer is a term for Magickind who can read and influence the thoughts of others." She frowned. "You have no idea what you are or what you're capable of, do you?"

Nyx hesitated. She had always wondered about where she had come from before she ended up with Harland and why she had been cursed. "How could I be a mind whisperer? I don't have any magic. The fae cursed me."

Traveller snorted. "Did that brute slaver at the tavern tell you that? What rubbish. He knows you have magic. That's why you're so profitable to him, as are the other two girls there. He uses you to find other slaves, doesn't he? Ones who have magical abilities?"

She bit her lip. She never told anyone about any of the things Harland made her do. He often took her and her foster sister, Domnu, to slave auctions to find the best slaves. Nyx had recently stopped going, though. Being around too many people overwhelmed her to the point she couldn't do anything.

"Where do mind whisperers come from, then?" Energy vibrated between her fingers, itching to get out. She wanted to touch Traveller's mind, to use her influence and find out everything the woman knew about mind whisperers.

"I don't know. They were supposed to have been wiped out a long time ago. I do know they came from lands far from here in the upper realm."

Her heart sank. Nyx had always dreamt of finding someone who might know about where she came from and who might have abandoned her. "I'm cursed, that's all I need to know." Nyx shook her head.

"That doesn't mean you're not in danger. You've been lucky, being secluded here all these years. But the time for anonymity is over. If you stay here, you will die." A piece of wood from the fire burst apart, sending sparks everywhere.

She shivered. Why would she need to leave? This realm had been her home for as long as she could remember. "I can't leave. Nor would I ever leave my sisters behind. Why would anyone come after me? I'm no one of consequence." Nyx held out her hand. "Please just give me the Nilanda." If she couldn't get any answers from the trader, then she would at least get what she came for.

Traveller turned and rummaged in her pack. She then pulled out a small vial. "Take it and heed my warning. This place is no longer safe for you."

Nyx grabbed it and gaped at it. It was half the size she usually bought. "Is this all you have? I need more." Her heart pounded in her ears. What would she do if she couldn't get enough of the drug? She didn't take it out of choice but necessity. It was the only thing that helped dampen her senses enough to avoid getting overwhelmed by the amount of people's thoughts going through her head.

Her curse proved unbearable at times and sometimes overwhelmed her to the point where she couldn't do anything other than huddle up in a corner. Sometimes she thought she would go mad from all the voices.

"It's all I have. You should go." Nyx held out the bag of coins and Traveller shook her head. "Gold won't do me any good now. Not with what's to come."

Nyx strapped the pouch back onto her belt. If Traveller didn't want the gold, then she wasn't about to throw away good money.

"Remember my warning. Leave while you still have the chance."

Nyx hurried out of the cave. Her mind raced with unanswered questions. What was Traveller afraid of? And why would anyone come after Nyx?

No one would want a cursed foundling. Would they?

She spread her wings as a chill came over her. The night seemed to have grown darker. It would be better if she got home before someone noticed her absence. Then warnings would be the last of her problems.

CHAPTER 2

Darius Valeran stared at the tiny village full of wooden shacks and wondered what he had done to be sent to this part of the lower realm. He ached to be back among the green wilds and floating mountains of his homeland. Worse still, he hadn't been able to bring his dragon companion with him either. People in the lower realm feared dragons, and he hadn't wanted to draw any unwanted attention to himself.

"This part of the lower realm looks so poor." His friend Ranelle frowned. "Don't they have any economy here?" With her fiery red hair, she would stand out no matter what she did. But he hadn't been able to say no when she had insisted on coming with him. Ranelle was training to become a scholar, and despite her love of books she always enjoyed getting out of the library and exploring the rest of the world.

"The lower realm, especially this part, is mostly made of tribes who are governed by their own rules," Darius replied. He hated seeing the poverty here, yet he knew there was little he could do about it. Still, it did strengthen his resolve in working with the resistance as much as possible.

His other friend, Lucien, shifted from foot to foot and ran a hand through his mop of curly brown hair. As an apprentice overseer and healer, Lucien had insisted on coming as well in case anyone got injured. Darius knew better though. Lucien had come along so he could find rare herbs and other things he could study. "Are you sure there is a mind whisperer here? There hasn't been one of those in centuries. Your grandfather had them wiped out."

Darius flinched. He didn't want to be reminded of his family's past crimes. "We will find out when we find her." He repressed a sigh. His elder brother, Gideon, had sent him all the way from Andovia to the lower realm to find this supposed mind whisperer and had ordered him to bring her back with them.

"We don't know she is a mind whisperer. Hearing people's thoughts is a skill that can be taught," Ranelle pointed out as she pushed her long hair off her face. "You druids have been doing it for centuries now. And your mentor taught us how to do it."

"Mind whisperers are unique, and they can do a lot more than hear people's thoughts. They can compel people to and if they choose to, enslave them. That's why they're so dangerous." Darius had no idea what he might find, or how powerful this mind whisperer might be. He cursed his brother again for sending him. Mind whisperers were some of the most dangerous of all Magickind. Why did Gideon think he would be able to capture her?

"How is a mind whisperer going to help with the crack in the veil between the worlds?" Lucien wanted to know.

Darius shook his head. "I have no idea." Since they had first discovered a rift in the veil a couple of days earlier and had seen that evil spirits had been coming through, he and the others had been researching on how to solve the problem. He had warned his brother about it but of course, Gideon didn't believe him.

Gideon had heard through one of his slave trader contacts about a mind whisperer living here and using her abilities as a thief. Or so a man named Harland was boasting about her. Darius wanted to find the mind whisperer and leave as soon as possible. This place set his senses on edge. Something didn't feel right here. Besides, he had much bigger problems to deal with at home and couldn't convince his brother to do anything about them.

"Rae, Luc, go and check around the area," he told them. The sooner they found their target, the sooner they would be able to leave. Once he gave his brother what he wanted, Darius could get back to more important matters.

"I thought the mind whisperer lived in a tavern?" Ranelle asked. "What does she look like anyway?"

"Yes, but I want you to check for any sign of tears in the veil." He shrugged. "I have no idea what she looks like. Her name is Nyx.

Ambrose said we would know her when we see her. She will probably be the only one with any real power in this province anyway. So she shouldn't be too hard to find."

"You really think this is a problem?" Lucien frowned. "Causing a tear in the veil in more than one place is almost impossible. To do so would require an incredible amount of power. Perhaps the rift we found on Eldara was the only one."

"For once I agree with Wolfsbane. For such a thing to happen is —" Ranelle said.

Darius repressed a sigh. After knowing them for a few months, he had hoped the two of them would have put their differences aside by now. But he guessed centuries of feuding between their two races in their homeland would take longer for them to deal with.

"Just look around. I'll go to the tavern. We can cover more ground that way." Darius pulled up the hood of his coat. He missed the familiar weight of his sword and bow. They hadn't brought the weapons because they wanted to blend in. They all had their different abilities to defend themselves if they needed to.

"Typical, why do you always get to go to taverns?" Luc grumbled.

"I thought you hated taverns, Wolfsbane?" Ranelle smirked. "You vowed to never drink again after we raided the Archdruid's cellar."

"Call me if you find anything." Darius took off in the opposite direction and left them to their usual bickering.

He kept his senses on alert as he passed through the village. Darius knew the tribe probably wouldn't be welcoming to a stranger. People here in the lower realm never were. Years of slavery and slave trading had seen to that. He hoped his expensive clothing didn't make him stand out too much, but he had no time to change. Gideon had insisted he leave at once and even ordered the ship to take him.

You could get things done fast when you were the heir of the Archdruid and the fae Queen. Unlike Darius, who was second born and had a sorceress for his mother.

The tavern stood nestled amongst the ramshackle houses. If it hadn't been for an old sign, he wouldn't have known it was the place he was looking for.

Darius pushed the tavern door open and winced at the stench of sweat and cheap ale. Only a few patrons were inside. A few men sent curious glances his way. He didn't look at them and headed straight for the bar. Dust covered the floor. All of the wooden tables and chairs were old, cracked and worn from frequent use. The wind whistled in through the shuttered windows and the stone fireplace was empty of wood.

A blonde-haired girl stood behind the bar. Her hair hung in rattails and her dress had holes in it, but her green eyes were clear. Darius scanned the tavern with his mind. The people here barely had any magic. They were little more than humans. Yet the blonde girl had power. It shone around her like sunlight.

"What can I get you to drink?" the girl asked. She looked no older than about fifteen. Only a few years younger than himself.

"Are you Nyx?" Darius scanned her deeper with his mind. Ambrose, his mentor, had said he would be able to sense the mind whisperer when he saw her from the feel of her power.

She had power, to be sure, but was she the one he had been sent to find? Her eyes widened. "Who wants to know?" She looked him up and down. The flow and hum of her power remained steady.

Darius couldn't understand why she didn't scan him with her senses. Unless she didn't know how to. Living here, he doubted there would have been anyone to teach her how to use her gift. Curse it, he should have planned this out better. "I need to find her." He sent his senses deeper, urging her power to reveal itself.

If this was the mind whisperer, he should get a reaction from her. Darius doubted she would hear his thoughts. His father had put a powerful mental shield on him to prevent anyone from ever penetrating his mind. The Archdruid feared mind whisperers more than anyone since their power rivalled his.

The girl froze and gasped as her eyes snapped shut. Her brow creased as though she were in pain. She was having a vision. He had met enough seers during his nineteen-year life to recognise the look.

Not a mind whisperer then. Harland hadn't been boasting when he said he had he found the best slaves.

Darius reached out to touch her. That way he might glimpse whatever she saw.

The girl's eyes flew open before his fingers had a chance to make contact with her skin. "You," she gasped as she stared at him.

"What do you see? Where is Nyx? I have to find her. It's important." He gripped the edge of the bar.

She glared at him. "You stay away from her."

Darius frowned. Had he said something wrong? He opened his

mouth to ask her again about what she had seen in her vision. Had she seen something that made her view him as a threat?

Someone stomped over and put a heavy hand on his shoulder. "What did you say about my Nyx?"

The blonde girl paled and backed away.

The hand belonged to a tall, muscular man with a shock of white hair. His icy blue eyes were lined with age, but he still had a strong grip.

Darius knew this must be Harland. Gideon had talked about the man enough times. Harland was infamous for finding slaves with strong magical abilities.

Judging by the girl he had just met Darius knew how he did it. Harland had little more than a spark of magic, so he must be using that seer or perhaps even the mind whisperer herself to find people.

Harland glowered over at the other girl. "Did you see something, Domnu?"

Domnu shook her head and backed away further. Work now... "He — he startled me." She motioned towards Darius.

"I'm looking for Nyx."

Harland's eyes narrowed. "Nyx doesn't help people, and she isn't for sale either."

"But —" Darius wished he had come up with a better excuse before coming here. But he couldn't say, "I'm here looking for Nyx because my brother ordered me to fetch her."

Harland gave him a shove. "If ya know what's good for ya, boy, clear off. No one comes sniffing around my girls."

Two burly looking men joined Harland. Both wore rough woollen clothing and stank of sweat and ale.

So much for not drawing unwanted attention. Darius backed away. He didn't want to cause any more trouble, but he had to find the mind whisperer.

He scanned the tavern deeper with the senses. The seer had retreated to another room and someone else with power was nearby. Their energy felt stronger, but he got the impression she might be a healer. If so, where was Nyx?

Something dark moved in the corner. An iciness washed over him. The shadow hovered behind Harland, yet the man seemed unaware of it.

Holy spirits, a darkling. Darius would recognise the strange, dark entities anywhere. Why had one come here? And why did it seem focused on Harland?

"Are you deaf, boy?" Harland demanded. "I said get out of my tavern."

The darkling hovered around Harland, its darkness wrapping around the old man's body like wisps of smoke. Its dark energy expanded and wrapped around the two other men at Harland's side.

Darius raised his hand and lightning sparked between his fingers.

Harlan's companions both drew weapons.

Darius braced himself and prepared to attack the darkling. Darius had never dealt with a spirit like this head-on, but he wasn't about to let these people die.

"If you want to fight, boy, you won't win," Harland growled.

"No, you don't understand —"

The darkling shot away from the men and disappeared through the back door. Someone screamed.

Darius made a move to follow as its men barred his way. One of the men grabbed his arm. "I can take you, boy. Magic or not."

Darius sighed and raised his hand, blasting all three men across the room. He didn't have time to waste, not with the darkling here. When he reached the door, he pushed it open. The men would be unconscious for a while. He hadn't hurt them; they were only stunned.

The blonde girl cowered in the corner and the darkling darted away.

"What happened?" Darius asked.

The girl trembled. "Please don't hurt me."

Darius went over and yanked her up. "I'm not here to harm anyone."

"That shadow —"

"It's a dark spirit. Did it hurt you?"

She continued to shake. "No, it came near me and it… Felt so cold. It's looking for someone — I could sense it."

Darius had a good idea who that someone was.

CHAPTER 3

Nyx decided to fly around for a while to clear her head. The wind had picked up and rushed around her, hard and fast.

Traveller's strange behaviour had disturbed her. Why had she been so intent on getting Nyx to leave?

Nyx had always dreamt of running away and starting a new life somewhere. She had been saving as much money away as she could. Her sisters, Domnu and Kyri, never believed her when she told them they would escape from Harland.

They had all been with him from a young age and his abuse had grown worse over the years. He lost his temper over the smallest thing nowadays.

Harland wanted Nyx to go to the city with him in a couple of days. She couldn't be around large crowds of people. Their thoughts overwhelmed her so much she couldn't move.

The Nilanda was the only thing that helped dampen the senses. Yet the tiny amount Traveller had given her would barely last a few hours. Probably less.

Nyx circled the forest a few more times, but the flight did little to ease her racing thoughts. Leaving Harland had always been the plan, but she doubted she had enough to buy travel papers for all three of them. Let alone enough to get safe passage out of the realm.

What should I do? Her mind continued to race. Leaving without a proper plan and resources could be just as dangerous as staying.

An iciness washed over her. Nyx glanced around. She had never felt anything like it. What was it? Was that why Traveller had cast wards near the cave?

Nyx shivered. The iciness grew more intense, but she couldn't tell where it was coming from. The only good thing about her curse was the fact it warned her of things. Like if someone had an aura of danger.

A faint buzzing echoed through her mind. Someone was nearby, but she couldn't quite make out their thoughts.

Two presences were close. One male and the other female. What were they doing here? No one from the village ever came out here at night. Had someone come to trade with Traveller? It didn't happen often, but it wasn't impossible.

She darted over to a nearby tree and concealed herself in its branches as the thoughts grew louder.

That mind whisperer must be around here somewhere, the female thought. *The sooner we find her, the sooner I can get away from that wolf. Why did Darius have to leave us alone together?*

The male's thoughts were somehow muted, so she couldn't tell what he thought.

Traveller had called her a mind whisperer. Although she still had no idea what it meant. Traveller had insisted she wasn't cursed either. How was that possible?

Harland had always told her she was a cursed thing and that was why she had been abandoned in the woods as a child. She had never found out where she had come from or who had abandoned her there. Nyx wondered if she could be a mind whisperer. She had been around the age of seven when she had been found. Soon after Harland had taken her home and forced her to become a thief.

Aside from her sisters and Mama Habrid, he was the only other person who knew about her curse. Yet Traveller had somehow known about it too.

The question was, how?

Nyx had been careful over the years to keep her curse hidden. It often proved hard not to blurt out a response to what someone thought but it was the only way out of trouble. Whenever she used her influence on people she always made them forget about it.

A dark shadow darted among the trees.

Nyx froze and pulled her wings tighter around her body. What was that? Goosebumps spread over her arms and she shivered. The shadow darted from tree to tree.

Was it looking for something? Or someone?

Maybe those strangers she had heard had sent it to find her.

She drew back. Should she fly off or remain where she was?

Her heart pounded in her ears. If that thing had come for her, she had to hide. Too bad her curse didn't defend her or give her a means of defending herself. Sure, she might be able to use her influence on people if they were a threat. But she couldn't do anything against a shadow.

"Remember a place of safety. Retreat to that place whenever you're in danger," she remembered someone telling her.

Nyx imagined a grove of trees around her inside her mind. Massive branches engulfed her on all sides. Her heart rate slowed, and she closed her eyes. This was a safe place. It had been with her for as long as she could remember. Nothing could harm her here. The iciness washed away like water flowing back into the ground. After a few moments, she opened her eyes and found herself back in the tree in the darkened wood.

"You sure you haven't lost her scent?" a female voice asked.

A male voice cursed. "I haven't. She was here. I know she was." He sniffed.

Nyx's blood went cold. They were nearby. She could feel them. *Oh, good god, they're still looking for me.*

The shadow thing from earlier had vanished. The iciness had faded too.

What did those people want?

She pictured the grove again and retreated to her place of safety.

"Curse it, I had her scent but it keeps disappearing," the male said. "How does she keep vanishing? She can't move around that fast."

"I can't sense any power either. Which is odd since her power is like a beacon."

Both of them came into view. They looked younger than she had expected. Maybe around the same age as her. The girl had long flaming red hair and wore a long tunic and hose. The boy stood a head taller than her, with a mop of short brown hair and a muscular build. He wore a brown jerkin and dark trousers.

"I think we are wasting our time," the boy said. "Darius should be the one here. He probably has immunity to her power given how much his grandfather feared mind whisperers. We don't have that."

"Ambrose said not to let her touch us. We'll be fine."

"We don't know how dangerous a mind whisperer can be."

"If you're so worried, why don't you shift?" She gave him a shove. "You're such a coward, Wolf's Bane."

He scowled at her. "Why don't you fly around and look?"

The girl's massive wings unfurled from her back. Unlike Nyx's wings, they were dark and leathery.

What was that girl? It almost reminded Nyx of images she had seen of the Archdruid's infamous Dragon Guard.

Could the girl be a dragon?

Nyx pictured her protective grove again. The last thing she needed was for them to find her.

"Wait, I think I have her scent." The man turned and headed in the direction of the tree Nyx was perched in.

I am safe. The grove enveloped her in its protective energy again. Somehow, she knew the grove was real. Somehow. Whenever she pictured it, no one could find her – not even Harland when he searched high and low.

The grove's energy enveloped her. She concentrated and kept her eyes open this time.

"She's gone again," the boy cursed. "How does she keep disappearing?"

Nyx smiled but almost faltered when she spotted the glowing white energy around her body. That had never happened before.

Was it some kind of magic? If so, where had it come from?

Harland always said they had cursed her because she was an abomination. They had done it to make her suffer. Now she didn't know what to believe.

Instead, she focused on the grove. If the light faded and she lost the image they would find her.

"She must be around here somewhere." The girl circled the tree line.

Nyx grew back. She had to get out of here soon or else she'd be stuck here all night. Then she would be in even more trouble when Harland found out she was missing. And he would punish her sisters for it.

Nyx took a deep breath. The other girl could fly too. Nyx would have to fly fast to get home without them trailing off her.

She unfurled her wings and prepared to take off when screaming ripped through the night.

Gods, Traveller. The woman's fear hit her in waves.

It's found me. Good god... Traveller's thoughts echoed through her mind. The words echoed in her mind. Whilst Nyx had never heard Traveller's thoughts before, she knew deep within from the tone and the pitch of the voice, those were Traveller's last words.

"Darkling," the boy called out to his companion.

"Where?" The girl hovered close to him.

He pulled her down into his arms, making her yelp. The two of them disappeared in a blur of light.

Nyx's mouth fell open. How could anyone move so fast?

It didn't matter. If Traveller was in trouble, she had to help her.

Spreading her wings, Nyx took to the air and headed back towards the cave.

CHAPTER 4

Darius, we've found the darkling, Lucien called in thought.

After Darius had left the tavern he had gone through the village and looked everywhere for the darkling. It had proved harder to track than he had anticipated. As had the mind whisperer. Her presence had come and gone so many times he had been forced to choose what to track first: her or the darkling. He had chosen the latter since it proved a much greater threat.

Have you found the mind whisperer? Darius asked his friends.

No, she keeps disappearing, Ranelle replied. *I think she's shielding herself somehow.*

I'm on my way. Darius scratched runes onto the ground and drew a transportation circle. He didn't have time to run to the woods even if it wasn't far away.

Light glowed around him as he chanted words of power. For a few seconds, his body became weightless and incorporeal. Then he reappeared near a scattering of trees.

Darius flung his senses out like a net and sprinted off in the direction of his friends. As he ran, he felt iciness wash over him — the darkling no doubt. So did something else. A stronger, more potent energy that beckoned to him like a beacon.

The mind whisperer. He glanced skywards since the presence didn't seem to come from the ground. There was no sign of anyone. Darius picked up the pace and a faint light came into view. Ranelle and Lucien were inside the cave. Something hovered just outside the cave. Someone with large wings.

The mind whisperer.

Darius raised his mental shield to cloak his presence. He didn't know how she would react to seeing him or what she might do. He wished he had listened to his father's lectures on the dangers of mind whisperers and how to avoid them.

Darius crept closer and sent his senses out. Both to alert him to the danger and to hear what was going on inside the cave. He winced as the feel of ice hit him. Dark magic. He'd been raised around enough of it to recognise its awful presence.

"Good god," Ranelle gasped. "This woman is hurt — hurry up and heal her."

"You know I can't heal anyone yet," Lucien grumbled. "I haven't mastered that ability." He sniffed. "We're too late. She's already dead."

Nyx edged deeper into the cave and Darius trailed behind her, careful not to get too close for fear of alerting her to his presence.

He moved closer still, keeping close to Nyx as she flew close to the cave ceiling. He was surprised she hadn't noticed him yet. His shield wouldn't hide him forever — he knew that from the strength of her power. Her energy set his teeth on edge.

Lucien and Ranelle came into view. Lucien turned the body over. Ranelle gasped when she caught sight of the gaping hole in the woman's chest.

Nyx stifled a cry of alarm and plunged to the ground as her wings lost all momentum.

"Nyx?" Darius made a move towards her.

Her eyes shot to him. She didn't look quite how he had expected. Her brown tunic and hose were rough and bedraggled. Her long hair flashed with a riot of colour and bits of leaves stuck out from it. Dirt covered her pale skin and her eyes were pale blue. Her wings stretched out before her blue like painted glass with white spots on them.

"You – you killed her!" Nyx's power raged to life like an inferno ready to boil over.

"No, I came to find you and —" Darius began.

Nyx pulled a sword from her back and pointed it towards him. "You stay away from me."

"Nyx, we're not here to hurt you. We —" Darius knew he had to keep her calm somehow. Her power flowed out like a dam ready to burst.

Nyx used her free hand and clutched at her head. No doubt she would pick up on Luc and Ranelle's thoughts. His mind would have been hidden behind his mental shield.

Her powers jarred against him. Spirits help him, Darius needed to contain her power before she hurt someone. Or worse, enslaved or killed them. Her power was too dangerous to risk unleashing it.

Darius raised his hand and cast a web of energy around her.

Her sword fell from her hand and clattered to the ground as she screamed. Her power exploded around them.

Darius gasped as the force of it pinned him to the cave wall. Her energy rattled against his bones like a clap of thunder without sound. Lucien and Ranelle screamed and clutched their heads. Blood roared through his ears, then drowned out by the screams.

Nyx's eyes turned black. "Why did you kill her?"

Darius opened his mouth, but no words came out. He thought he heard Luc and Ranelle call out for help, but he couldn't be sure. His web of energy faltered as her power came at him hard and fast.

Nyx approached him with her hand outstretched.

Now he knew why his grandfather had tried to wipe out the mind whisperers. Her power felt incredible — like it could rip him apart if she wanted it to.

Darius couldn't form any words to a spell. As though pushing through a gale force wind, lightning sparked between his fingers. A bolt shot across the cave and hit the wall behind Nyx, sending shards of rock flying.

She stumbled and her power lessened.

More lightning sparked between his fingers as he prepared to fight again.

Darius wouldn't kill her. He never killed unless he had to. Besides, she was too valuable for that.

Nyx glowered at him, turned, then took to the air. After a few moments she had vanished, and Darius took in lungfuls of air.

Luc and Ranelle were both on their knees.

Ranelle wiped her streaming eyes with her sleeve. "I've never felt anything so awful."

Luc slumped back against the wall. "I felt like her power would rip me apart. Now I understand why they were so feared."

"My grandfather was a power-mad tyrant who feared mind whisperers," Darius growled. "She thought we killed that woman." He motioned to the body. "Spirits, I didn't expect her power to be so bloody strong." He leaned back against the wall.

The Archdruid had spent decades waging war against mind

whisperers until he thought they were all gone. Darius's father had done the same.

How had someone as powerful as Nyx slipped through the cracks? She looked young, too. Maybe younger than him. How she got here didn't matter. Finding her again would have to wait.

"Are you both alright?" Darius headed over to the body.

"We'll live," Lucien breathed. "God, I hope I never have to feel that again."

Ranelle sniffed. "Who is the woman?" She motioned to the body.

"No idea. Someone has removed her heart." Lucien ran a hand through his hair. "We sensed the darkling come this way. The mind whisperer wasn't here."

"The darkling must have done it." Darius grimaced and reached out for his mentor with his mind. *Ambrose?*

After a few moments, Ambrose's familiar presence came to him. *Yes, boy? Have you found her?*

Yes, and more. There is a darkling here. It killed a woman and removed her heart.

Ambrose groaned. *It's as I feared. The killing has begun.*

Where are you? Darius winced at the sight of the body.

Also in the lower realm, tracking areas where the veil may be broken. I've found two small rifts so far.

We could use your help. He hoped his mentor could come and help them with this mess. Ambrose would be much more likely to attract the darkling and perhaps figure out why this woman had been killed.

Examine the body as best as you can, but I won't be able to reach you until the morning.

Darius sighed. *Understood.* As much as he wanted the other druid here, he did understand Ambrose had to track the rifts.

The mind whisperer escaped from us. Darius rubbed the back of his neck. He was glad Ambrose couldn't see his embarrassment. *Her powers are incredible. She is fae — but I can't tell what kind.*

Find her. You need to bring her back to Andovia before your father finds out about her.

Darius knew that better than anyone. If the Archdruid found out about Nyx he would send his best assassins out to find her. Or worse still, he'd capture her and force her to become his slave. Fergus would love to have someone with her power under his control.

Darius shuddered at the thought. One way or another, he had to convince Nyx to leave with them. He had to get to her before something else went wrong.

CHAPTER 5

Nyx's mind raced as she flew back towards the village. Who were those people? What did they want? Hot tears stung her eyes at the thought of Traveller. They might not have been friends, but they had a mutual respect for each other.

Perhaps Traveller's warning had been right all along. She needed to leave. Those strangers had power – especially that boy who had tried to hit her with a lightning bolt.

Magical abilities might be rare here, but she had seen them over the years. No one she had encountered had power like that. What was he, anyway?

He had known her name too. Had someone sent him to arrest her?

There was no Guard here in this part of the lower realm. No rule of law either. The different tribes made their own laws and took justice into their own hands. She had never been caught stealing before and had always been careful to cover her tracks. Somehow she doubted they had come for her because of the petty theft.

They had called her a mind whisperer too, from what she had picked up from their thoughts.

Nyx had to get home and grab whatever she could. She would have to convince her sisters to leave with her.

Nyx breathed a sigh of relief when she reached her window and climbed inside.

"Nyx?" Domnu rushed over to her. "Where have you been?"

"Out. I had to get something. Dom —"

"A boy came here looking for you. He said he needed your help then…" Domnu shivered. "Something was here — a strange shadow creature. I thought it was going to kill me."

All colour drained from her face. That boy had come looking for her here too, gods above.

"What happened? Did anyone get hurt?"

"He used magic on Harland and two of his men. I don't think it hurt them. The shadow almost attacked me, but he came in and it vanished." Domnu ran a hand through her long dirty hair. "I had a vision and saw the newcomer in it. You — you were being burned at the stake."

Nyx gasped. "When will it happen? Why would…" She shook her head. "Never mind. That vision isn't going to come to pass. Traveller is dead. I think the shadow creature killed her. Dom, we have to get out of here. It's not safe anymore."

"We can't leave. We don't have identity papers or any money."

"I have some money, and we can buy forged papers. Hopefully, it will be enough. Go and get food from the pantry, and hurry. Make sure we have everything we need."

"If we get caught —"

"I can't stay here. Those people are looking for me. I have to get out of here before they find me again – I barely got away earlier."

"You should go. We would only slow you down."

Nyx gaped at her sister. "What? No. I would never leave you behind." She gripped Domnu's hand. "Nor will I leave you to endure Harland's wrath either." She knew full well what their foster father would do to them once he found out Nyx had gone missing. If she weren't there to rein his temper in, both of her sisters would probably die.

"Your safety is important, Nyx. I will not watch you die. Get —" Domnu was cut off by a scream from the other room, followed by the sound of a crash.

Oh no, Harland had told off Kyri again. She had heard her sister screaming enough times to recognise the sound and sense Kyri's presence nearby.

"Stay here. I'll take care of it. Just get ready. We are leaving." Nyx grazed Domnu's shoulder and hurried out of the room.

She rushed down the hall to the room where Domnu and Kyri slept.

Harland shouted at Kyri, demanding to know where Nyx was.

"Harland, stop." Nyx pushed her way into the room. "I'm right here."

"Stupid girl, you are good for nothing. You can't even serve drinks downstairs." Harland continued to berate Kyri. "Can you do nothing right?" He backhanded her.

"Harland, stop." Nyx's hands clenched into fists as energy roared to life from deep inside her. She had already lost control of her curse once tonight and didn't want to do it again.

"Finally, you're back." Harland spun around to face her. "Where have you been?"

"I — I went for a walk. Had another bad headache but I'm here now." Nyx raised her chin.

Too bad he didn't stay unconscious. She and her sisters had to get out of here before those people she had seen in the cave came back.

Something moved in the corner of the room. The shadow creature. It shot into Harland. The old man gasped, and his eyes turned black.

"You," he hissed. "You're the one."

Nyx stepped back. "Harland?"

Harland lunged at her. Her senses screamed at her. She ducked and dodged the blow.

Now, this was not Harland anymore. It was the shadow creature.

"Harland, stop!" Nyx reached for the familiar weight of the sword at her back. She gasped as she realised it wasn't there. She must have dropped it back at the cave. The eyes staring back at her were black as night. "Stay back." But he lunged her again. "Kyri, run!"

Kyri remained curled up in the corner and whimpered. She didn't move.

Nyx scanned the room and looked for any kind of weapon but found none.

Harland grabbed hold of her arm, and heat seared through her skin.

Nyx yelped from the pain. "Kyri, help."

Her sister remained where she was.

Nyx drew back her free hand and punched Harland in the face. Pain exploded in her now-bruised knuckles. Harland didn't so much as flinch despite the blood pouring from his face.

Curse it, she had to do something to make him stop. Icy energy washed over her, clawing at every fibre of her being.

It slammed against her mind, trying to force its way in.

"Stop." She used her free hand to grasp Harland. "Let go of me."

Energy reverberated through her hand, blasting Harland across the room from the force of it.

Nyx sank to the floor. Blood pounded in her ears as her energy drained away. Her influence always sapped her energy, but now it might be the only thing that could stop him. She often used it to get him to calm down and stop him from attacking her sisters. She had never had to use it to defend herself, though. Harland feared her and her curse, she had always known that.

Harland scrambled up and screamed, clutching at his face. "What have you done to me?" he screeched, his voice unholy and unnatural. He stumbled towards her again. "I'll kill you, mind whisperer. The prophecy will never come to pass."

When he reached for her, Nyx screamed and raised her hands to shield herself. More power slammed out of her and into Harland. Like thunder without sound.

Her vision blurred. Blackness beckoned to her and Nyx had no choice but to give in to it.

Someone dragged Nyx to her feet.

"You killed him; you wretched girl! You killed him!" someone screamed and shook her.

Her head pounded like a heavy drum. It took a few moments for the room to shift back into focus. Mama Habrid stood before her, clutching Nyx by the collar of her tunic.

Kyri was sobbing in the corner.

"What's going on?" Nyx murmured, still dazed.

Two men came into the room. Mama Habrid shoved Nyx towards them. "Here she is. She killed my Harland."

What? Nyx shook her head. How had she even got into Kyri's room? The last thing she remembered was running away from the cave. Then what happened?

Her mind had gone blank. She gasped when she caught sight of Harland slumped against the far wall. His glassy, blood-smeared eyes stared back at her. Almost in an accusing way.

"Harland? No, I didn't do this."

"You killed him!" Mother Habrid snapped. "I always knew you were unholy scum." She spat in Nyx's face. "I will see you die for this."

The two villagers took hold of her arms.

"Wait, no. I didn't do anything. Let go of me!" She waited for her influence to work.

It didn't. Exhaustion hung over her like a heavy blanket.

The men dragged her downstairs and then outside. The villagers came out to see the men dragging her away.

She caught sight of the blue-eyed young man among them. His expression was grim.

"You did this! You killed him!" she screamed.

But despite her protests, no one stepped forward to help her and the blue-eyed stranger had soon vanished.

They brought Harland's body out on a cart.

When Jarrod, their village elder caught sight of it, he struck Nyx so hard she fell to the ground. "Witch," he spat. "You will burn for this. It's time you paid for your dark deeds."

CHOSEN SEER

CHAPTER 1

"How much do you want for them?" the slave trader asked. The rotund man with greasy hair and beady eyes towered over them.

Mama Habrid, the woman who had reluctantly taken care of them since they were children, tapped her chin. Her brow creased. "They are strong girls – my husband never bought weak slaves. I'll accept no less than fifty gold coins for each of them."

Fifty gold coins? Domnu would have laughed if the pit of fear in her stomach didn't weigh on her like a heavy stone. The price was outrageous, and they all knew it.

The slave trader laughed. "No girls are worth that much. Look at them, they are skinny. They won't cope well with hard labour."

"These two are special. They have been touched by the gods and have unnatural abilities. The one with the red hair can see the future. Her visions always come true. And the other one can heal people with her touch. Imagine the money you could make off them."

Domnu looked away and her long red hair fell over her face like a heavy curtain. Her visions didn't always work. Most of the time, she couldn't even control them.

If they could make someone so much money, why wouldn't Mama Habrid let them stay at the tavern? It wasn't much of a home, but it was the only one they had ever known.

"Fine, let's see their powers. Tell me, girl, what do you see in my future?" The man sneered at her and grabbed her by the collar of her tunic.

She almost gagged under the stench of his foul breath. "I don't see anything." She almost wanted to have a vision just to get the awful man away from her.

"Hold her hand. She has a much better chance of getting visions if she touches someone." Habrid motioned towards Domnu.

The man grabbed her by the throat. "Tell me what you see, girl."

Her sister, Kyri, whimpered in the corner and buried her face in her knees where she sat in the ground.

She gasped as pain shot through her head and her eyes snapped shut. An image of a boat rising out of the water came to her. At the helm stood a dark-skinned man with a glowing orb above his head.

A few moments later, the vision faded. She winced as her ears rang and pain stabbed through her skull.

Gods, what did that even mean? The vision had barely shown her anything, and what she had seen made no sense.

"Well, what did you see?" The man shook her hard.

"I saw you in the tavern tonight having a drink." She glared up at him. "That is all I saw."

The man gave a harsh laugh and shoved her backwards. "Perhaps you are gifted after all. I will give you fifty coins for both of them." He tossed a coin purse at Mama Habrid. "That's all you will get for them. Slaves with magic can be harder to sell."

The old woman's eyes gleamed. "Good riddance to them. Those girls have been a plague in my life since the day my husband brought them home. I always said they would be the death of him, and I was right. Kill them both for all I care." She slammed the door shut in their faces. Leaving Domnu to wonder what would happen to them now.

Domnu kept her eyes on the ground as the trader dragged her into Joriam's slave market. The stench of sweat, animal manure, and heat filled the air. Shouts rang out and people hurried in all directions.

She couldn't believe it. Harland, the man who'd bought and raised her, was dead. Her foster sister, Nyx, had been accused of his murder. It didn't matter she had been innocent, and Domnu had told them that. They had wanted Nyx and Domnu gone for years. Being gifted with magic when you lived among a tribe of humans never boded well.

Nyx had been sentenced to death; her execution was supposed to have been carried out by burning her at the stake. Domnu had helped her to escape. Nyx was long gone. A druid had come and arrested her. Then the tribesman kept saying the druid had killed her. Domnu didn't want to believe that, though. Nyx had always been the strong one, the one who protected them from Harland's abuse. Domnu had no idea if they would see her again. She would have to be the strong one now.

Kyri whimpered beside her. The sound grated on her nerves. Fury burned through her. At Nyx. Harland. Mama Habrid. At all of them.

Her visions, or curse as Harland called it, had helped bring in coins. Whether it was telling fortunes in the tavern, or picking pockets on the streets with Nyx.

"Hush, Kyri," she hissed. "We don't want to draw attention to ourselves." She knew they had to keep their heads down.

Their hands had been tied behind their backs, so neither of them could use their power. Why hadn't her visions warned her Habrid had called a slave trader? Mama Habrid had always been jealous of the attention Harland gave them. Habrid had grinned with glee when the slave trader handed her a bag of gold for them.

"Dom, where's Nyx? Why hasn't she come back for us?" Kyri sobbed. "I don't understand. She said she would come back to help us."

"Because she can't. Now keep your mouth shut." Domnu wanted to comfort her sister, but she was still furious with her. Kyri never spoke on Nyx's behalf. But deep down, she knew it wouldn't have made any difference.

"What do they do with us?"

"What do you think they'll do?" Domnu snapped. "People come here to buy slaves. No doubt we'll be sold to someone else or forced to work for someone."

"They will let us stay together, won't they?" More tears streamed down Kyri's face.

"Don't bet on it. Now keep quiet. Don't draw any attention to us."

"Quiet down." The slave trader gave Kyri a hard slap across the face. The girl cried harder.

Domnu gritted her teeth and looked away. She wished her power would give her some sign of what would come next. Or a glimpse of what happened to Nyx. The tribe said the druid had killed her, but she didn't believe it. She had seen how much that druid wanted to find Nyx. Why go to so much trouble just to kill her? It made no sense. But her power remained quiet and showed her nothing.

She cursed under her breath and willed her power to show her something.

Anything.

Touching things made it easier to trigger her curse. Sometimes she didn't need to.

Come on, show me something. Anything. She prayed to whatever gods might be listening.

Her eyes snapped shut. The druid stood beside Nyx and held her arm tight. He waved his hand and her appearance changed into that of another woman.

A few moments later, another girl that looked like Nyx ran towards them. The druid threw a fireball at her. The girl screamed as she exploded in a burst of flames.

"Get moving!" The slave trader pulled her out of her vision.

Domnu gasped as the vision faded.

What did that mean? Nyx was dead? No, Nyx had changed. Or at least Domnu thought she had. Curse that man. If only she could have seen more.

One by one, different groups of slaves were dragged onto a dais and examined. People inspected them, poking and prodding at them, then handed over their money. Domnu wanted to scream. They were people, not cattle. What gave them the right to sell people?

She and Kyri had no rights. No slave did. Not even if they were freed or had the money to buy their freedom.

Domnu glanced around at the other slaves. Men, women, children of various ages. Most skin and bone. No doubt she and Kyri would be more desirable since they were skinny but not haggard.

Domnu wished she could cover up her bright red hair. It made her stand out. Her tribe had called her a witch because of it.

If Nyx was alive, why hadn't she used her curse to escape and come find them? Nyx was powerful. She could hear people's thoughts and compel others to do things with a single touch.

Domnu blew out a breath. She had to put all hope of rescue aside.

The slave trader grabbed their arms and dragged them onto the platform.

"Two young, strong girls here. Perfect for labour. Start the bidding at twenty gold coins each."

"Twenty for each? They are skinny. Plus, they're cursed," one man growled. "Look at them. No doubt they have magic."

Domnu gritted her teeth. Why did all humans think magickind were cursed? Most of Erthea had hundreds of races of magickind.

It was too bad they couldn't use their powers to help them escape. But their abilities weren't defensive. At least hers weren't.

"Kyri, use your power. Try to heal one of the men," she whispered.

"What? Why —?"

"Do it. Instead of healing, use your touch to burn one. We have to get out of here."

"I can't."

"Yes, you —"

"Quiet," the slave trader snapped.

"If they have magic, let's see it." A young man with a mop of dark blond hair stepped forward out of the crowd. Power clung to him and his clothing cost more than Domnu could make in ten lifetimes.

Only royalty wore fabric that expensive. But that made no sense. Joriam was a small island. It had no royal family.

The slave trader shoved Domnu forward. "Show him."

"We can't. We don't have any magic." Domnu raised her chin. "If we did, don't you think we would have used it by now?"

The prince stepped onto the platform and moved closer to her. "Harland kept slaves with magical abilities. What's yours?"

"Harland's dead, in case you hadn't heard." Strange, she almost missed the old brute. At least if he were alive, she and Kyri would still have a roof over their heads. And the pretence of safety.

The prince narrowed his eyes. "I heard Harland had three girls. One a seer, one a healer, and the third could hear things and compel others. The third is gone. So, which one of you is the seer?" He glanced between them.

"We don't have magic," Domnu repeated.

"We shall see." The prince chanted something in a strange tongue and grabbed her by the shoulders.

The image of Nyx being changed and killed flashed through her mind again.

"You're the seer. Good, take them both." He tossed a coin purse to the trader. "Bring them to my ship."

CHAPTER 2

Domnu nearly screamed when the ship rose into the air. She and Kyri sat huddled in the hold. Their hands were still bound.

"Kyri, listen. We have to find a way out of here."

"How? We're on a ship. We have nowhere to go."

"You need to stop the whimpering. You're not a child. Why didn't you speak up when they took Nyx? We both know she never killed Harland. That shadow creature did." She shuddered at the memory of the shadow creature she had seen upstairs in the tavern.

"I never meant for Nyx to die. I was —"

"She's not dead. I had a vision. That druid faked her death and took her away."

"Why would he do that?"

Domnu shrugged. "Nyx is powerful. I think he needed her help for something."

"Where are they taking us?"

"To Andovia, from what I've heard. That prince is the son of the Archdruid. God knows what they want with us." Domnu tugged her bonds. *"Sombre."* Fire sparked around her wrists and burned through the rope. She rubbed her wrists. "Much better."

"Dom, we can't jump out of the ship. We'll die."

"Maybe not. They must have lifeboats. If we can get to one of them, we can escape."

"But where would we go? We are slaves."

"We'll go find Nyx. The druid that came for her came from Andovia, too. If we can find a way to get there, we can find her."

Domnu burned through Kyri's bindings. "I don't know how long it will take us to get to Andovia, but we need a plan."

"We're not jumping off. We'd die."

Kyri had a point. They couldn't jump while the ship was in the air. There weren't any guards near the hold. If they could sneak on deck, maybe they could find the lifeboats and go from there. Domnu didn't know much about steering a boat. Would a lifeboat even be able to float in the air like this vessel could?

"We'll need weapons. Look around and see what we can find."

"Weapons?" Kyri gasped.

"That prince doesn't have anything good planned for us. Do you want to die?" Kyri shook her head. "Good. Look for potential weapons."

Domnu opened one of the chests and gasped at the sight of jewels and gold. She rummaged through, looking for something sharp. She found a jewelled pendant with sharp points on it and shoved it, and some other jewels, into her cloak. They'd need money if they managed to escape.

She shoved some into Kyri's hands and her sister put them into the pockets of her dress.

"I found this." Kyri held up a hammer.

"Good. Hide it."

Footsteps echoed above them.

Domnu grabbed Kyri's arm and yanked her back over to the spot where they'd been left. "Quiet," she hissed in her sister's ear.

The door to the hold opened, and the prince came down.

"You're the sisters I've heard about. Nyx's sisters."

"Nyx, is she —?" Kyri beamed.

"She's in Andovia. My brother brought her there as my prisoner. I have been looking for a mind whisperer for a very long time."

The prince clasped his hands behind his back. "I'm Gideon Valeran, heir to the Archdruid."

"What is a mind whisperer?" Domnu kept her face impassive, but her heart pounded in her ears.

"Someone who can hear thoughts and compel people with their touch. I've heard many stories about her. When I met her, her power seemed… Negligible. So, tell me more about your sister. What can she do? Are you like her?"

Was that why he wanted them? Because of Nyx? If so, why? She couldn't understand what purpose that would serve. They didn't have abilities like Nyx did.

"We're not related to her by blood." Domnu shook her head.

"But what are her abilities? Can she enslave others with her touch?"

If he already had Nyx, why would he need them? Was it to force her to do something? That would only increase the need for them to escape. She didn't want her or Kyri to be used as leverage to force Nyx to do anything.

"Nyx is cursed like us," Kyri said in a small voice.

"Cursed?" Gideon laughed. "Who told you that?"

"Harland did. We were cursed by the gods because we are slaves."

"None of you are cursed. You are both magickind. Where did you and Nyx come from?"

"From Joriam. We've been with Harland since we were children," Kyri replied.

Domnu gritted her teeth. Why couldn't Kyri keep her mouth shut?

"What about before that? Who owned you?"

"We were born into slavery." Domnu raised her chin. "We don't know who our parents are. We were with Harland for as long as we can remember."

Kyri nodded. "That's true. Most slaves never know who their parents are. They died when we were young."

"What about Nyx? She was older when she came to you."

"She was around ten. She had no memory of her life before," Kyri answered.

Domnu wanted to slap her. How could she tell this man so much about their sister? Had she gone mad?

Nyx would always be their sister. Nothing would change that.

Whatever the prince wanted with Nyx couldn't be good, and Kyri backed away. No doubt the prince wanted to use Nyx's powers. But what would he do with them after he learnt everything he wanted to know? Would he kill them or use their powers for his own gain?

The sooner they got away, the better. Her mind flashed back to the vision she'd had when the slave trader had come to collect them the day before. She had seen a vision of a ship sailing on the high seas. Could it have warned her about the ship? If so, what did the vision mean? What was her power warning her of?

Cursed visions. Why couldn't they give her simple explanations?

"But Nyx can influence others with her touch?" Gideon persisted.

"Of course not. If she could, she wouldn't have been stuck in a dingy tavern," Domnu snapped.

She, Nyx, and Kyri had always planned to run away together. They had been saving every penny they could to buy safe passage out of the realm. Her chest ached with the thought of that never happening now.

Gideon's eyes narrowed. "I think it's the perfect place to hide the three of you. How long have you had your gift?" Gideon turned his attention to her now.

She shrugged. "I'm cursed."

Harland had warned them to never tell anyone about their abilities. They were cursed by the gods, and that was all they needed to know. Domnu had never believed that.

Gideon scoffed. "You don't believe that. You seem to have some control over your visions." He turned to Kyri. "What are you? Do you control your gift?"

Kyri dropped her gaze to the floor. "I don't have a gift. It's a curse. I have no control over it."

"Show me." Gideon pulled out a knife and slashed the blade across his palm. "Heal me."

"I can't." Kyra shook her head and her body trembled.

Domnu wanted to reach out and comfort her, but she couldn't. If she did, it would probably only lead to Gideon striking her down. Her mind raced. She had to do something to get the prince away from them. But what?

Gods, please help us out of this. Help protect me and my sister. Tell me what my vision meant.

"Show me. Or should I start cutting your sister instead?"

Tears filled Kyri's eyes.

"She can't heal cuts that deep. Her power only works on minor injuries." Domnu knew she needed to keep Gideon's attention on her. She often did that with Harland when he got angry and took the blows to protect Kyri. She closed her eyes and gasped. "Danger is coming. Someone is going to attack your ship." She wished that were true just to get Gideon away from them.

Gideon scoffed. "You expect me to —"

"My lord, we need you on deck," someone called out.

CHAPTER 3

Light flashed around Gideon's hand, and the wound closed. He grabbed Domnu by the arm and pulled her and Kyri on deck. "What's going on?" Gideon demanded.

Domnu winced as the prince shoved her and Kyri aside. She quickly placed her hands behind her back to make it seem as though they were still bound. It was a good thing the prince hadn't had time to search her and Kyri and find their hidden loot.

"We are having to descend. There's too much wind to fly safely. We will have to continue on the water instead." The captain was a large, muscular man that towered over all of them and had dark skin. A skull with two bones through it was emblazoned on his large hat.

"Look over there," she whispered in her sister's ear and inclined her head towards a set of three small wooden boats. "It's the lifeboats. If we can make a run for it, we might be able to get off the ship once we are closer to the water."

Are you alright? A voice rang through Domnu's mind.

Domnu glanced around. *Who said that?*

Only Nyx could talk to people in thought and that didn't sound like her voice.

I did. The captain flashed her a smile.

But how —

Gods, how could that man hear her thoughts? Was he like Nyx? The prince had called her a mind whisperer. If the captain was powerful like her sister, why hadn't he done something to stop the prince before now?

Do you need help? The captain swung the ship about as it descended lower.

"What do you mean? Keep us in the air," Gideon demanded. "We can't go through The Strait. Those waters are too hostile."

The Strait? It took her a moment to remember it was a stretch of water that ran through the lower realm. Legend stated it was filled with mermaids and other magickind that filled the undersea realm.

"Sorry, my lord, we've got no choice. It's too dangerous to fly in these winds."

"Fly lower. We're not entering those waters. I know what the merfolk are like."

Please, you have to help me and my sister get away from the prince, Domnu said. *He'll imprison us or worse if you don't.*

Domnu knew the captain helping them was unlikely, but she had to try something. They were on their own. He could be taking them anywhere.

The ship descended lower. Waves crashed against the ship from all sides as he hit the water. Domnu winced as the spray stung her eyes.

More waves rose higher and hit the ship so hard it banked to one side. The prince and his men cried out as they went crashing into the water. Domnu and Kyri grabbed onto the ship's rail to stop themselves from being thrown off.

"Watch out!" the captain yelled.

The captain brought the ship around, and it rose into the air.

"Stop!" Gideon yelled.

"Sorry, your highness, but this is where we part ways." Bones gave him a mock salute. "I'm sure you can find a way back to Andovia. But these former slaves are no longer your prisoners." He turned the ship's wheel. Wood and metal ground as it rose into the air again and floated away from the yelling prince as he threw bursts of energy after them.

"I don't understand. Why would you help us?" Domnu asked. "Did you hear my —"

"I'm Bones, captain of The Bounty." Bones tipped his hat. "You could say I'm somewhat of an outlaw in these waters. No, I can't hear your thoughts, but I can use mind speak. Don't worry, you don't have anything to fear from me or my crew. We work with the resistance, helping former slaves like you and your sister."

"We need to get to Andovia to find our other sister."

"We won't be able to go there for a while. Not until I get some new crystals fitted to my ship."

"The prince was right. Where can we go?" Kyri asked. "I doubt there is anywhere safe for us."

"We are headed to Doringa, near the Dragon Islands next. You're welcome to join us."

"We need to find our other sister. The prince's brother took her," Domnu explained.

"From what I hear about Darius Valeran, she should be fine. He works with the resistance."

Kyri touched her arm. "Nyx said she would come and find us. Maybe we just need to wait for her."

Domnu shook her head. Something didn't feel right about this. Complete strangers didn't help people out of the goodness of their hearts. The world didn't work like that. Especially not for slaves like them.

She narrowed her eyes at the captain. "Won't the prince come after you for what you did?"

From what she knew about the Archdruid's family, they weren't the forgiving sort of people. They would do everything in their power to avenge the affront of dumping Gideon right in the middle of the sea.

Bones laughed. "The prince won't drown. He's a Valeran, and he's very powerful. Someone will come and get him soon enough."

"Can you prove yourself at the nearest port?"

Kyri scrambled to her feet. "Wait, why are we still headed in the same direction. Aren't we still heading towards Andovia?"

Domnu frowned. "You said you were headed towards the Dragon Islands. They are south of Andovia. We're heading in the wrong direction." She had always collected maps whenever she could so she could get a good idea of the different realms. She knew the layout of the lower realm well enough. "Where are you taking us?"

"Clever girl. We are headed to Andovia. Jinx!"

A glowing orb of light appeared as a small woman, a Pixie or Sprite, with pointed ears and fluorescent wings appeared. Light flashed around the sisters as the Pixie threw bolts of energy at them.

"Sorry, girls. You are now prisoners of the Queen of Andovia. It's up to her to decide what to do with you now."

WARRIOR OF ELMYRA

CHAPTER 1

Kyri trembled as *The Bounty* docked in Andovia. She didn't know if it was from the cold air when they reached the surface or because of fear. Maybe both. Being on a ship that could move underneath the waves with a magical air bubble terrified her.

Her sister, Domnu, seemed more angry than anything. They had escaped from Prince Gideon — the man who had bought them at the slave market in Joriam. Being in their old realm felt like a lifetime ago. So much had passed in the last couple of days.

Their foster sister, Nyx, had been accused of murdering Harland, the man who had owned them. Their tribe had sentenced her to death by being burned at the stake.

Domnu, a seer, insisted Nyx had somehow escaped from what she had seen in her vision. She said Nyx had been saved by Gideon's brother and taken to Andovia. Gideon had intended to take Kyri and Domnu there. Instead, the captain of the ship they had been travelling on had dumped Gideon and his guards in the middle of the sea. Kyri had thought the captain had meant to help them. But he'd claimed them as prisoners for the Queen of Andovia instead.

Kyri didn't understand what that meant. The Archdruid ruled Andovia, not a queen. Captain Bones had told them that but not much else.

"Who is the Queen of Andovia?" Kyri spoke up. "I thought the Archdruid ruled this realm?"

Domnu shot her a warning look. "Be quiet," she hissed.

"The Archdruid does rule here. The queen is a long story." A sprite with purple hair landed on the helm. "The queen ruled this realm a century ago until the Archdruid overthrew her. Now she is in exile."

"But why does she want us?" Domnu demanded. "We're slaves, we're not fit to serve anyone."

"You're both magickind with strong gifts. The queen ordered me to bring you to her," Bones replied in a booming baritone. The big man towered over them, his body all rippling muscle. His dark skin shone like ebony and his dark eyes fixated on them.

"And what will she do with us?" Kyri's blood pounded in her ears along with her racing heart.

Bones shrugged. "I can't say."

"You lied when you said you worked with the resistance." Domnu glowered at him. "They help free slaves. They don't pass them on to new masters."

"I do what I can for the resistance, but I can't ignore orders from the queen."

"Why not? You ignored the prince's orders," Kyri pointed out. Her long blond hair blew over her face and she clutched her stomach. She hated the roll and sway of the ship. How could anyone stand being stuck at sea for more than a few moments?

Bones rumbled with laughter. "No one can disobey the queen. She can command others with her touch and walk through your mind as easily as breathing."

"Is she a mind whisperer?" That was what Gideon had called Nyx. The term still sounded strange to her. Kyri had seen Nyx compel people then make them forget about the event.

Bones nodded. "She is the first mind whisperer, from what legend says. She's immortal." He tossed them some apples. "We'll be going to see her soon. Here, you'll need your strength."

They took the apples as Bones disappeared below deck. "What are we going to do?" Kyri whispered to her sister.

Domnu narrowed her blue eyes and pushed her long blood-red hair off her face. "I say we make a run for it. We're close to land now. We can find our way to the capital and get Nyx. Then get out of here. We have the jewels." They had found boxes of treasure below deck and managed to smuggle some of the loot into their cloaks. They would need as much gold and jewels as they could get. Travelling as former slaves wouldn't be easy in the lower realms.

Kyri glanced over at the sprite that still stood on the helm. "How do we get past her?"

"My power isn't defensive, but yours can be. Use it."

Kyri tucked the apple into her dress. "I've never used it to harm others." She swallowed hard; her mouth now dry. As a healer, she never wanted to hurt anyone.

"We don't have a choice. Concentrate your power on the sprite."

"I need to touch her for it to work. You know that."

Domnu blew out a breath. "Come on."

They both got up and headed to the helm. "Play along," Domnu hissed and said, "I never expected to see a sprite on a pirate ship."

"It's easier to travel by ship. Even for me." The sprite stared up at them with big almond-shaped eyes.

"Are you a pirate like the captain?" Kyri asked.

The sprite tinkled with laughter. "Hardly. I'm more than that. My name is Jinx. You girls better not think of running. You won't get far."

"Why not?" Kyri furrowed her brow.

"Because the old city is shielded and cut off from the rest of Andovia. You can't escape. Only the queen allows people in and out."

Domnu scoffed. "You expect us to believe that?"

"Believe what you like. It's the truth. Once Azura gets here, we'll take you to —"

Kyri drew magic. Her palm flared with light and she grabbed hold of Jinx. She didn't fully know how her power worked. Normally she just let instinct take over. Her power reacted to her emotions.

Freeze. You cannot move and you cannot stop us from leaving… You will not scream or call for help… She released the sprite and Jinx stood there, mouth open in a silent scream.

"Let's go." She tugged at Domnu's hand. They hurried to the side of the ship. "We'll have to jump." Kyri scrambled over the railing followed by her sister.

"Hey, where are you two going?" A silver haired young woman appeared below them. Water rose as she raised her hands and tossed them back onto the deck. Her magic drenched them with water. The woman jumped out of the sea, using the water to propel herself with magic.

Kyri gasped. "That's a mermaid."

The mermaid's iridescent blue tail shone with light as she changed into human form. She landed on the deck on two legs. "You must be the new prisoners." The woman's azure eyes narrowed, and she tossed her silver hair over her shoulder. "What did you do to Jinx?" Light flared around her hands as she picked the sprite up. "Are you alright?"

Jinx screamed, then gasped for breath. "What did you do to me?" She shook her tiny fist at them.

Kyri's mouth fell open. Her magic had worked, she'd felt it. What had that mermaid done? Kyri blanched. "I'm sorry, but we are not becoming your queen's slaves."

"You're not going anywhere." The mermaid glared at them. "You have to be brought before the queen. She is demanding to see you. Let's go."

Bones, Jinx and Azura led them off the ship and into an enormous great hall. Its high vaulted ceiling glimmered with chandeliers that sparkled like diamonds. The gleaming oak floor shone so bright they could almost see their reflections in it.

A dark-haired woman sat perched on a golden throne on a raised dais at the end of the hall. Tree branches and flowers were carved into the ornate gold.

"My queen." Bones and his companions bowed before her. "We have brought you Gideon's prisoners as you commanded."

Bones remained down on one knee, but Azura rose and Kyri thought she caught a flash of defiance in the mermaid's gaze.

"It took you long enough." The queen rose from her throne, her black robe billowed behind her. Her face appeared pale and striking. Her bright blue eyes narrowed on them, and her long raven hair fell past her shoulders.

Kyri resisted the urge to reach out and grab Domnu's hand. She kept her eyes on the floor, counting the lines there.

The queen laughed as she approached them. "I love it when people try to hide their thoughts from me. As if you could." She circled around them. "So you are the two slaves that were owned by Harland. I've been eager to meet you for some time now."

"We — we're no one important." Kyri couldn't keep the tremor out of her voice. "We won't be of any use to you, believe me."

Domnu shot her a glare as if to say, *what are you doing?*

Gods, she sounded pathetic.

Memories of Harland hitting her flashed through her mind. The familiar sliver of fear shot down her spine.

"You are a seer." The queen put her finger underneath Domnu's chin, forcing her head up to meet her gaze. "The sight is strong in you."

"My visions are unreliable." Domnu met the queen's gaze head-on. "I won't be of any use to you."

That earned them another cackle.

"Don't bother lying to me, girl. Mind whisperers can see the truth." The queen gave Domnu a shove so hard Domnu stumbled. The queen turned to Kyri. "A healer. Interesting." She laughed and forced Kyri's head up as well.

Kyri trembled. This woman could look into her very soul. Power rolled off the queen like thunder. "I'm — I'm not very good."

The queen snorted. "We both know that's not true. You saw how you could use your power today. It excited you, didn't it? To feel in control, to control another? I know that feeling well enough."

"No — no. I...I hated it." She remembered the feel of her power; the control she had over Jinx sickened her. She wanted to help others, not harm them. That wasn't what healers were meant to do.

"Time to see if you're both as powerful as the rumours say you are. I know Harland had a knack for finding powerful slaves." The queen gripped Domnu's shoulders. Domnu gasped and Kyri knew she was having a vision. "Good, you've shown me what I'm looking for."

The queen had seen Domnu's vision. Gods, Kyri thought only Nyx could do that. But Nyx had never been able to trigger visions the way the queen had.

The queen turned her attention to Kyri and Kyri's stomach dropped. Fire formed in the queen's hand then she threw it straight towards Kyri. Raising her arms, Kyri screamed. Heat washed over her but didn't burn her as she had expected. Instead, the fire dissipated and left her unharmed.

"I guess the two of you will have to do." The queen headed back to her throne.

"What do you mean?" Kyri asked and flinched when the queen's eyes narrowed at her.

"Azura, you and your crew are to bring me a dragon back from Elmyra. These two are going with you. Use them to bring me what I need."

CHAPTER 2

"I don't understand," Kyri remarked once they were back on board the ship. "How can we bring the queen a dragon?"

"My ship can move anywhere. It's why the queen uses us as her spies." Bones tapped the runes on the helm. "But we need you to help us find and capture a dragon." Azura pulled back the ropes that tethered the ship to the dock.

"How?" Domnu glowered at him. "We're slaves, not dragon hunters."

"You have visions. You can help." Bones turned the wheel and led them away from the dock.

"What good can I do?" Kyri wrung her hands together. "My powers are no good against a dragon."

"You are immune to the dragon's fire since you can heal yourself," Azura pointed out. "You can get close a dragon. Much more than the three of us can."

"I — I can't go near a dragon. I'm — I'm not a warrior."

"Your healing powers are just what we need. So start acting like a warrior," Azura said. "We'll arrive in Elmyra within a day. You too should get some rest. There's a cabin down below. You can sleep there."

Kyri followed Domnu to the cabin. "What are we going to do?" she asked.

Domnu shrugged. "We'll have to play along for now, I suppose."

"But we can't. I can't go up against a dragon. They're betting too much on my powers." She paced up and down. "I can't do this. I'm not brave like you and Nyx. My gift barely works even when I want it to!"

"You are brave. You're just as strong as me and Nyx. Now you have to believe that."

A tear dripped down Kyri's cheek. "I wish Nyx was here. She always protected us."

"Now we have to protect ourselves." Domnu wrapped her arms around Kyri.

"I never got a chance to tell her how sorry I am." When Nyx had been arrested, Kyri had been too afraid to say anything. She had let their human tribe sentence Nyx to death for a murder she hadn't committed.

"You were afraid. Nyx will understand that."

"Why me? I can't face a dragon. I run away from mice!"

"We'll find the damned dragon. Then we'll escape. The queen didn't use her touch on us."

"Please tell me you've seen us escape in your visions."

"Not yet, but I will find a way."

"Have you seen Nyx anymore?"

Domnu shook her head. "This may sound strange, but I think she will be safe with that druid."

Kyri couldn't imagine how that was true. Another druid had come to arrest Nyx and he turned out to be the brother of the man who had bought them. How could she be safe with him?

"What about the dragon? Have you seen anything about that?" Kyri clutched her sister's hand.

Domnu gasped as energy jolted through her. Kyri waited. Most visions didn't last long.

Too bad Nyx wasn't here. Sometimes Nyx could see into Domnu's mind and witness visions for herself. Kyri had always envied that about her.

Domnu opened her eyes.

"Well, what did you see?"

"Nothing."

"You must have seen something. I know what you look like whilst you're having a vision."

"I didn't see anything." Domnu shook her head.

Kyri put her hands on her hips. "Domnu, don't lie to me. You had the same look you always get when you have a vision."

"I don't have a look. And you don't understand. I didn't see anything when the queen touched me either. I think she did something to me. Like she somehow intercepted my visions so only she can see whatever they're showing." Domnu shuddered. "Gods, what if I can never see my visions again?"

"We'll find a way to overcome her. We just need to have some faith."

"Before we get to Elmyra, we need to learn everything we can about the ship and her crew."

Kyri didn't know how to feel as darkness fell over them like a heavy blanket. But at least the captain hadn't taken the ship underwater again yet. He'd only done that as they were leaving Andovia.

"Where is Elmyra?" she asked when she found Bones on deck.

"It's one of the dragon islands. Dragons are bred and raised there. Have been for millennia. The Archdruid controls the islands, but we'll sneak in and get one."

"You're putting a lot of misplaced faith in my abilities and in me." Kyri grimaced. "I'm no hero. Up until a few days ago, I worked in a tavern sweeping floors and serving ale." She had thought life had seemed hard back then. But now she longed to go back to her old life.

Gods, she would even be glad to see Harland again. It didn't matter he used to hit her and treated her the worst out of all her sisters. He always said she was slow and clumsy. Nyx had always been his pride and joy.

"We don't put faith in anyone but ourselves. If the queen thinks you can do it, you can. She is rarely wrong. Certainty is part of her gift."

"Why do you serve such a tyrant? Why don't you leave?" Kyri leaned back against the railing. Bones had been kind enough to give her something for her seasickness earlier so at least her stomach had settled.

Azura laughed as she came on deck. "You make it sound so easy."

"Good always triumphs over evil."

Bones boomed with laughter. "You have a lot to learn about the world, kid. We don't have much choice about serving the queen. I'm under her control, can't change that unless she dies."

"That will never happen. She's immortal. Even the Archdruid couldn't kill her," Azura said.

"There must be a way," Kyri insisted. "I know there are bad rulers all over Erthea, but there are good people too."

"Name one," Azura scoffed.

"The resistance. They fight against the Archdruid."

"Yeah, and they pay for it with their lives. We've helped them out a time or two, but there ain't no going against the Morrigan," Bones remarked.

"What about you?" Kyri turned to Azura. "Does she use her power on you?"

"No. I'm immune to that. Maybe it would be better she did." Azura grimaced.

"If you're not compelled by her touch, then why serve her? Why not run away?" Kyri and her sisters had planned on running away for months. They scrimped and saved every coin they could. That dream hadn't changed just because they had been separated from Nyx. Kyri knew she'd have to be strong. The weak didn't survive in this world.

"You ask a lot of questions, little mouse." Azura scowled at her.

"I'm not a mouse. And you didn't answer my question."

"I can't defy the queen. That woman — the body you saw today — that's my mother's body." Azura bared her teeth. "The queen — or at least her spirit — has possessed her on and off for an entire century. I won't lose my mother. One way or another I'll get her back."

"But — but how is that possible?" She couldn't fathom how a spirit could possess someone's body. Especially not for so long.

Weren't things like that just legends? Stories told around the campfire? The human tribe she used to live with had told such tales.

Azura looked away and a tear dripped down her cheek. "The Archdruid destroyed the queen's body, so her soul left it and took my mother as her host. I never had the chance to know her. Instead, I have to watch that thing wandering around as her."

"I'm sorry, Azura."

"Don't be. Just help me get her a damned dragon." Azura headed over to the rail and jumped overboard.

"Let her go. Talking about her past and her mama always upsets her." Bones tapped the runes on the helm.

"I didn't mean to upset her."

"She will get over it. That's why she serves the queen. In the hope the queen will release Lyra. Doubt that will ever happen, though."

"Why not?"

"Because Lyra was the queen's priestess and now she pretends to serve the Archdruid. Ain't no way the queen will ever give her up."

"I wish I could help her. Prove to her not all people are evil."

Bones chuckled. "It's a nice thought, mouse, but we know the way of things."

"What happens if you try to resist the queen?" Thinking of Nyx made her chest tighten with a pang of sadness.

Would they ever see their sister again? Would Nyx be safe in Andovia?

"If I resist, it drives me mad. So I can think of nothing else. To defy a mind whisperer's will will lead to madness. If that don't do it, the queen would kill my crew. They're the only family I've got."

Kyri shuddered. "Not all mind whisperers are bad."

"Oh yeah? Do you know a good one?"

"My foster sister."

"And what does she use her powers to do?"

Kyri bit her lip. "To steal things — but she doesn't harm people."

Bones snorted. "No mind whisperer is good, mousy. Remember that. In the old days they used to be a voice of justice on Erthea. If there are any left, they're dark, like the queen."

"Was the queen always bad?"

"Some called her a hero. She kept the peace in the lower realms — until the Archdruid came. Some say she went mad. The Archdruid murdered her daughters in front of her. No one could come through that as a whole person. He killed the other mind whisperers too. The queen is the last of her kind."

Kyri shivered. "One must have survived. Or my sister wouldn't be here."

"I doubt that. I was there the day Varden City fell. Watched the Archdruid slaughter every mind whisperer there. He'd never let one survive." Bones shuddered again. "If your sister's in Andovia, I doubt she will survive for long. The Archdruid won't stand for any threat against him."

"Don't be so sure of that, Bones." Jinx settled on the helm. "People have been talking about this new mind whisperer. They are saying she is part of the prophecy."

"What prophecy?" Domnu came out on deck.

"Some ancient prophecy says a child of the fae and one of the dragonborn will bring about a time of peace…" Bones boomed with laughter again. "Codswallop if you ask me."

"The prophecy also says the two chosen ones will bring about a time of great darkness," Jinx remarked. "Another dark age — they could go either way. The Archdruid would love that."

"Ridiculous," Domnu insisted. "Nyx couldn't do that."

"The Archdruid seems to think she can. That's why his sons want her. If she's the one, the Archdruid might use her," Jinx remarked.

"It's late. Kyri, come on. Let's get some sleep."

CHAPTER 3

"We are coming in to dock," Azura came into the cabin and found them the next morning with her arms full of clothing. "You two need to change your clothing. You can't go around looking like bedraggled slaves."

Why did it matter what they looked like? They were still slaves — now prisoners. That hadn't changed and wouldn't until they finally escaped.

Kyri prayed they could escape. She wanted to return to Andovia to find Nyx, but not at the expense of being the queen's prisoner.

"Put these on." Azura tossed them each a tunic, trousers and jerkins.

"But these are men's clothing," Kyri gasped.

"Women wear clothes just like this. Do you want to blend in or not?" Azura arched an eyebrow at them.

"We'll be ready." Domnu nodded.

"Please tell me you had a vision that showed we'll make it out of this alive," Kyri begged.

"I haven't seen anything. Get dressed. We'll be ready to run once we've found this silly dragon."

Kyri couldn't be sure about their plan. This realm was too unknown to them to ensure success. The dragon islands were said to be barren and uninhabited. What if they couldn't escape from here? She guessed they would have to wait and see how things played out.

She pulled the clothes on and plaited her long blond hair. Kyri would be ready for whatever came next.

Kyri's stomach churned the moment they stepped on land. She almost missed the roll and sway of being on the ship.

"Come on, mouse," Bones called out as they walked through the bustling dock.

People hurried past them carrying boxes and running back and forth. Kyri hadn't expected this place to appear so busy. Weren't most of the Dragon Islands meant to be uninhabited?

Azura, still in human form, walked alongside him.

"I wish you would stop calling me that," Kyri muttered under her breath.

"You might just focus. The sooner we find the dragon, the sooner we get out of here."

They had stored their stolen goods and what little they had brought with them near the ship. Kyri prayed no one would find it there.

Once they were clear of the dock, Azura used a potion to transport them into the middle of nowhere. Sand covered everything in a haze of white gold. Jinx stayed behind to keep an eye on the ship. Kyri couldn't imagine how a tiny sprite could defend an entire ship

"Now it's your turn, seer," Azura said. "Find us a dragon."

Did they really think they could find a dragon out in the middle of nowhere?

She has to be mad, Kyri decided.

Weren't dragons kept in breeding enclosures? Under armed guard? That was what they had told them on the ship.

"I can't control my power," Domnu protested. "Or what I'll see."

"The longer you take, the longer we have to be stuck here." Azura shuddered. "I hate sand, especially when there's no water around."

Domnu closed her eyes and blew out a breath. "I don't see anything."

"I thought dragons were locked up and controlled by the Archdruid's forces?" Kyri spoke up.

"Not out here. Dragons live in the wild here, but the Archdruid's forces do come and hunt them," Bones said. "That's where you two come in."

"I can't see anything." Domnu shook her head.

Azura gritted her teeth. "If you don't find this dragon, the queen will kill our friend."

"What friend?" Kyri frowned. "You never mentioned that before."

"Our crewmate Dahlia. Whose cabin do you think you've been staying in?" Bones demanded.

"I told you, I can't control —" Domnu protested.

Kyri took her hand. "Concentrate."

Domnu closed her eyes again. Energy jolted through her. "I — I see a dragon. Big, green, scaly. It's… Attacking Kyri…"

Kyri's heart stopped beating. Would the dragon kill her when she finally encountered it? Gods, she wished she could run away.

"But where is it?" Bones demanded.

"I don't know." Domnu shook her head again. "I only see glimpses of things. Like shimmers in a pond. Some things come true, some things don't."

"Then we'd better split up. Mouse, you come with me. Bones, you take the seer."

"Wait, why are you separating us?" Kyri glanced between them.

"Making sure you two don't escape."

She and Azura headed off in the opposite direction. They wandered around for what felt like hours but found nothing.

They finally reunited with the others around dusk.

"Maybe you were wrong about there being dragons here." Kyri slumped down beside her sister.

"We'll find one sooner or later. We have to. For now, we'll make camp."

Kyri's mind raced as she lay down beside Domnu. Despite her exhaustion, she couldn't sleep.

What if they couldn't find a dragon? What would happen then? Would the queen kill them?

Failure didn't seem like an option, not to these pirates.

She dreaded to think what the queen might do to them. Despite kidnapping them, she had no ill will to Azura or her crew. They didn't have a choice but to follow the queen's orders. If the roles were reversed, she couldn't say she wouldn't have done the same thing. Especially if the queen had someone she loved.

She sat up. Bones and Azura lay sleeping under their blankets. A full moon hung overhead like a lantern in a sea of darkness.

Something moved toward them.

What was it?

Kyri's heart pounded in her ears.

She reached out for Domnu, then hesitated. Instead, she crawled closer to get a better look.

A dragon. It loomed over her like a giant. A huge mass that blocked out the moonlight. The dragon's golden eyes stared back at her.

Kyri froze. What should she do? Call out for the others?

They hadn't said what they would do once they found one. Other than she would be the one to go after it.

She closed her eyes and reached out. A cold snout met her hand. She opened her eyes to find the dragon still staring at her.

The beast craned its head forward and sniffed at her. *You smell like mine. But you are not my kindred. Where is she?*

Kyri put a hand over her mouth to stifle her gasp. Good gods, had the dragon just spoken to her?

What…what do you mean? What kindred?

60

My kindred… I'm looking for a girl. Do you know where she is? She is a winged fae. I was given to her when she was a child. But we were separated many years ago. Where is my kindred? I can smell her scent on you. The dragon leaned forward and sniffed at her cloak again. *Why do you smell like her?*

Her mouth fell open. This cloak had belonged to Nyx, but Nyx never had the chance to take anything with her before she was taken.

I…I think you mean my foster sister. But how can she be connected to you?

Where is she? I need to find her.

She—

Bones sprang to his feet, throwing a net over the dragon. The beast roared and thrashed. "Good, we've got what we came for."

Kyri's heart sank when they returned to the ship. She'd been responsible for helping to capture that poor beast. That had been her job, but she hadn't expected to feel a kinship with the creature. Nor had she had the chance to find out how it was connected to Nyx.

"Here." Azura handed them their bags. "There's some extra coin in here and papers to help you get out of the lower realms."

Her mouth fell open. "I don't understand."

"You helped us. We owe you for that. You two are free to go."

"But the queen —"

"I can handle her. I'll tell her you two were lost in the fight to get the dragon. That's all needs to know. We like to help when we can."

"Thank you." Kyri clutched her pack to her chest.

She squeezed Domnu's shoulder as they watched the ship sail away.

For the first time in their lives, they were free. One way or another, they would get back to Andovia to find Nyx when it was safe to do so. But for now, they had their freedom.

IN DAWN'S LIGHT

CHAPTER 1

Calena Reevus muttered an oath as her long dress caught on the edge of the wall she had just climbed up. The night hung overhead like a heavy blanket, with only a scattering of stars and a few fine slivers of silver moonlight.

I knew I should have worn trousers and dressed like a man. But dressing like a man would have only drawn unwanted attention. If she had, she might never have escaped from the citadel. Being caught there didn't bear thinking about. Callie thanked the gods she and her brothers had escaped unscathed. It had been a long night after she had broken into the high lord's study and stolen what she needed.

Too bad there had been no time for her to change. But they had run all the way from the citadel to the great wall that looked over the city like a silent sentinel.

She and her brothers, Roderick and Tyrone, had to get into the old city and find the spell circle. It was their last chance. Magic was vanishing from the island of Entara, and what little remained would soon run out.

If they didn't reach that spell circle, the magic here would be gone forever and what remained of her people would die out. They needed the energy from the land itself to survive. Most had lost their magic already, while some were only able to use a limited amount. Callie and her brothers had spent weeks preserving whatever energy they could get. But they had been forced to use a lot to escape from the guard.

Callie prayed they would have enough energy left between them to cast the spell, or all of this would have been for nothing.

Lord Aron had already enslaved her people—the Entarans. He and his druid-trained guard were the only ones allowed to use magic. Anyone else caught doing so was either imprisoned or killed. The solstice was the last chance for them to bring magic back into their realm and use it to overthrow Aron and his minions.

Callie pushed her long black hair off her face. Before her lay ruins of the old city. Great stone buildings that stood out among the stark mountain peaks. This had once been a thriving metropolis—the biggest in the lower realm. People had flocked here from all over the lower realms thanks to Entara's famous mines of black stone. In the end, everything that made this land desirable had led to its downfall.

Since Aron came over a decade ago, it had fallen into ruins. No one was allowed to live there now. Entara's stone mines were running out too. Her brothers had told her how their workload had grown less over recent weeks. You couldn't mine what wasn't there. Taking away so much stone had depleted the earth of its natural resources.

Her heart ached at the sight of it. She had only been a small child when she had been forced to flee. Most of her family were all gone now. All she had was her three brothers. Her youngest brother was elsewhere.

"Come on, Callie." Roderick tugged at her arm. "We can't linger." His dark hair looked almost black against the night sky.

"Hurry," Tyrone hissed from below. His dark clothing made him blend in with the rest of the great wall. She could only just make out his pale skin in the blackness.

Callie moved, but something pulled her back. The hem of her dress had caught on one of the jagged stones that made up the great wall that stood between the old city and the current city of Lyris. They had to get moving. Guards frequently patrolled the walls in case people tried to escape through the different sectors in the new city. Sectors meant they could keep small groups of people in one place, which made them much easier to control.

Callie didn't want to ruin the dress, either. It was the only piece of clothing she owned. Her life as a fugitive didn't allow for luxuries. She tugged the dress free and winced as part of it ripped off.

Then she jumped. Callie breathed a sigh of relief when her feet met the solid ground.

Moving through the empty streets felt like walking into a different world. Houses still stood; carts lay abandoned. Doors remained open. As if time had stopped and nature had crept in. Dust covered everything, weeds and brambles covered what had once been prominent homes.

Still, Callie felt safer here than beyond the wall where a perfect city stewed with its towers of stone. Stone that was draining the very magic from these lands.

None of them said anything as they passed through the eerie streets. Other than the taps of their feet against the hard stone, no sound echoed around them.

Callie almost wished she could go in search of their childhood home. To see if it still stood and have a chance to remember the few happy times she had there. She barely remembered what the house looked like or where it had stood. Her brothers had told her stories of it and she ached to go back. She half feared what she would find, though. Her home had always been a safe haven in her mind. Seeing it destroyed would only bring more heartache.

Callie shook her head. No, it would have to wait. This was their last chance. If they succeeded, perhaps there would be time for that later. If not, she reminded herself it didn't matter. Seeing the house again wouldn't bring back her lost loved ones, nor would it change anything. It would only remind her more of the life she had lost when her father had been killed and she and her brothers had been forced into servitude. That part of the past was best left forgotten.

They turned down another street. Bits of old clothing and other debris still lay across the cobblestones. No doubt remnants left over from where the Entarans had been herded out by the guard when Aron had claimed this realm. They had swarmed over the city like a plague, rounding up the dragons that had once lived peacefully there. The high lord's strange magic had controlled the creatures and forced them into servitude, too.

"Where is the circle?" Tyrone asked, all colour draining from his face.

The spell circle had been a prominent feature in the heart of the city. Dozens of people had come from all over the lower realms to witness magic performed inside it by the high lord and other leaders back when the city had been thriving. It had been the centre point for all of Entara. Every year, the high lord had used an ancient spell to imbue the land with renewed growth and energy. Using the very magic that had blessed their realm since the creation of their people.

This street stopped at a dead-end. Aside from a few broken-down ruins, there was nothing here. Only remnants of buildings that had long since been destroyed and had their black stone walls harvested for the magical properties that lay within.

Callie groaned. "We must have taken a wrong turn. Rod, I thought you knew the way."

Callie had been too young to remember how to navigate the old city. Her memories of her past life here were vague at best. Roderick and Tyrone were both several years older than her and remembered things in much better detail than she ever could.

Rod and Tyrone had worked in mines. Callie had worked as a maid at the high lord's kitchen. Together, they had worked in secret, along with the resistance. Although most of the resistance here had either been killed or imprisoned over recent months. None of them had been able to accompany them that night, and their friend had been killed when they had escaped from the citadel.

Anyone who went against the Archdruid and a select group of High Lords and Ladies were imprisoned or executed.

They didn't allow anyone to oppose them.

"I do. I thought this was the right way." Roderick ran a hand through his long black hair. His dark eyes were sunken and hollow. The last few days of planning everything and preparing their escape from the citadel had taken its toll on him the most.

Weariness hung over Callie as a heavy cloak. She would have liked nothing better than to curl up and sleep. Of course, there had been no time. It had been hard to escape the citadel to get to the great wall and past any guards that had been patrolling it.

"We'll double back." Callie motioned for them to follow.

The more they wandered around, the less time they had to prepare the circle. She would need time to cleanse it and make sure everything was ready. They had a few hours before dawn when the spell would be cast. She didn't want to lose any of that precious time.

All the streets blurred together. Any signs having long since vanished.

The knot in her stomach tightened. The guards were already looking for them after Callie had stolen a powerful orb from Aron. Patrols would be looking everywhere.

Callie peered around another corner and gasped. There it stood; a circle etched into the foundations of the city. "We're here," she whispered to her brothers.

It remained intact, even after all these years. Callie couldn't believe it. Somehow, she thought it would have been destroyed long ago, like the rest of the old city. She remembered her parents bringing her here when her father, Baltazar Reevus, had led them and performed magic.

Tears stung her eyes at the memory, but she brushed them away. "Spread out. We need to purify the circle."

The circle had to be cleansed and prepared so magic could be channelled through it. Any debris or anything negative lying in it would impede the effect of the spell. Everything had to be perfect for this to work. Otherwise, everything would have been for nothing.

Callie took off her pack and pulled out the orb she had stolen. It was small and fit into the palm of her hand. Without it—and the dragon bones, the spell wouldn't work.

"Rod, start the cleansing. Tyrone and I will hide the bones and the orb." She clutched the orb. If the guards came here, she would not allow this to be found. They were too crucial to the spell, and they still had several hours to go before dawn arrived and the spell could begin. These items were too important to be found or worse, destroyed.

Callie went over to the wall and pulled a stone loose then shoved the orb behind it. Once it was out of sight, she fumbled in her pack and sprinkled a salt circle.

Kicking off her shoes, she felt the faint vibrations of power as it hummed against her bare feet.

She wished she could use her magic, but she needed to preserve it for the spell.

Tyrone came back over to her. "The bones are hidden."

She nodded. "Good, help with the cleansing."

Callie moved around the ancient circle. The vibrations felt weak and jagged. She needed the circle to be in perfect working order.

"The salt isn't cleansing much," Rod observed. "We need to use magic. It's the only thing capable of truly cleansing the place."

Callie bit her lip. The friend who had helped them escape the citadel had dodged everything he could to contact the resistance and ask them for aid.

"You know we can't. The guard would be alerted, and we would all be captured," she protested.

"What other choice do we have?" Tyrone hissed.

"He's right, little sister. If we don't do this, we'll never bring magic back."

Callie ran a hand through her hair. They were right. They had to make sure the circle was in full working order. The future of their race was at stake. But at the same time, she didn't want to risk it.

"If the guard does come, we'll split up. We all know how to cast a spell," Tyrion said. "As long as one of us survives, we can do this."

Callie's chest tightened. She didn't want to lose either of her brothers. They were all she had left.

Everyone else, friends, family, anyone she had ever cared about had fallen under Aron's regime. But if they didn't risk themselves for the realm, who would?

No one else knew how to cast the spell except for them.

If they died, the secret would die with them.

Callie nodded. "I know… Let me do it."

"No, I'm the eldest. I'll do it." Roderick raised his hand, and Callie held her breath. She and Tyrone retreated, both prepared to run if they had to.

Slowly, blue light enveloped the circle. Line by line, it washed over the cracks like freshwater.

Rod smiled. "It's okay. It worked. Callie—"

An arrow shot through the air and hit him in the back. Rod's eyes widened, and blood dripped from his mouth.

"No!" Callie tried to scream, but it came out as a whisper. She couldn't believe it. They had come so far. He couldn't die. Not now. She still needed him to help perform the spell.

"Run, Callie," Tyrone called out to her.

Callie stood there, frozen.

Guards moved out of the shadows, and more arrows shot through the air.

Then instinct took over. Callie dropped to the ground and rolled, avoiding the arrows as they struck the earth. Grabbing her fallen pack, she leapt to her feet and ran.

Another scream was like a knife to her heart.

She turned. Tyrone fell to the ground. Three arrows protruded from his back.

No! She wanted to scream, to weep. She didn't.

Instead, Callie hitched up the hem of her dress and took off running. Thank the gods she had put her shoes back on when she stepped out the circle.

She had to hide. Where didn't matter.

More shouts came from behind her, along with the thud of heavy footsteps and the flank of armour and steel.

The guards didn't know the city like she did. Some of it looked familiar to her.

Callie rounded a side street and came face-to-face with Thane, Aron's general. The very man who had murdered her family. His face had haunted her dreams for most of her childhood.

Thane towered over her. His long grey hair hung loosely around his angular face, and his grey beard blew in the faint breeze. His eyes were like steel and he wore the silver armour of the guard, along with a red cloak.

"Going somewhere, Calena?"

Callie fumbled in her dress for a dagger. "Stay back."

Thane laughed and hit her with a bolt of energy. They wouldn't kill her, that much she knew. Not until they recovered the orb first, at least.

She cried out and sank to her knees. It was no use. These were Druid warriors. Their magic wasn't tied to one place the way the Entaran's was.

"Lord Aron will be most pleased to hear we caught you alive," Thane said.

Two more guards pulled her up by her arms. "Now, where is the orb that you stole?"

Callie hung her head. She had failed. Worse still, her brothers were dead. Dead because of her. Bile rose in her throat and she vomited onto the ground.

Now she wondered if there was any hope left.

CHAPTER 2

Aidan Wilson swore under his breath as he took another wrong turn.

Holy spirits, where is that tavern? He wanted to get settled and make sure he had a room to stay in, since he didn't know how long he would be staying here. It could take a few hours or even days to find the person he was looking for.

He glanced down at his map again. The man who had hired him had given it to him, along with the promise of fifty gold coins if he found and brought in the fugitive. Aidan had found it odd someone had paid him that much to find one person. Stranger still, he hadn't seen the man's face, and his voice had been distorted, too.

He thought the man had been trying to trick him at first. But the map of the city and some of the gold he'd already received had been real enough.

Aidan unfurled another scroll. There was a drawing on it of a young woman with long black hair and blue eyes. She would have been pretty if she didn't have a frown on her face.

Calena Reevus, wanted for stealing a precious artefact from the high lord.

Aidan had never liked coming to the realm of Entara. It was an odd place, split into different sectors and had a high wall around the entire region that kept people in and separated. Lyris was unlike the cities he usually worked in and he had been all over the lower realm and beyond. Even as far as the five lands of Almara. He went wherever the promise of good coin took him. Tracking down rogues and fugitives paid well, and he never liked to be stuck in one place for too long.

His benefactor hadn't told him much about Calena Reevus. Other than the fact she had stolen a powerful orb and it was paramount, he recovered both of them. Aidan didn't know what the orb was or did. It didn't matter to him either.

Aidan had already been passing through one of the sectors when he'd met a cloaked man who insisted he wanted to hire Aidan.

Entara wasn't a great place to find work. Aidan only stopped there last night because it had been too late to catch a ship to the next realm.

He ran a hand through his short, curly blonde hair and sighed. If he couldn't find the tavern, he would set off for the citadel. That was where Calena had last been seen.

Aidan would find out what he could about her, knowing things about people such as where they liked to frequent and who they cared for helped when tracking them down.

Aidan passed through streets that were lined with dozens of beggars. Filthy people with empty eyes and thin frames.

He hated slavery. It was something all druids were raised to oppose. At least they were supposed to be. Archdruid Fergus Valeran had created many new slavery laws, often enslaving entire races. The fact Aidan had once worked for the man still bothered him. Back then, he hadn't known better though. He thought he'd been fighting for a better future. How naïve he had been.

Aidan didn't like it, but he knew there was nothing much he could do about it. He'd had encounters with the resistance and things never ended well for them. They usually ended up dead, but that didn't stop him from working with them when he could. A good friend had introduced him to them, and he felt like he could make a difference in a way he could never have during his days in the Dragon Guard.

He stalked through the streets and covered his nose at the stench. He had heard the old city had been clean and thriving. They had erected everything here on the cheap. Buildings were made from either wood or cheap grey stone—nothing like the shiny city of black stone that this realm had once been renowned for.

Legend had it that the stone used to build the old city had held magical properties, like the stone from the mines. After Aron had come to rule here, places had been knocked down and the stone mined. Over the years, the mines had run out. Or soon would, from what he'd heard.

The citadel loomed like a dark beast at the centre of the new city of Lyris. Its walls shimmered with the ancient onyx stone that hummed with energy. That stuff had made Entara such a desirable realm. Blackstone held and retained energy the way most rocks on Erthea couldn't.

Aidan headed back to the entrance of the citadel and waited until a guard he knew that worked there came out. A few moments later, a scrawny looking man with misty brown hair came out.

"I need to know everything you can tell me about a woman named Calena Reevus. She worked here as a maid." Aidan leaned against a wall and took out a few coins. "There's some gold in it for you, if you can help me find her."

The guard gave a harsh laugh. "Oh, I know who you mean. Just heard she's been captured." He grinned.

"By whom?"

"The guard, of course. Doesn't sound like they found the orb she stole, but they'll get answers from her. Then the witch will burn."

Aidan's shoulders slumped. That meant there wouldn't be a payday. Spirits damn it. He had been so sure he would be able to find Calena before the guard did. Finding people was what he was good at. It set him apart from other mercenaries who usually never followed through on their hired jobs.

Unless he found the orb first, the man who hired him wanted both Calena and the orb.

"Where was she captured?" Aidan asked.

Maybe all hope wasn't lost yet.

"In the old city near a circle. The high lord suspected she'd go there." The guard looked around, uneasy. Aidan knew he would get in trouble if either of them were caught, but he didn't sense anyone nearby. They were safe enough for now.

"Thanks." He tossed the guard a couple of coins, which only earned him a grumble from the man. What did the guard expect? If he couldn't get hold of Calena, he wouldn't get the gold he had been promised.

Aidan headed back up the street, careful to avoid the beggars and crowds of people on their way in and out of the citadel. The old city was off-limits and surrounded by the great wall.

The wall remained guarded at all times. There were too many patrols around there to get through undetected.

Aidan knew the risk involved, but he didn't want to let down the person who hired him. They had sounded desperate. Although he couldn't be sure if it had been because they had wanted to find Calena or the orb. He guessed it was the latter.

He never failed a job before and wasn't about to start now. Aidan always got his quarry. No matter what went wrong.

He would bribe a few guards if he had to. Aidan knew the wall well enough to know a possible way to sneak into the old city. Perhaps the orb would still be there if they hadn't found it yet. At least then he could complete one part of this job.

Aidan hurried through the streets, keeping to back alleys. The cover of night kept him hidden. It would be several hours before dawn came, so he had time.

Up ahead, he spotted a group of three guards dragging someone along.

The person had a bag over their head and was thrashing against them.

Aidan stopped and hid behind the wall of a house. Judging by the skirt, he guessed it could be a woman.

Was it Calena herself?

"Hold her still," the first guard said.

The woman spun and kicked the first guard in the gut. The man doubled over in pain.

The hood fell off her face, but Aidan couldn't make out her features.

She spun again and kicked the second guard in the face, loosening her ropes she raised her hand and hit the third guard in the face with a bolt of purple energy.

Then she turned around and ran in the opposite direction. Aidan had to admit she had fought well. He admired her tenacity.

Since he was headed the same way, he took off after her. If he caught her, he might get some extra coin and didn't like to throw away a golden opportunity.

He spotted the woman ahead. She was about to climb over the wall of a house.

The woman scrambled to get her footing on the wall then slipped.

"Need a hand?" Aidan asked.

The woman whirled around, and Aidan gasped.

Her dark hair was wild around her face, eyes wide and cautious. Calena Reevus. The woman he'd been hired to find.

What were the odds of running into her?

"The guards are behind you." Aidan inclined his head in the opposite direction.

Calena narrowed her eyes. "Please help me. The future of my people is at stake. I have to get to the old city."

Aidan hesitated. He could either hand her over to the guards or go with her until he could find the orb.

Helping a fugitive could land him in even more trouble. It was a crime punishable by death. Yet the man who'd hired him had insisted he do whatever it took to find Calena and help her, if necessary.

Was it worth a few dozen gold coins?

Then again, if he found the orb, he would be a hero to the high lord. Maybe that would be enough to spare him execution.

"Please, I can't do this alone," Calena said. "They already killed my brothers."

Aidan sighed. "We need to move. I know another way to get to the wall. Let's go."

They fled down a nearby alley. Shouts echoed in the distance, along with the sound of running footsteps. Aiden kept one hand on the hilt of his sword and his senses on alert as they moved.

Around another corner, they came face-to-face with two guards.

Aidan drew his sword. Steel clashed as the guards drew their weapons.

Aidan didn't have time for this. More guards would be on their way.

Get back, he told Calena in thought. He had no idea if she would hear him but said it anyway. *Cover your eyes.*

Aidan raised his hand and chanted words to a spell.

He shielded his own eyes as a burst of light exploded around them.

Calena yelped.

Aidan lowered his arm. Both guards now lay on the ground, unconscious.

The third guard lunged at Calena, dagger in hand.

Calena muttered something; the dagger flew into her hand. The guard lunged at her and she stabbed him in the stomach in one swift move.

Aidan gasped. "You killed him."

She narrowed her eyes. "The only good guard is a dead one." She made a move to do the same to the other two.

"Leave them. Spirits, you'll be in even more trouble now if you're one of them."

"But they'll follow—" she protested.

"We're already being followed. Let's go."

They hurried around another bend and found it ended at a dead-end. Nothing but a stone wall stood in their way.

"Take my hand," Aidan said.

Calena frowned. "Why?"

"Just trust me."

Calena grasped his hand. Aidan chanted words of power and together they passed through the wall that blocked their way.

CHAPTER 3

Callie gasped as they passed right through the wall. Her head spun from the odd sensation. "How…?"

"No time to explain. We need to move, or the guards will find us."

"But—" she wanted to ask him dozens of questions. Like how he'd spoken in her mind and how they had passed through the wall. There was no time for any of that. She stopped for a moment to catch her breath. "Thanks."

Callie had no idea who this man was, but she thanked the gods he had come her way. Most people would never have bothered to help her. They were too wrapped up in their own problems to care about others. Allies were rare except for her resistance contact, who had been killed earlier that night. She had never even known his name or had a chance to thank him.

The newcomer had surprised her when he'd come with her too. Although she hadn't been happy when he stopped her from killing those other two guards. Nor could she understand why he'd stopped her. Guards were a danger. Callie didn't like to kill, but she never had a choice.

Besides, she was already a fugitive. One more crime would do nothing to her.

All it would do was annoy the guards a little more. Any strike against Aron was worthwhile in her opinion.

"We need to keep moving," he insisted, his eyes darting in every direction. "Come on."

Callie spotted a discarded shawl and picked it up. Maybe it would help to disguise her. So, she wrapped it around her head. "Do you have a name?"

"Be quiet." He glared at her.

Argh, he had a winning personality; it seemed.

"We're going the wrong way. The wall is in the opposite direction."

"We are not going to the wall."

"And where are we going?" Her hand went to the dagger she had stolen earlier. Callie couldn't afford to keep using magic. If she did, she wouldn't have enough to perform the spell. Somehow, she doubted her rescuer would lend her any energy to aid with it either. His help wouldn't extend that far. "We have to go. I have to get into the old city. It is of vital importance."

"We'll hide out somewhere safe then—"

"You don't understand," Callie snapped. "If I don't get into the old city, I'll lose the one chance I have of saving my people."

"Stop arguing with me. I don't think you realise how much trouble you're in, woman," he hissed.

Callie put her hands on her hips. "You don't realise how important saving my people is. Dozens of people will die if I don't get to the city."

"You didn't have a problem extinguishing that guard's life."

"Guards are not important. My people are. Guards are the enemy. They kill people here every day and—" Callie stopped as he grabbed her arm and pulled her to the ground with him. A bolt of energy shot over their heads, hitting the side of the house behind them.

Guards swarmed around them, each with a staff weapon. Wonderful, it was the elite guard. They were much more well-armed than the ones they had dealt with earlier. That made them harder to escape from and even harder to kill.

"Stun them," Callie whispered. "Like you did earlier.'

"There's too many. I'll distract them. Be ready to move."

Callie nodded.

"Avock!"

Light burst around them. Bright as the midday sun. Callie squeezed her eyes shut against the glare and stars danced across her vision. She wished she had had the foresight to shield herself with her arm before he'd done that.

He grabbed her arm and pulled her up. Together they ran.

More blasts darted after them.

Callie cried out as heat seared the back of her shoulder. She stumbled and fell to her knees as another grazed her back.

He stopped and dragged her up. "I know somewhere safer first." He raised his free hand. The side of the wall exploded, sending piles of rubble over the alley. The pile of stones would slow the guards down for a while at least. Either that, or they would find another easy way around.

Together they went through the deserted streets, then ducked inside a tavern. Callie grabbed an old shawl along the way and used it to cover her face.

The smell of smoke hit her and made her cough along with the stench of cheap ale and watered-down wine.

"Why are we here?" Callie hissed. "You said you could get to the great wall." She didn't have time to waste. Why had he brought her here? Did he plan to attack her?

No, this didn't seem like an ideal place to do that with so many witnesses around. Still, Callie would keep an eye on him. No doubt there was a high price on her head.

If only her resistance contact had managed to get aid. If she and her brothers had more help, things might have turned out differently. Her brothers might still be alive, and they might have been able to sense the guards before they surrounded them.

Callie sighed. No point in dwelling on what might have been. She couldn't change the past, only the outcome of the future. If that was still possible.

"That changed when you killed that guard."

Callie didn't like killing, but she never had a choice. It was to kill or be killed when it came to the guards.

With his short, curly blonde hair and blue eyes, he looked very different from the usual men she encountered in Lyris. He wore a yellow tunic, brown jerkin and black trousers. His sword was well made, and he looked too clean for someone of this realm.

His energy didn't feel like that of a sorcerer either.

Then what was he?

Her newfound helper approached the bar and asked for a room.

The tavern keeper disappeared.

"Why do we need a room?" Callie hissed. "We need to leave."

"We need to lay low. You're injured."

Callie pulled her shawl tighter. "We don't need a room."

"You're injured. You need tending to. Plus, we need to lay low."

Callie winced at the pain from her injuries. "I don't have a lot of time."

The tavern keeper gave him a key once he handed over a few coins.

They headed up to a small room with little more than a bed, skinny window, and a bowl for washing.

"I'm Callie."

"I know who you are."

She froze. "How?"

"You're a fugitive."

"And you are?"

"Aidan." He fumbled around in the small pack he carried and tossed her a small jar. "Here. It's a healing balm." He then turned around.

Callie unscrewed the jar and winced at the smell. "Why did you help me?"

"I have my reasons."

Callie rubbed some of it onto her shoulder and the other places where she had been struck.

"Why are you so desperate to get to the old city?" Aidan asked.

"There's something I need there." Warmth spread over her shoulder, and the pain lessened. "What is this ointment?"

"It's made by the druids."

"Is that what you are?"

Few druids came to this part of the lower realm. But that would explain his strange powers. Their magic came from Erthea itself. It wasn't tied to one realm like the Entarans was.

Callie had always envied them for that. As long as their world existed, the druids would never have to worry about losing their powers.

"Why are you in Lyris?" She sat and rubbed some of the ointment on the back of her legs. Her dress had holes in the skirt and on the back of the shoulder from where she had been hit.

"For work. Can I turn around now?"

Callie hesitated. Although he had helped her, she didn't know whether she could trust this man. "I'm done." Callie screwed the lid back on the jar.

Aidan turned around and raised his hand. With a few strange words, ropes wrapped around her wrists.

"What the... What are you doing?"

"I was sent to find you. I'm a mercenary. You are Calena Reevus, wanted for theft and illegal magic," Aidan said. "Once I turn you over to the person who hired me, I won't have to worry about getting into any more unnecessary trouble."

"But... But... Didn't you hear anything I told you?" Callie's dark eyes flashed.

"Yes, I heard the nonsense you said."

"It's not nonsense." She tugged at the rope but couldn't move her hands. "It's true. If I don't cast the spell, magic will vanish from Entara. My people are tied to this land. If the magic dies, so will we."

Aidan scoffed. "That's ridiculous. There are dozens of people—"

"Yes, and they're all forced to answer to Lord Aron. He is ravaging the realm of its natural resources." She fumbled with the ropes again.

"That's not my problem. I only saved you to get the gold."

Callie's mind raced. She couldn't miss a chance to get to the circle or her people were doomed. What could she say to convince him to do the right thing?

"You can have even more gold if you take me to the old city." She didn't have any gold to give, but she had to say something. If she had a way to get away from him, if he didn't help her, then he was no use to her.

Aidan raised an eyebrow. "How?"

"There's something important there. If you let me go and retrieve it, you will get double what you were offered. No doubt about it."

Callie had no idea who, or why, anyone would pay for her capture. It must be because of the orb. Aron knew how valuable it was.

It could only be used on the day of the solstice.

81

"Take me to the old city. We both know it's not only me you were hired to retrieve."

Aidan sighed. "Don't think of escaping. I'm in enough trouble because of you already."

"Then you know a sacred artefact is the only way to redeem yourself." Callie would take him with her, for now.

"You better not be lying. Let's go."

CHAPTER 4

After leaving the tavern, they hurried back through the deserted streets. They were careful to check for any potential guards after what had happened earlier. Aidan kept his senses on alert as they went. He didn't want to be caught by surprise again, but he knew the ways of druid-trained guards. They would do everything to shield themselves until they were right upon them.

"How did you do that?" Callie stared at the wall in disbelief.

Aidan's head spun. He hadn't used that kind of magic in months, but it did come in handy at times like this.

"A little magic I learnt in my days in the Dragon Guard." Aidan let go of her hand. "Come on, show me where the orb is."

"It's not that simple." Callie scowled at him.

Aidan wondered why he had agreed to this. Sure, extra gold would be nice, but this woman was more trouble than she was worth. She had already killed one guard and dragged him into her mess.

Why had he agreed to help her?

He couldn't be sure. Aidan didn't believe the nonsense she had said about saving her people. It sounded too impossible to be true.

Aidan would get her to retrieve the orb, then hand her and it over to the man who had hired him. Then he could finally leave this spirit forsaken realm for good.

There were plenty of realms that had jobs that were far less troublesome than this.

"You? In the Dragon Guard?" Callie scoffed. "Guess I shouldn't be surprised. I heard how much they terrorise people."

Aidan's jaw clenched. He shouldn't have to defend himself to her, of all people. "You don't know anything about the guard. Not all of them are bad. We worked for honour and—"

"And decimated entire towns on the order of the Archdruid," Callie snapped. "A man who enslaves entire races. And he put Aron in power here."

Aidan opened his mouth to protest and closed it. He couldn't deny the Archdruid had done all of those terrible things. And much worse. The current Archdruid was just as bad as his father had been, perhaps worse. It was one of the many reasons he had chosen to leave the guard and helped the resistance as much as he could.

"Not all druids are bad," he growled. "Don't be so quick to judge." He had a good friend in the resistance, Darius Valeran, the son of the current Archdruid. But he couldn't mention that to Callie.

Any ties he had to the resistance would have to remain secret. His connection to them wasn't as strong as Darius' anyway. He helped when he could, but didn't make a show of it. Getting too involved would get him killed.

The Archdruid had clamped down on anyone being part of the resistance over recent years. Anyone suspected of involvement was usually tortured until they confessed then executed.

Callie fiddled with the ropes on her wrists. He caught her doing it whenever she thought he wasn't looking. She wouldn't get free. The ropes were spelled so only he could remove them.

"Where is the orb then?" Aidan didn't like wandering around in the dark. It felt like the shadows were watching their every move. There could be guards too, lurking around every corner. Or for all he knew, Aron could have spies positioned around the city. The spirit is nearly Archdruid and has spies everywhere in almost every realm.

The guard would know they would come here, since this was where Callie had been captured. He scanned the surrounding area again and checked for any trace of different presences. Just because he didn't sense anything, didn't mean people weren't there. He knew how the guard worked and acted.

Callie's eyes narrowed. "I am not going to tell you that. You'd probably kill me and take the orb for yourself."

Aidan gave a harsh laugh. "I don't kill unless I have to, and I won't kill you for a few extra coins either." He might be a mercenary, but he still had a conscience.

Callie scoffed. "Then what do you call turning me over to the guard? You'll be condemning both me and my people to death."

He sighed. "Not this again. Look, what happens to you isn't my concern."

"Only the gold matters, right?"

"No." His jaw tightened. "Maybe you should have kept your head down instead of stealing from the high lord."

Callie's mouth fell open as she glowered at him. "Aron stole everything from my people. Our culture, our resources, our very lives," she snapped. "Using the orb is the only way to stop him."

"How will the orb do that?"

Callie hesitated and fell silent.

"Tell me then." Aidan didn't believe much of it but enjoyed a good tale. He might as well hear her out.

"When Aron arrived, he overthrew the old Lord of Entara. The city was so different then." She shook her head. "The orb is used as part of a spell that can revitalise the land. It can only be cast on the eve of the solstice."

"That's today."

"Yes, I'm the only one left who knows how to cast it. Aron wants to use the orb for his own means. This is the last chance I have." Callie looked away. "There's no one else left. I lost my brothers today."

Guilt swelled in his chest. He had lost his family as a boy when his village had been attacked.

"I am—I'm sorry for your loss." He averted his gaze. What else could he say? No words were enough to make up for losing loved ones.

Steel sang as she yanked his sword from its sheath.

"Hey," Aidan gasped.

Callie pointed the sword at his chest. "I'm going to cast that spell. If you get in my way—"

Aidan pushed the tip of the sword away and tried to disarm her.

Callie blocked his attempt.

Aidan raised his hands in surrender. "Okay, let's talk about—"

"I don't have time to talk. You've done nothing but get in my way." Callie aimed the sword at his chest again.

"Wait, let's not do anything drastic. Give me the sword and I'll—"

"Turn me over to Aron's men," she finished for him. "I should kill you." The sword quivered as her hand shook.

"Callie, killing me won't help you save your people." Aidan looked for an opening. A way of getting the sword out of her grasp. He found none. If he provoked her, she would stab him.

"Get on your knees," she ordered.

"What?" Aidan racked his brain for a way out. Now, what was she planning to do?

How could he have let his guard down around her? He knew better than that. Aidan didn't think she would kill him, but he couldn't be certain. She had no qualms about killing the guard who had just been doing his job and following orders.

Aidan recognised the desperation in her eyes. He had seen it during his days in the guard.

Callie swung the sword and used the hilt to hit him across the head.

Stars flashed across his eyes as he slumped to the ground face first. He groaned as his head pounded like a heavy drum.

Aidan murmured words of power. The aching eased—part of him wanted to give in to the blackness that threatened to drag him under.

He scrambled up, and it took a few moments for his vision to become clearer. Callie had already run off. He couldn't see any sign of her.

He had to get his sword back. That thing had been part of him since his days in the Dragon Guard.

Besides, he was already in trouble. What else did he have to lose?

Aidan finally spotted Callie up ahead as she weaved in and out of the ruins. Slivers of moonlight made the remnants of black stone glisten like tiny diamonds.

Callie stood rummaging round the side of a broken wall. "The orb is gone!" she cried. "How can it be gone? I left it here."

Aidan rubbed his aching head, then used his free hand. "Sword." His sword laid at Callie's feet, flew through the air towards him. He caught hold of it, glad of the familiar weight in his hand.

Callie spun around. "You again," she groaned.

"Me again." He flashed her a weak smile.

"The orb is missing." She ran a hand through her long black hair. "It can't be gone. I hid it."

Aidan cast his senses out and scanned the wall with his mind. If the orb was here, he should sense something. Nothing came to him. "Is the orb warded or shielded somehow?"

Callie glowered at him. "My brother cast runes over it. I don't know how effective they would be. Someone must have taken it."

"You didn't bother to ward it?" Aidan gaped at her.

"I don't have unlimited power like you do it. My magic is weak. It took me weeks to gain enough power to do the spell, and I've wasted so much of it on you and—"

Several guards emerged from the shadows—staff weapons aimed at them.

Spirits, why hadn't he sensed them? He kept his mind on alert for any sign of another presence nearby. Either he was losing his touch, or they had become much better at shielding themselves.

Aidan's hand went to the sword, but he knew full well he wouldn't be able to take all of them down. A few light tricks wouldn't work against them this time, either. Something did prickle at the edge of his senses, though. Something powerful.

One guard grabbed Callie and yanked her hands behind her back.

They would need help to get out of this.

If anyone can hear me, this is Aidan Wilson, I am in Antara. Send help as soon as possible. He put one hand behind his back so he could use his magic without being seen.

General Thane appeared. "You led us on a merry chase, Calena. Now it's over. Take them away."

CHAPTER 5

Callie couldn't believe they had captured her again. Worse still, she had lost the orb. For a moment, she had almost thought they would make it to the spell circle and succeed in casting the spell.

She couldn't understand why Thane kept demanding she tell him where it was. He'd questioned her for a while earlier before throwing her in this cell and taking Aidan out. No doubt to interrogate him as well.

Shadows danced around the tiny cell. It stank of dampness and she shivered as water dripped down the dark grey stone walls. She wished they had let her keep her cloak so she would have some kind of warmth. Callie could no longer use her magic either, since she now had spelled metal bonds around her wrists that bound magic and prevented the user from using it.

Callie had hidden the orb in the wall. The only other people who had known about it were her brothers. Her heart ached thinking of them. She only had one brother left now. Nate, he was barely more than a boy. Now she would probably never see him again.

Callie slumped back against the wall. She had failed her people. Her family. Everyone.

If that damned druid hadn't waylaid her, perhaps she would have had a chance. No. Succeeding in casting the spell had been near impossible from the beginning.

Now she had lost everything.

Callie pulled her knees up to her chest and buried her face in her hands. I'm sorry, Papa. I know I promised you I would do everything I could to protect our people.

The cell's outer door opened.

They shoved Aidan back inside.

Odd, she expected them to kill him already.

He slumped down on the dirty floor beside her. The only light came from a flickering torch outside the cell. The door only had a small narrow slit for bars.

"I'm sorry you got dragged into this," Callie murmured. "I only wanted to keep my vow to my father." She leaned back against the wall, ignoring the drops of icy water that slid down the back of her neck. Did it matter? They would kill her soon enough. That much she knew. There was no hope now—no chance of getting out.

Callie resigned herself to her fate. She only hoped the execution came sooner rather than later. At least once in death, she would be reunited with the rest of her family. She only hoped they could forgive her for her failure. What would they say when they found out she didn't cast the spell?

It didn't matter. At least she would be with them again, in a world much better than this one.

Aidan frowned. "What vow?"

"To help our people. After Aron killed him, my brothers and I vowed to do everything in our power to save them from Aron's tyranny." She sighed. "Roderick and Tyrone are dead. Soon I will be too. And Nate…" Tears dripped down her cheek. "At least he is far from this realm. Perhaps the Reevus bloodline may continue with him."

"Wait, Reevus, I know that name from somewhere." Aidan furrowed his brow. "Lord Baltazar—Baltazar Reevus. That's your father, isn't it?"

Callie nodded. "He was a great man. He treated my people fairly until Aron…" She shut her eyes. "It doesn't matter. The mines are almost empty. There is no hope left."

"What does the spell do? The one you mentioned?"

She hesitated. She had always promised never to reveal that spell to anyone. It had been handed down in her family for generations.

"It draws magic back into the land to the one who blessed this realm. Through Naga, the first Dragonkind." It didn't matter if she told him. The secret would die with her anyway.

"A dragon? That's what this is about?"

"Dragons came here from the lower realm. Naga blessed this island with her fire." Callie rested her head on her knees. "It's why the Blackstone only comes from this realm. Dragons were kept here for centuries until Aron killed them all. I need the orb and the bones of a dragon in the spell circle for the spell to work. That was the plan."

"We need to work out a way to get out of here."

Callie lifted her head and frowned. "You know that's hopeless."

"No, it's not. I'm sure we can figure out a way if we put our heads together."

She scoffed at that. "You said you didn't want help. All you care about is the bounty on my head." She gave a harsh laugh. "I doubt you will get that now. Not now the orb is gone." Her mind raced. It still bothered her how the orb had somehow disappeared. Her brother may have spelled it, but she should have been able to sense it. Now she might never know the truth.

"I'm not heartless. I know what it's like to fight for honour."

"You left the Dragon Guard."

Aidan looked away. "I had to. There was so much corruption. And the way they treated the dragons…" He shook his head.

"It doesn't matter. It's too late. The spell had to be cast at dawn on the solstice. The light of the rising sun is the key." Callie didn't know what time it was, but dawn would be fast approaching by now.

She had run out of time. Even if they escaped, it would be too late. The solstice wouldn't come for another year. By then, it would be far too late to imbue the land with dragon magic or revive the old dragon again.

"Dawn is a couple of hours away. We—"

The door that led into the cell block creaked open.

Thane himself approached.

Callie groaned. She didn't need to ask to know he had come to interrogate her about the orb's whereabouts. He could torture her all he liked. She couldn't answer what she didn't know.

"Come, Calena." Thane inclined his head.

Get ready, Aidan's voice rang through her mind.

Callie frowned at him; sure she had imagined it.

A blond-haired young woman rounded the corner. Her long hair fell past her shoulders and she wore a black tunic, black leather jerkin and black trousers. "They're coming with me." She flashed Thane a smile.

Thane narrowed his eyes. "Who are you?"

"I'm no one." She grasped his throat and her blue eyes blurred to black. Energy reverberated from her into Thane. "Release the prisoners."

Callie stumbled as the concussive force of the girl's power rattled against her bones.

Thane stumbled too.

He stood there, dazed, before he drew a knife and unbound Callie and Aidan's bonds.

"Thank the spirits, you got my message," Aidan breathed. "I thought we'd never get out here."

"Don't thank the spirits just yet," the girl said. "We still have to get out of here. Are you both alright?"

Aidan nodded. "We are now."

Callie's mouth fell open. "Wait, what's going on? I don't understand."

"I called the resistance, just before they bound my powers. I thought we might need help," Aidan explained.

"Explanations will have to wait. Let's go." The girl motioned them out. "What's your name?" she asked the commander.

"Fenwick Thane," he answered.

"Alright, Thane. You're going to lead us up to the roof. Let's go."

The four of them hurried out of the cell block.

Callie noticed the girl had disappeared into the shadows when several guards appeared.

"I'm taking the prisoners for interrogation," Thane told them.

Callie froze. Was Thane helping them? Gods, what had the girl done to him? Had she compelled him somehow?

The first guard hesitated. "But, sir, Lord Aron wants the woman in his meeting chamber. That's the opposite way."

All the guards had their hands on their weapons, ready to fire on them.

How would they get past all these men? She doubted even Aidan had the power to do that. But would the strange newcomer help?

Callie still had no idea what the goal was or what her strange powers did. She had never seen anything like it. Such magic was impossible even for sorcerers. No one, save for the Archdruid or those who practice dark magic, could bend someone to their will. At least that was what she had been taught.

"The orders have changed, Captain. Stand aside," Thane ordered.

"I'm sorry, sir, I can't—"

The girl appeared again. "I knew I was going to have to use more energy," she groaned. "Aidan, Callie, stand back."

Both of them drew back. Callie didn't know what the girl was going to do, but she didn't want to get in the crossfire. Her magic was strange and unnatural. Yet somehow Callie didn't think it was dark. At least not in the way she was taught to fear dark magic.

"What is she?" Callie hissed to Aidan. "What is she doing?"

"My guess is a mind whisperer. She works with the resistance."

Mind whisperer? No, it was impossible. They had been wiped out centuries ago by an Archdruid. Mind whisperers had been able to listen to people's thoughts and somehow influence them. Callie supposed the girl matched the stories she had heard about them. But how could one still exist after all this time?

"Her name is Nyx," Aidan added.

Light flashed in Nyx's eyes as waves of energy blasted through the air. Like thunder without sound.

Callie winced, the force of Nyx's power shaking her to her core.

"Alright, boys. You're going to let us go on our way and forget you ever saw us," Nyx told them.

Callie clutched her head, the pressure threatening to overwhelm her. Good Gods, her head pounded from the incredible currents of magic. How did Nyx withstand feeling it? If it were Callie, she knew the force of such magic would tear her body apart.

Nyx stumbled under the force of her power. "Thane, let's move."

Callie and Aidan hurried after them.

"How did you do that?" Aidan asked Nyx. "Only druid-trained warriors have mental shields. I should know, I used to be in the Dragon Guard."

Nyx waved a hand in dismissal. "That's the thing, they're not Dragon Guard. They had basic shields."

They headed to the end of the corridor until they found a set of stairs that led to the roof.

"Thane, you are to go back to your chamber and forget you ever saw us. As far as you know, the prisoners are in their cell. You don't remember being told to retrieve Callie, either," Nyx instructed.

Thane nodded and wandered off, still looking dazed.

"Come on, I don't know how long my power will last on them." Nyx pushed the door open.

Cold air hit Callie's face as she hurried outside.

A dark shadow loomed up ahead.

Callie gasped when she realised it was a massive dragon. Beside it stood a young man with long, black hair tied at the nape of his neck and he had piercing blue eyes. He wore a dark tunic and trousers. A forest green cloak adorned his shoulders.

"Holy spirits, Darius." Aidan grinned and clapped the other man on the back. "I had no idea you would come."

"Ambrose said you needed a quick getaway." Darius motioned to the dragon. "We got here as soon as we could."

Callie's mouth fell open. No, it couldn't be the Archdruid's son. That was impossible.

"You're—" she gasped.

"An annoying druid, I know," Nyx smirked. "Ignore him, I usually do."

"We need to get to the old city. Fast," Aidan added.

The first slivers of light had already appeared on the horizon.

"Dawn is almost here." Callie shook her head.

Darius and Nyx scrambled onto the dragon.

"Come on." Aidan motioned for Callie. "We don't have the bones or the orb. Nor do you have time to search for them." The orb could be anywhere now. It would take too long to search the citadel.

"Do you mean this?" Darius made a small orb appear. "Someone sent this to me earlier."

Callie gasped. He had the orb she had stolen.

"That would be me. Come on, Callie." Aidan climbed on and gave her a hand up.

"I don't understand." Callie bit back a scream as the massive dragon took off. Its wings flapped, moving through the air as the prison vanished behind them.

It took only minutes to get to the old city. Fragmented ruins glittered like tiny stars below them.

Aidan explained as they flew how Darius was a friend and worked with the resistance.

Aidan had called for help and shielded the orb before the guards had come, when he'd sensed them closing in.

Callie's head still spun. She barely believed it when the spell circle appeared.

The dragon descended and Darius handed Callie the orb.

"I don't have the dragon bones. I never found out where my brother hid them." Callie glanced around, half expecting her brother's bodies to still be there. "My brothers…"

Thane and the guards would have left their bodies to rot. They never would have bothered to bury them.

"I cast a spell and moved them. They're buried close by," Darius explained. "Aidan relayed to my mentor about what happened. I'm sorry for your loss."

Callie's chest tightened. She wanted to fall to her knees and weep. But grief would have to wait.

"The spell you're going to use, it imbues the land with energy through a dragon, doesn't it?" Darius asked. "We have a dragon right here." He motioned to the massive beast that stood behind him.

"I need bones, not a living animal," Callie insisted. "That's how the spell works."

"In the light of dawn, on dragon's breath, so shall cover the land with life," Darius recited the old tale. "In its wake shall Blackstone shine and—"

"Life shall flow once more," Callie finished for him. "How do you know that?"

"My mother insisted I have the same education as my older brother—he was my father's heir. I had to learn the history of every realm," Darius explained. "The spell calls for a dragon. It doesn't have to be bones."

Callie opened her mouth to protest. She didn't have time to argue. "Get the dragon in the circle."

Darius raised his hand and chanted a cleansing spell.

All the dust and debris within the circle blew away in a gust of wind.

Callie placed the orb in the centre of the circle and began the chant. Purple light illuminated the circle as the orb flared to life.

A dark shadow blotted out the first rays of dawn's light. A dragon was coming towards them—a rider atop its back.

"We've got company," Nyx remarked.

"It's Aron. I can sense him," Darius said. "He must have realised you escaped."

Callie almost faltered as Aidan took hold of her hands. Strength flooded through her. She realised he had joined his magic with hers.

"Keep going." Darius drew magic. "Kellan, stay," he told the dragon.

Callie continued the chant and more power flared within the circle.

Darius threw a bolt of energy at Lord Aron as he neared them.

"Let life flow back into this land," Callie said.

"Kellan, breathe fire into the circle," Aidan called out to the dragon.

Kellan reared up and shot a plume of fire into the circle. The purple light exploded, sending lines of energy zigzagging round the barren earth.

The great dragon took to the air and hit Aron with a plume of fire. The high lord screamed in agony as flames licked at his flesh, then his body blew apart.

The other dragon screeched, circling around in confusion.

Callie sank to her knees as magic expanded outwards.

Aidan let go of her hands and whistled. The other dragon circled once more then landed by him with a loud thump. "Little trick for the guard."

Light from the circle expanded, rushing over the ruins like a tidal wave. Callie knew the magic was back.

Maybe there was hope for her realm after all.

"It's so pretty," Nyx breathed as sunlight shimmered over remnants of the stone.

"It is." Callie wiped tears from her eyes.

"Aron is dead now. No doubt, my father will send someone to take his place." Darius grimaced.

"Magic flows freely again. My people and I will take back what is ours," Callie said. "Thank you, all of you. I couldn't have done it without you."

"It is what we do," Nyx said.

"Call us if you need anything else. Our contacts within the resistance will be happy to help," Darius said. "Aidan, do you need a lift anywhere? We're headed back to Eldara."

Aidan shook his head. "I think I will stay here for a while. They have a dragon that needs help." He motioned to the one Aron had been riding. "Plus, I think things will be interesting."

"Don't be a stranger." Nyx waved as she and Darius climbed back onto Kellan.

Callie gaped at Aidan. "You're staying?"

"As a criminal, I can do some good here. And you need someone to watch out for you. That's what friends do."

"Friends," Callie murmured.

She hadn't had one of those for a long time.

As they watched the sunrise, it brought new hope to her and her people in the dawn's light.

DANGEROUS TIDES AHEAD

CHAPTER 1

Yasmine stalked into the tavern called the *Flying Dragon*. What a stupid name. Couldn't they come up with something better? Then again, dragons were popular here in the islands of Andovia. Especially with the Archdruid's Dragon Guard ruling the skies.

Iron chandeliers lit the darkened room, music drifted through and the smell of cheap wine and ale struck her nose.

Yasmine couldn't believe she had set foot on Eldara. As a pirate, she never set foot in high-risk places like this. Eldara was the realm of the druids, but a lot of the Forest Guard and the Dragon Guard came here. But Yasmine didn't have a choice. She had lost her ship and her crew. Now she needed someone to help her get them both back.

She scanned the bar area but found no sign of her quarry. Typical. She stalked up to the bar and kept the hood of her cloak over her face. Her long brown hair fell in loose waves and her blue eyes scanned everything.

Gods, why couldn't that druid be here when she needed him? She kept her senses on alert as she did another scan of the tavern. If someone recognised her, she would soon earn a trip to the hangman's noose. She usually met Darius Valeran in less public places during her dealings with the resistance. But she needed to find him, and fast.

Yasmine knew he worked in the Forest Guard, but she couldn't just ask anyone where she could find him. She had no glamour spell to disguise herself with, and there was a pretty large price on her head. It made her laugh to think they considered piracy a crime. Especially after all the awful things the Dragon Guard were infamous for.

At the bar, a young man with a mop of dark hair and amber eyes came up to her.

Yasmine still found it strange to be around other druids again. Not that she considered herself one now. She didn't quite follow their ways, nor would she follow the Archdruid either. People would be much better off not listening to anything the Archdruid said and to steer clear of anything he did.

"Can I get you anything?" the man asked.

He looked no older than nineteen. Only a few years younger than her. He wasn't a druid and didn't look fae either. He moved with grace. A lykae, perhaps. She had encountered a few of them in Almara. What was one of them doing in Eldara? Lykaes kept to themselves and didn't associate with other races.

"I'm looking for Darius Valeran," Yasmine kept her voice low. "You're a friend of his, aren't you?" She knew she'd seen the lykae with Darius before. Yet his name eluded her.

The lykae narrowed his eyes. "Who wants to know?"

Yasmine leaned forward. "I need to see Valeran now. It's urgent."

He inhaled. "You smell like a druid, but saltier. You… likely spend a lot of time at sea."

"I'm Yasmine Oberon. Valeran knows me. Just tell me where I can find him." She gripped the edge of the bar and fought to keep her temper under control. Why couldn't he just call Valeran and get him here? Why did she have to wait and answer stupid questions?

He leaned closer. "Why?"

"I help the resistance. I'm the captain of the *Vanity*. I need his help to get my ship and crew back. Please tell me where he is."

She would search the entire island if she had to. It wouldn't be that hard to find the son of the Archdruid. Everyone knew who he was. Someone must have seen him.

"Darius will be here soon. Can I get you a drink?"

Yasmine took some coins out of the pouch at her hip. She only had little money with her. Everything she had *earned* had been on the

Vanity. That ship was her home, and she would not give it up without a fight. "Give me an ale."

Once she had her drink, she stalked over to a dark corner where she could sit out of sight and away from the tavern's other patrons.

Her mind raced. How someone had been able to take both her ship and crew, she couldn't fathom. Her crew was the only family she had ever known, and they wouldn't leave her.

A while later a young man with long blond hair came over. He wore the dark uniform of the Forest Guard with a white tree emblazoned on his tunic.

Darius Valeran, second son of the Archdruid. Captain in the Forest Guard and friend to the resistance. He looked even more handsome than when she had last seen him. His fair blond hair was tied back at the nape of his neck and his cool, blue eyes roamed over her. Although only nineteen, he was turning into a strong, handsome man.

A young woman came up beside him. Yasmine didn't recognise her. She had long, bright pink hair that fell in a plait at her waist. Large purple wings were felled at her back. Her piercing blue eyes scanned Yasmine.

Somehow, it felt like she was seeing into Yasmine's soul. An aura of power clung to her; unlike anything Yasmine had seen before.

Holy spirits, what was she? Yasmine could tell she was some type of fae given her wings and appearance, but why was she so powerful?

"Yasmine, it's been a while." Darius sat down. "I didn't expect you to come here. Especially without a glamour. This is Nyx Ashwood."

Nyx sat down beside Darius but said nothing. Her gaze bored into Yasmine.

"I need your help. Will the Black stole my ship and my crew."

"What does that have to do with me?" Darius asked.

Yasmine stared at him in disbelief. "Have you forgotten my ship is one of the few the resistance has access to?"

If he refused to help her, she didn't know who she would turn to. Most of her allies lay far beyond this realm. It had taken her a couple of days to get here by stowing away on another vessel.

Darius shook his head. "That's not true. We have access to a couple of others."

Yasmine scoffed. "Yes, small ones. Have you forgotten how many slaves I've helped you rescue, Valeran?"

"Are you sure someone kidnapped your crew?" Nyx spoke up. "Are they free to come and go? Or are they slaves?"

Yasmine scowled. "I despise slavery and yes, Will the Black did kidnap them." She heaved a sigh. "Who are you anyway?"

"Technically, I'm his servant." Nyx scowled.

"She works with me," Darius added. "How do you expect me to help?"

"You are the Archdruid's son. You have an entire fleet of ships at your disposal."

Darius laughed. "No, I turned my back on that life, remember? My father would never give me a ship. They use ships here for trade and transport, not pleasure."

Yasmine gritted her teeth. "I don't have anyone else to turn to. There must be something you can do. I thought you were my friend, Valeran."

"Yas, I'm sorry. There's no way I can get you a ship. Nor are you going to steal one. You know how well guarded the docks on all four of the Andovian islands are."

Yasmine sighed. Maybe she had been a fool to come here. She had no other friends with the kind of influence Darius had. Pirates were not friends with each other either. She could steal another ship, but she wouldn't leave her crew to rot. To find them and get them back, she would need help. She couldn't take down Will's crew by herself.

"I can steal a ship easy enough," Yasmine said. "I just need a few people to serve as crew until I find Will and my ship."

"No, you are not stealing anything." Darius gripped the table.

What had she been thinking? She should have known his damned morality would get in the way. He always was too moral for his own good.

"She's telling the truth." Nyx turned to Darius. "Maybe we should help her. I've seen how many people she has helped. Her ship and her crew will be a huge loss to the resistance if we don't get them back."

Yasmine's eyes widened. "You saw? Are you a seer?"

Nyx snorted. "No, I'm a long story."

101

"Yasmine, we can't take the risk—" Darius protested.

Nyx cut him off. "Everything we do is a risk, druid. We don't even have to steal a ship. I can use my influence and get a captain to line up one for us for a few days. We can find her ship, save her crew, and be back in time."

Yasmine didn't know what to make of the strange fae friend but was glad Nyx seemed to be on her side. At least more than Darius was.

"You're going to seduce a captain?" Yasmine frowned. "Don't get me wrong, you are pretty but—"

Nyx's lip curled. "No, not seduce. Yuck! The captain will give us their ship."

Darius shook his head. "No. No, we are not—"

"Do you have a better idea, druid?" Nyx arched an eyebrow at him.

Darius opened and closed his mouth. "Fine, we'll help you, but you owe me after this, Yasmine."

CHAPTER 2

Darius wondered how he'd gotten roped into this, as he and Nyx's headed down to the docks the next morning to meet Yasmine. Rays of sunlight splintered over the morning sky, and clouds hung heavily over the blue waves.

If they got caught, there would be no end to the trouble he would face. But Yasmine was an old friend and had been invaluable to the resistance over the years. Especially by helping to move slaves around the islands.

Still, he didn't like the idea of Nyx using her abilities. As a mind whisperer, she could not only hear thoughts but also compel others to do her bidding. He had tried to talk her out of it, but she refused. He couldn't come up with a better way of helping Yasmine either.

Thievery was never his first course of action. To Nyx, it came naturally since she had grown up as a thief.

"Would you stop looking so nervous?" Nyx hissed. "You are usually good at hiding your emotions."

Darius flinched. He was immune to her powers, so she couldn't read his thoughts. Somehow, he could neutralise her powers as well.

"I can't help being anxious. This whole thing is madness."

Nyx placed her hands on her hips. "Do you doubt my powers now, druid?"

Darius snorted. "No, but we can't rely on your powers for everything."

He had seen some of the things Nyx was capable of doing first hand but it still worried him. Darius had considered using his magic to convince the captain to let them borrow a ship, but that meant using high magic. He toed the line of darkness whenever he used such magic.

"You could just ask a captain and use your rank to get a ship," Nyx pointed out.

Darius shook his head. "Word would get around and then we'd all be in trouble." He ran a hand through his long hair. "I still can't believe you volunteered us to go with her. I have duties here too."

Nyx waved a hand in dismissal. "Your general will understand. You can tell him you had business with your father."

Sometimes he hated how well she knew him, even though they had only known each other for a few months.

Darius scanned the dock, but there was no sign of Yasmine. He didn't sense her presence either.

"So, Yasmine is a druid?" Nyx asked as she arched an eyebrow.

He nodded. "Yes, I've known her since childhood."

Yasmine was older than him, but Darius's nursemaid had taken her in and they had become friends. She had left a couple of years ago to travel, and he'd only seen her a few times since then; during missions with the resistance.

"She was telling the truth. I saw it in her mind. You don't have to worry about her deceiving us."

Darius shook his head again. "I'm more worried about exposure. We agreed to keep your powers hidden. Maybe I should—"

Nyx scowled at him. "No, you're not using high magic. We both know you might lose control."

"I am much more in control of my powers than you are of yours." Darius had spent years training and learning how to use high magic. Nyx had only recently started learning how to control her powers a few months ago.

"I have better control now than I used to." Nyx crossed her arms. "I haven't lost control in quite a while, nor have I used my influence on anyone."

She had a point there.

"Where is that pirate?" Nyx glanced round. "I thought she would be here by now given how desperate she was for help."

Darius cast his senses out. Yasmine was never late, and he knew how desperate she'd been.

A cloaked figure advanced around the dock. Moving past each ship.

"There she is." He inclined his head towards the figure. He would know Yasmine's energy anywhere.

"She's inspecting ships," Nyx lowered her voice as they headed towards the figure.

"Yasmine?" Darius approached her and Yasmine spun around. Her long brown hair spilled out from her hood and her blue eyes narrowed for a moment.

"Don't sneak up on me like that, Valeran." She glowered at him. "And don't call me by name either. There are always guards patrolling around the dock. If someone sees me, I'll be arrested and executed for piracy."

"You should always be alert. Ambrose taught us to be better than that." He had already told his mentor, Ambrose, about helping Yasmine. The other druid had agreed they should help the poor. Though, Darius would have been even more grateful to his mentor if he had instead come up with a reason for them to not help Yasmine. Or at least found another way to help her that didn't involve him travelling into unknown lands to find her ship.

Yasmine scowled. "Now you sound just like the old goat."

"Do you see anything you like?" Nyx motioned towards the fleet of ships.

Most of them were large trading vessels. Only one was a large warship meant for carrying troops that had come in for repairs. All the ships could sail by sea as well, thanks to the same ancient magic that allowed them to float in air.

"Don't even think about the warship," Darius warned. "It belongs to my father. Stealing that will lead to nothing but a death sentence."

"But a warship would be a lot faster than any of these leaky tubs." Yasmine grinned. "I could blast that other pirate to smithereens."

"Yasmine!" Darius frowned at her. She should know better than that. If she set even a single foot near that ship, he would be tempted to call one of the guards and have her locked up. He wouldn't do that of course. He would never sentence a friend to death, but nor would he let her anywhere near that ship either.

"You are no fun, Valeran."

Darius prayed to the spirits she was only joking. Stealing one of his father's ships would cost them all their heads. He wouldn't put it past her trying to get to that ship, though.

"Pick something small and inconspicuous." Darius crossed his arms.

Yasmine shook her head. "You don't know the first thing about ships."

True enough, but the three of them couldn't man a large vessel by themselves.

"Small means slow," Yasmine snapped. "No, let me do the choosing, Valeran."

Darius and Nyx followed her around the deck, twice. Darius couldn't understand why she couldn't just pick one and be done with it. This was getting tiresome. They stopped by a small vessel with only two levels. It stank of fish.

"This looks suitable," Darius remarked as they were on deck.

"It's a fishing boat." Yasmine glowered at him. "It doesn't even fly. We need a ship that flies to get past the Ring of Sorrow. I'm not taking this anywhere near the Undersea Realm."

"How far are you planning on going?" Darius asked. "You said you were unsure where the Vanity was."

"I have a good idea where to find her. But I'm not taking this thing." Yasmine jumped on over to the deck of a much larger vessel next to the fishing boat.

Darius raised his hands and formed steps in the air to get on deck.

Nyx rolled her eyes, spread her wings, and flew past him.

"Show off," he muttered under his breath.

"This looks a little better," Yasmine conceded.

Darius went to the helm and spotted the runes that allowed the ship to fly. "This one can fly."

An old man joined them on deck. "Thought I heard something. What are you lot doing on my ship?"

"Will this one do?" Darius asked Yasmine and rubbed his temples. He was tired of looking at vessels. It would be easier to buy her one using his own coin, but it would take time to negotiate everything. And it required paperwork that might raise suspicions. No, Yasmine would never go for that.

Yasmine sighed and turned to the captain. "How well does this thing sail?"

"As well as the day I got her. Been trailing back and forth within the slave islands for years."

Nyx flinched. As a former slave, Darius knew that would make her uncomfortable.

"But my ship's not for sale," the captain added.

"When are you next due to sail?" Darius asked.

"Not for another two weeks. She's just had some repairs done and I—" the captain stopped dead. "Lord Valeran… Forgive me, sir. I didn't expect you to—"

Nyx, get to work, Darius told her in thought.

Nyx stepped forward and grasped the man's throat. Energy reverberated through the air like thunder, but without sound, as her eyes glowed.

Darius winced. His bones felt like they rattled, and Yasmine yelped in alarm.

"You are going to let us borrow your ship for the next few days," Nyx instructed. "If anyone asks you about it, you will tell them you lent it to some friends. They are going to return your ship safely back to you. You will forget about seeing Darius, and you won't remember what we look like either."

The man stumbled back, dazed. "Friends…"

"Now go to the tavern and get yourself a drink." Darius handed the man a handful of coins. He hoped it was enough to cover the cost of the ship.

The man wandered off without saying another word.

Yasmine gaped at them. "What was that?" She turned to Nyx. "What are you?"

Nyx glanced at Darius. "I am a mind whisperer."

I told you not to mention that! Darius warned her.

You said we can trust her. I don't sense any threat from her.

Darius sighed. *Fine, but we need to stay on our guard.*

"Mind whisperer?" Yasmine gasped. "They were all but wiped out centuries ago."

"All of them."

Yasmine shook her head and glared at Darius. "You're full of surprises, Valeran. Right, let's sail."

Another man climbed on deck. "Need another pair of hands?"

107

"Who is this?" Yasmine scowled. "You are the lykae."

"This is Lucien. He's a friend. I called him," Darius explained.

Yasmine blew out a breath. "Fine, all hands on deck. Let's get this bucket moving."

CHAPTER 3

Nyx climbed onto the bow of the ship.

"I still say you could have picked something smaller," Darius grumbled.

"Hush up, Valeran. I have no idea what condition the Vanity will be in. And a slave ship is fitting." She spat on the deck in disgust. Yasmine stood at the helm and guided the ship through the air as it bounced along.

Lucien already had his head over the side. "Why must we fly?" he groaned.

Nyx wondered why Darius had invited him along. She knew full well how sick he got.

"Nyx, get on the deck," Yasmine ordered. "Now is not the time to dawdle."

Nyx pouted. She didn't get to enjoy the experience the last time she had flown on a ship when she had first travelled to Andovia. That time, she had been a slave, falsely accused of murder. It still surprised her how much her life had changed since then.

"Valeran, take the helm," Yasmine ordered, and went over to the pack she had brought on board. "Here." She tossed a small jar to Lucien, who caught it in one swift move. "Drink that. I need all hands working, not being sick. You need to find your sea legs, lykae."

Lucien stared at the jar. "What is this?"

"It will settle your stomach. We head straight to Alvon."

Nyx's mouth fell open.

Alvon, one of the neighbouring realms to Joriam—her former home.

The idea of being so close to her old realm left her with mixed feelings. Joriam had never felt like a real home. She had only gone back a few months ago, hoping to find her foster sisters.

She pushed those thoughts away. Her sisters had been sold after she had been taken to Andovia. Every time she and Darius went anywhere that had slaves being held, she looked for them.

Nyx tied a rope down to the mainsail.

Darius stood at the helm and looked at ease there.

"Do you know who took your ship?" she asked Yasmine.

"Yes, Will the Black." The pirate scowled. "I've never met him before, but I know him by reputation. I don't know why he'd steal my ship. He already has his own ship—the Bounty." Yasmine rolled her eyes. "What a stupid name."

"We should arrive in a few hours," Darius told them.

"We need to get there and see what state the ship and the crew are in, then plan our next move." Lucien had perked up.

"It's simple. Find my ship and blow that other pirate to kingdom come."

"We are not killing anyone," Darius said. "Not on purpose at least. That's not the way we do things."

"No one steals from me," Yasmine growled. "That ship is my home. She's more than just wood and rivets." She turned to Nyx. "How did you end up as his servant?"

"I was falsely accused of murder. His brother heard about me, and Darius brought me to Avenia. But my powers were considered… negligible."

Nyx had been lucky to keep the true extent of her powers a secret so far. She knew that wouldn't last forever. Now she was trying to find her place in the world.

Yasmine's eyebrows rose. "You have a lot of power judging by what you did to that captain. How did you end up as a servant though?"

"It was either that or be sent to the slave islands to suffer a slow and prolonged death. I was a thief before that."

Yasmine grinned. "A girl after my own heart. I'm surprised Valeran let you be one of his servants. He hates people waiting on him."

Nyx shrugged. "I'm not a real servant. We work together now. I go where he goes. I love working with the resistance, to feel like I can help."

She had never liked stealing, but it had been necessary to survive. Her foster father had taught her that was all her abilities were good for. Things changed when she had met the druid and his friends. Instead, she felt like she had a real purpose now. Although she still didn't know much about her missing past before she had ended up being a slave.

She and Yasmine chatted more over the next few hours, and she decided she liked the pirate. All the awful tales she had heard about pirates and how dishonourable they were seemed untrue.

When they arrived at Alvon, ships filled the large port. All of the vessels flew the colours of different islands from around the lower realm and beyond.

Yasmine wanted to storm off the ship and search for the Vanity and her crew.

"Maybe you should stay here," Darius suggested. "There are a lot of guards stationed here. What if someone recognises you?"

"I'm not sitting here and doing nothing, Valeran," Yasmine snapped. "I need to find my crew and make sure they're alright."

Nyx winced from the intensity of Yasmine's anger. She understood the pirate's need to find her vessel. It meant a lot to her, but they had to be cautious in this strange new realm. Especially until they knew what they might be up against.

"I'll fly around and look at the ships," Nyx offered. "I can see more from the air. Can you show me what your ship looks like? Picture it in your mind."

Yasmine frowned. "You're going to read my mind?" She took a step back. "Will it hurt?"

"I only want to see your ship. I won't intrude on any of your other thoughts. And no, it's not painful. You won't even know I'm doing it." Or at least Nyx hoped she wouldn't. Although she had better control over her powers now, she couldn't always prevent herself from picking up on things.

Nyx reached into Yasmine's mind with her senses. Yasmine didn't have a very strong mental shield. Strange. She had thought all the

Druids were taught to protect their minds.

The image of a large ship with deep red sails came to her. Along with images of her crew. Two large men, both giants, came through strongest in Yasmine's thoughts. They were both burly looking men and looked like they could break things apart with their bare hands given their enormous size. Nyx had never seen giants before. Although, she had heard a lot of stories about them back when she had lived with her human tribe.

Nyx had never been one to judge the other races, but she had also heard tales of giants being complete brutes. She didn't sense any fear from Yasmine towards them. She had learned a lot over the past few months. Not all people were what they seemed to be.

She wrapped a glamour spell around herself, unfurled her wings, and took to the air.

Nyx glided around the different ships and took in the sights and sounds. She breathed in the salty sea air. It felt so different being here compared to the forests on Eldara that she had grown so used to.

Circling around the vessels, she checked the different flags. So many of them had symbols painted on she had never seen before.

Nyx hoped whoever had stolen the ship hadn't changed the sails. But she wouldn't be surprised if they had. Whoever had stolen it, would probably have done their best to make the ship look different.

If only she could use her powers to track the crew. But she couldn't trace someone she'd never met or heard before.

There were too many sounds here for her to focus on. If she lowered her mental shield, she would get overwhelmed by all the voices.

Still, she could try.

Nyx hated letting her shield down. It had taken her months of training to form it by working with Ambrose and Darius. It was the only thing that allowed her to be around a large number of people. Before that, she had drugged herself to dampen her power. Or she would become overwhelmed and useless.

Thoughts buzzed through her mind like bees.

She quietened her thoughts so things would become clearer. *Vanity. Where is the Vanity?*

Darius walked along the deck below her. He gave a slight wave. No doubt he would see straight through her glamour.

Nyx waved back and circled around the ships again. If the sails had been changed, maybe she could still spot the name on the side of the ship.

Nyx flew from ship to ship. Some had names that had been scratched out.

By the time she circled the entire dock, she wondered if Yasmine had brought them to the right place.

The Vanity could have sailed to any realm by now. There were numerous islands nearby, or it could be out at sea.

Druid, I don't see any sign of the Vanity, Nyx told him.

Neither do I, but Yasmine insists it's here. She cast a spell on her ship so she could always locate it. The spell is pointing here.

Spells could be broken or changed. She had learnt that much in the time she had spent with the druid and his friends.

Does Yasmine see anything? Nyx asked. If her spell was working, shouldn't it give her a signal, or a sense of direction to wherever the ship was?

She focused on the pirate, but Yasmine's thoughts were too chaotic for her to make out.

She says she can't see anything either. You and Lucien found anything?

Not yet. Lucien is trying to track the crew. Yasmine had some of their clothing and he's trying to follow their scent.

Nyx lowered her mental shield once more.

More voices droned around her. There was a strange buzzing sound.

It wasn't the buzz of thoughts. It sounded different from that.

Nyx furrowed her brow and swooped lower. The sound grew louder. It sounded far above people's thoughts.

Nyx, have you found something? Darius asked.

She barely heard him and didn't bother to reply.

The buzzing grew in intensity as she focused her senses on it.

What was that?

Nyx reached for the sound with her mind.

The sound grew so loud that she screamed through her mind.

Nyx covered her ears. What the heck with that thing?

She lost momentum and fell into the water.

CHAPTER 4

Darius and Lucien helped Nyx back onto the deck. He and Nyx were both dripping wet now.

"What happened?" Darius asked her.

He had seen Nyx flying around the dock. But then, out of nowhere, she had fallen into the sea. Which had struck him as odd.

Nyx shivered. Her long pink hair stuck to her back and face. She shivered. "Something… The noise. Don't you hear it?"

Darius heated the air around them to dry her and himself off.

"What noise?" Darius frowned, glad to be dry once again.

"That buzzing sound." Nyx waved her arms in exasperation.

"I hear nothing," Lucien remarked. "I would hear it if there was anything. All I hear is the sounds of the sea, people, and the cry of gulls."

"The buzzing!" Nyx clutched her head. "It hurts!"

Darius gripped her hand. Energy tingled against his skin the moment his fingers touched hers. The sensation had always struck him as odd before. But after months of being with Nyx, it didn't feel so bad. Whenever he touched her, he somehow neutralised her power. They had never been able to figure out why, though.

"Has it stopped now?"

Nyx breathed a sigh of relief and nodded. "Thanks. I have never heard anything like it."

Yasmine furrowed her brow. "What sound? Did you see anything?"

Nyx shook her head. "No, none of the ships here look like yours."

The pirate groaned. "Then where is the Vanity? She must be around here somewhere. My spell wouldn't lead me wrong. It never has before."

"Maybe we should split up," Lucien suggested. "There are several taverns nearby. And sailors like to talk. Especially when they're plied with drink."

"She's here somewhere. I just know it." Yasmine stalked back off along the dock.

"Lucien, go with her. Make sure she doesn't get into trouble," Darius told him. "I know she's desperate to find her ship and crew, but we can't afford to be reckless with everything going on here."

Lucien nodded and blurred away.

"I still don't know what that sound was. All I did was use my senses." Nyx ran a hand through her long hair.

"Did you lower your shield? Maybe you got overwhelmed by the number of people here." Darius kept hold of her hand as they headed along the busy dock. People ran past them and carriages raced along the street.

"Yes, but it wasn't someone's thoughts I heard. There was an awful sound that echoed through my mind." She shuddered. "It paralysed me."

Darius frowned. "I have heard stories of there being weapons and devices that could be used against mind whisperers. They can overwhelm their senses." He rubbed his chin. "But I don't see how one could be here. Everyone considers mind whisperers to be extinct. Most people wouldn't have heard of them outside of Andovia."

"We both know they're not extinct. Or at least I'm not. If I exist, then there could be more." She gripped his hand a little tighter. "How do the devices work? How can they be stopped?"

Darius shrugged. "No idea. The stories never mentioned that."

Darius wished he could tell her more. But all the lore about mind whisperers had been erased.

They headed into the nearest tavern, The Black Penny.

The stench of unwashed bodies and cheap ale hit him. Dust and dirt covered the blackened floor. Some of the tables and chairs were propped up by books or bits of wood.

115

"This place looks even worse than where I used to live," Nyx observed. "At least that tavern was clean."

Darius remembered the place he had found her in. It hadn't looked much better than this.

He hoped they didn't have to stay here long. Being in dank taverns always led to unwanted trouble. Plus, he always feared someone might recognise him. Maybe he should have activated his glamour before entering, but it was too late to do so now.

"Will you be alright if I let go of you?" Darius arched an eyebrow.

Nyx hesitated. "I-I don't know. What if I am overpowered by that noise again?"

They weren't far away from the dock, but she hadn't been able to pinpoint where the sound had come from.

As travellers, they would stand out. But as two people holding hands, they would stand out more.

Darius let go of her, ready in case he needed to help her again.

Nyx blew out a breath. "I can't hear it anymore."

"Good. Let's ask around then."

Nyx put her hand on his arm. "Won't that arouse suspicions?"

"I know how to be discreet." Darius headed over to the bar and pulled out a few coins. Money got people to talk.

A burly man with only one eye and several missing teeth came over. "How can I help you?"

"I'm looking for someone. Goes by the name of Will the Black." Darius slipped a few coins onto the bar. "Do you know where I might find him?"

"Not seen Will in these parts in many moons. Who wants to know?"

"Let's just say I have business with him. Have you seen any other pirates come through here on a ship with crimson sails?"

The man picked up the gold and stared at it. "Andovian gold with the Archdruid's insignia. That's even rarer in these parts."

Damn, he should have known to bring non-Andovian minted coins. But to most people, it didn't matter. Gold was gold.

"Not that unusual." Darius leaned forward. "Have you seen the ship or not?"

"That's a pretty girl you've got there. I'd be much more likely to trade information for her."

Nyx scanned the bar's patrons, and Darius knew she was listening to all of their thoughts.

Nyx shot a glare at the barkeep and shifted her focus away.

"She is not for sale. Trust me, you wouldn't want to go near her." Darius placed a few more coins on the bar. "Have you seen the ship or not?"

Darius wanted to ask Nyx if she had found anything, but decided against distracting her.

He wanted out of the seedy place and back to their vessel. He belonged in the forest. Not in places like this.

Another couple of men came up to the bar. A dark-haired, scruffy man grabbed Nyx by her hair and slapped her backside.

"I've always wanted myself a pretty fae." The first man grinned.

Oh no. Darius' hand went to his sword. "I would unhand her if I were you."

"Why? What are you going to do?" The second man sneered.

Metal sang as Darius pulled out his sword and thrust the tip under the man's chin. "Step away from the lady. Or do I need to start cutting pieces of you off?"

Darius didn't want any trouble. Usually, the threat of a sword got most men to back away.

Nyx slapped the first man around the face. She twisted and then grasped both men by their necks. Her eyes flashed with blackness. She muttered something under her breath and both men started screaming.

Darius stared at Nyx, and she flashed him a smile.

Darius turned back to the bar.

The barkeep glowered at them. "Get outta my tavern. I won't have witchcraft in here."

Darius sheathed his sword and sighed once they were outside. "What did you do to those men? We are supposed to blend in whilst we are here."

He knew she had used her powers. But he hadn't felt the full force of them.

Nyx snorted. "I told them I cursed them with impotency and if they ever touched a woman again without her permission, their manhood would fall off."

He chuckled. "I can't take you anywhere, can I?"

Nyx shrugged. "They started it. At least I didn't use my full power."

Darius rolled his eyes. "Can you please try not to compel everyone in this realm? We need to find that ship and get back to Andovia."

"Sometimes I think you have no sense of adventure, druid. This could have been fun."

"We don't have time for fun. I'm risking a lot by being here. If my father found out—"

"He's off on another realm. And from what I've seen he doesn't pay much attention to what you do anyway."

Darius was grateful for that, but luck wouldn't always be on his side like this time.

One day word would get back to his father about his work with the resistance. One deed and he knew he couldn't walk away from them either. The resistance grew every day, and one day he hoped they would be able to overthrow his father once and for all.

CHAPTER 5

"I came for my ship and my crew." Yasmine sighed. "Damn it, they must be here somewhere."

She and Lucien had already been in two different taverns and had no luck in finding out anything about her ship, or her missing crew. Her patience was wearing thin.

"Maybe someone tampered with your locator spell," Lucien suggested.

Yasmine shook her head. "Not possible. Every part of that ship is covered by my magic—it's a part of me."

Nyx and Darius headed back over to them.

"Did you find anything?" Yasmine demanded, hardly daring to hope.

Darius shook his head. "Nothing. No one here is talking."

"I couldn't get anything from their minds either. All we found was a bunch of lewd men." Nyx crossed her arms. "Maybe it's not at the dock."

"It must be. Where else would they put it?" Yasmine crossed her arms.

"First rule of being a thief. Once you steal something, you spend your entire life trying to keep it," Nyx said. "The best place to hide something is in plain sight."

"Try casting your locator spell again," Darius suggested. "If it is here, we should see something."

Yasmine recited the words to her spell and felt a surge of magic rush through the air. She glanced around, waiting for something to happen.

Lucien cocked his head and his eyes flashed with amber light. "I see a ship. Although, it's hidden behind a glamour."

Yasmine's head shot from side to side, looking for the familiar sight of her ship. But found nothing.

"Over there. See where those gulls are circling around?" Lucien pointed in the opposite direction.

"That must be it." Yasmine raced down the end of the dock and scoured for a way to her ship.

Lucien blurred to her side. "Allow me." He offered her his hand and led her to the steps.

Nyx and Darius followed behind them.

Static rippled against her skin as she passed through the glamour. Her ship was here!

Yasmine's heart soared. Now she had to find her crew and make sure they were alright.

A dark-haired woman spun around to face them. Her long black hair fell past her shoulders, and a red jewel glistened around her throat. She had to be a few years older than Yasmine herself.

"Who are you and what are you doing with my ship?" Yasmine pulled out her sword. She scanned the vessel with her mind but detected no signs of anyone else on board.

Where were her men? What had happened to them? If this woman had done anything to harm them, she would pay with her life.

The other woman frowned. "How did you get on here?" she demanded. "This ship is cloaked. You are not welcome aboard."

"I asked you a question. I'm the captain of the ship and no one steals from me."

The other woman grabbed a sword from the stack of boxes. "The ship is mine now. You're not taking it anywhere."

Yasmine shifted into a fighting stance. She swung her sword at the other pirate.

The other woman parried the blow.

"Go and search the ship. See if you can find my crew."

The men wandered off, but Nyx remained on deck.

Yasmine and the other pirate continued to block and parry blows. A clash of steel against steel.

Darius and Lucien soon appeared on deck again. "There's no one on board," Darius told her.

"Where's my crew?" Yasmine lunged at the other pirate again.

The woman dodged the blow, spun, and knocked the sword from Yasmine's grasp.

Yasmine stared at her hand in dismay.

"Nyx, use your powers on her," Yasmine snapped. "Find out what she's done with my crew. I need to know where they are."

The other pirate raised her swords as Nyx approached her. "Stay back."

Nyx waved her hand as an invisible wave of energy sent both blades flying across the deck.

"My friend here is a mind whisperer." Yasmine smirked. "So, I'd start talking if I were you."

Yasmine, I'd appreciate it if you didn't tell the whole world about Nyx, Darius warned. *If word spreads about her, we will have even more problems on our hands.*

"Her name is Will," Nyx announced. "She is Will the Black."

Yasmine's mouth fell open. "What? How can that be? She's a woman."

"So are you, Captain," Will added.

"She took your ship because she needs to pay off the debt to a man she works for. Captain Gold. She owed him after she lost one of his ships helping to smuggle some slaves away." Nyx furrowed her brow. "Your crew are Gold's prisoners. From what I can see in her mind, she doesn't really live up to her name. She doesn't seem to do bad deeds."

Yasmine wondered how Nyx could know that. She thought Nyx had to touch people to get answers out of them. Like she had done with that old captain.

Will gaped at Nyx. "How do you know that?"

"Because I can read your thoughts." Nyx crossed arms. "Like the captain said, I'm a mind whisperer."

Yasmine went and picked up her sword. "If you needed help against Gold, why didn't you ask for it?"

Will scoffed at that. "As if you would have helped."

121

"We'll help you now," Darius said. "Where is Gold holding the prisoners?"

Will shook her head. "You can't go up against Gold. His men are too well-armed. He'd kill all of you before you had—"

"My friends and I can handle it. Take me to my crew," Yasmine demanded.

Will led them to a small cove that had a network of caves nearby. Two guards stood outside.

"Excuse me." Lucien shot towards them and knocked them both unconscious. They headed through the network of caves until they finally found a group of several people chained together.

"Olaf, Ike." Yasmine beamed "I have found you at last."

Lucien knelt and yanked on the chains, but they wouldn't break. "They are spelled."

"What are you doing here?" A man with a long black beard approached, along with several other armed men. "We came to rescue my crew and free their lives." Yasmine drew her sword. "We'll also be taking back the Vanity."

The men started throwing blasts of energy at them.

Yasmine ducked.

Lucien blurred every time the men came at him.

Darius got to work on the chains.

Nyx waved her arm and sent two men flying.

Yasmine lunged straight for Gold.

Will went for him too. She seemed to want the man gone as much as Yasmine did. So, she guessed they were allies for now at least.

Lucien and Nyx took down the other men.

Yasmine knocked Gold unconscious. Part of her might have wanted to kill him, but they were fighting for the greater good. And that sometimes meant killing wasn't always the best way.

EPILOGUE

"Thanks for your help," Yasmine told Darius. "I couldn't have saved my crew and all these other slaves without you."

"Any time." Darius gave her a smile. "Try not to lose your ship again, though."

Yasmine laughed. "I won't." She glanced over at Will. "I still think we should have handed her over to the authorities with Gold and his crew."

"Why don't you let her sail with you? She's trying to find where she belongs. Reminds me of a girl I once knew." Darius squeezed her shoulder.

"Sail with me?" Yasmine gaped at him. She couldn't say she liked the idea. But maybe she would see how it went. In the end, Will had helped her to get her ship and her crew back.

"Wait, Valeran. I thought you should have this." Yasmine held out a gold amulet. "We found this in Gold's loot. It says something about warding off mind whisperers. I thought it would be safer with you since it affected Nyx."

He took it and nodded. "Thanks. It's always an adventure with you around. Take care of yourself, Yas."

Yasmine helped him. "You too, Valeran."

Yasmine marched over to the edge of the deck and sighed. "Come on then."

Will arched an eyebrow. "Me?"

"Yes, you. Who else would I mean? All hands on deck. We have to get these former slaves to safety. There are still dangerous tides ahead, but my ship and crew can weather any storm."

Will grinned and followed her on deck.

Maybe it was the start of a new beginning Yasmine decided as she took the helm and guided her ship away from Alvon.

GUARDIAN OF VARDEN

CHAPTER 1

Velestra sensed the presence of intruders within Varden Forest. Some strangers had entered the forest without permission. She'd better find out who it was. She grabbed her staff weapon and mounted her horse, Lightning. She couldn't believe someone had dared to enter so close to the Varden's home without invitation. They hadn't had any trouble from the Archdruid or anyone else for a while, and she planned on keeping it that way.

Who would dare to come here? Why would they come here again? To get to the old city? No one had tried going near that in years. But deep down, she always knew it would happen again at some point.

Velestra prayed it wasn't the Archdruid's forces. He had tried attacking the city several times over the last century after being forced out. During that time, the city shield held strong and prevented anyone from going into the abandoned city anymore.

She urged Lightning onward, and they raced through the forest.

One of the pixies darted out of a tree and flew along with her. Aviva, the pixie, sparkled like a glowing orb. Her long blue hair and pointed ears were almost invisible from the sheer sheen of her gossamer wings.

"Aviva, fly ahead. Find out who is here," Velestra told her and urged Lightning to move forward.

Aviva nodded and flew off, leaving a trail of pixie dust in her wake.

Velestra wondered if she should have flown herself. The Varden protected the old city. It was their sacred duty to guard it and defend the lands that once belonged to the true Queen of Andovia. It was a miracle the Archdruid hadn't destroyed the entire realm by now. This was a small part of the realm that had been left intact.

Legend said their queen would one day return to them. A century had passed since her death. Velestra wondered if it was true sometimes. Even if it weren't, she wouldn't let anyone lay waste to their home again. One day, they would get back into the old city and reclaim it. She believed that much, at least.

Branches whacked against her head and against Lightning's flanks, but she ignored them. She kept on the narrow path because it was the fastest route. She pushed her long brown hair off her face and folded her purple wings on her back. Besides, no matter how much they cleaned the trails, they always became overgrown again overnight. She was used to such things, though. The trees moved and talked to each other in a language only the fae understood.

Velestra kept her senses on alert as she rode. Taking in every scent and sound as she went. Two unknown presences came to her. Stronger than before. Magic crackled through the air. She looked up and spotted a young woman with large purple butterfly wings.

Good goddess, an Andovian. A true Andovian.

Since their queen's demise, the fae had been enslaved. Few Andovians got to fly anymore. There were laws against it.

A figure clad in black leapt from tree to tree as they chased after the fae girl. And they dared to carry weapons here too. Judging by the shape of the figure, Velestra guessed the assassin must be female.

Why had they come here? Didn't they know this part of the forest was off-limits?

She gritted her teeth. Younglings never did as they were told. She would catch up with them and give them a good piling. It would serve them right if they headed too close to the old city. It would amuse her to see them repelled by the city's shield. No one could get through that. Not even the Varden themselves.

The winged fae disappeared over the treetops.

Velestra stopped and raised her hand, so the leafy canopy parted. Both the winged fae and her pursuer had disappeared.

How had they moved so fast?

Aviva flew back towards her in a cloud of pixie dust. "I found them. One is an assassin. She is trying to kill the other girl."

"No one is spilling blood today," Velestra growled. "Keep after them. I'll follow. Maybe I should fly."

"The winged fae is a fast flyer. I had trouble keeping up with her. Stick to the horse. They are headed towards the old city." The pixie flew off in a trail of dust.

"Slow them down if you can," Velestra called after her. She urged Lightning into a gallop and raced towards the city.

Trees finally moved aside, allowing her and her mount a clearer path. She caught sight of something that glinted in the sunlight. Throwing knives.

The assassin's dark form perched on a branch and magic carried on the wind. This assassin was skilled both with magic and weaponry—that much she could sense. But that didn't make her welcome here. Or free to harm anyone. The winged fae hovered up ahead.

Velestra kept to the trees so she could watch.

The winged fae had magic of her own, it seemed. Again, that was unusual to see in this realm. Most of the enslaved fae were stripped of their powers or bound. She raised her hands and pushed the blades back as they hovered in front of her. The assassin pushed back as well. Now a true battle of wills had begun.

Aviva flew down and perched on Velestra's shoulder. "You need to do something. That assassin is well armed. I smell poison on her, too. She will kill that girl."

Velestra raised her staff, about to fire upon the assassin. Light flared overhead as the winged fae traced runes in the air. The blades fell away.

Velestra turned her attention to the assassin.

"Keep an eye on the girl," she told Aviva and rode towards the tree where the assassin perched. Lightning moved swift and silent. As only a fae steed could.

Velestra fired her staff weapon, a blast of light aimed straight for the assassin.

The assassin screamed as she lost her balance and fell off the branch. She raised her arms and somehow controlled her descent. Incredible. Velestra had never seen anything like it. The assassin landed on another branch and her icy blue eyes glared down at Velestra.

Come on, kid. I've got a hundred years on you. Velestra longed for a good fight. *Don't think you can take me.*

She fired again.

The assassin jumped onto another branch above, then threw another blade.

Velestra rolled her eyes, waved her hand so the blade bounced away from her.

"Don't think your games will work on me, girl." Velestra glared up at her. "Why don't you come down here and fight like a true warrior?"

The assassin threw two more knives.

Velestra dodged them and sent out several bursts of light from her staff. One way or another, she would get that assassin down and give her a good hiding. The girl needed a lesson on following the rules and respecting her elders.

The girl leapt out of the way and straight onto a nearby tree.

Aviva whizzed back over to her. "Velestra, there's a man near the shield. He is dying."

"What? Who is it?" She furrowed her brow.

She hadn't sensed any other strangers come into the forest. Unless she had been distracted by the assassin and her target. Who else would have appeared? Outsiders rarely came into this part of Andovia. Other than the occasional forest guard, but Velestra got on with most of them.

"High fae would be my guess. The girl is with him. We need to hurry."

Velestra hesitated. As much as she wanted to go after the assassin, she had to find out who else was here.

"Follow the assassin," she told Aviva.

She pushed through the tree line. A yellow stone tower shimmered behind the leafy curtain. It had once been one of the city's watchtowers. Now it stood in ruin like the rest of the city. Protected by an impenetrable shield.

Nature had reclaimed the city over the decades and slowly swallowed it up.

Velestra hesitated as she got to the edge of the tree line.

The winged fae knelt beside a man as he lay slumped against a tree. "I don't, I'm going to help you."

"Listen to me. I kept your secret, but you cannot let her rise again. If she returns, she will destroy us all."

"What are you talking about?" The girl frowned at him. "Who can't come back?"

The man gave one last shuddering breath before his life expired.

CHAPTER 2

Velestra watched the girl a while longer, deciding not to approach and just observe for now.

"No, come back." The girl touched his chest then called out, "Druid, come on. I need you." She rose and glanced around, as if expecting someone to appear. "Druid!"

Velestra wondered who she meant to call. Perhaps Ambrose or one of the other druids.

"Damn it, druid, why won't you answer me?" She glanced around, then vanished in a flash of light.

How had she disappeared? Velestra doubted anyone could have transported themselves out. Not being so close to the city's shield. That alone would have prevented anyone from using such magic.

Staff in hand, she hurried over to the fallen body. Velestra knelt and touched his chest. He showed signs of torture. But where'd he come from? She hadn't even registered his presence. She did a quick examination of the body. Although he had signs of torture, she couldn't see any visible signs of what might have caused his death. His cuts were too shallow to cause major blood loss. But she was no healer, so she couldn't be sure.

Velestra didn't want to touch the body too much. She should report this to her people. Since he wasn't one of them, the Forest Guard would have to be involved. Velestra cringed at the thought. She didn't mind the Forest Guard since they kept the peace throughout the forests of Andovia, but she still hated having to deal with anyone who served the Archdruid. They weren't ruthless murderers like the Dragon Guard. But they were still loyal to the Archdruid. The very man who destroyed the old city.

The dead man had said, "She will rise again…"

What did that mean?

Velestra thought about the queen. So many years had passed since her demise. Many of her people doubted she would ever return. She studied the man's face. He reminded her of someone. Perhaps she had seen him as a child growing up in the city. He looked familiar, but she couldn't place him.

Aviva flew towards her and hovered. "The assassin got away. She threw a knife at me and pinned me to a tree." The pixie spun around to show her torn skirt.

Velestra gritted her teeth. "Are you hurt? She'll pay for that."

"No, but she cut my dress. It took me a while to get free."

Damn, that girl needed a good hiding.

"Stay close to the body. I'm going to scout around to see if I can trace the assassin." She leapt back onto Lightning's back.

She rode back through the forest, in the direction Aviva said she'd last seen the assassin. Velestra knew the girl would be long gone, but she had to search, anyway.

Velestra? a voice echoed through her mind.

She pulled Lightning to a halt. *Yes, Ike?* She had expected one of her people to call for her. Had word of the assassin spread already? No surprise there, given how much the dryads and other fae who lived in the forest liked to gossip.

We need you back in the village. The elder wants to talk to you.

I'm busy. Can't it wait? We've had trespassers.

Velestra—

She froze when a shadow moved ahead. She would know that shape anywhere. A dragon.

Whatever it is, Ike, it will have to wait. Alert the others. There is a dragon in the forest.

Ike cursed. *Find out who it is. At the first sign of the Dragon Guard, we will be out in force.*

Velestra gave a nod, even though she knew he couldn't see it.

She and Lightning kept pace as the dragon glided over the tree line. The dragon looked smaller compared to the Dragon Guards'

133

beasts. This one had pale silver-white skin. Hardly any good for camouflage. The Dragon Guard liked dark, hulking beasts that they broke in and turned into mindless killers. This dragon bore two riders. One male with long blond hair and a female with long bright pink hair. It was the same girl she'd seen earlier. As they drew closer, Velestra realised who the young man was. Darius Valeran, the second-born son of the Archdruid.

Gods below, why did it have to be him? He could lead the Dragon Guard straight here. She knew Darius lived among the druids rather than his father's court and worked in the Forest Guard, but that didn't make him any less dangerous. He was still a Valeran.

Darius landed and his fae companion landed a few moments later. Then they walked off and left his dragon alone.

Velestra had seen enough. She galloped towards them and aimed her staff weapon. "How dare you enter Varden territory, Valeran. You know our laws," she snarled.

Darius raised his hands in surrender. "Velestra, I'm not here to cause any harm. We're only here for him." He inclined his head towards the body. "I'm part of the Forest Guard. You can at least allow us to do that."

"You still came here without permission and brought a dragon with you."

"The dragon is not threatening anyone. Can we at least investigate and find out what happened to him?"

Something prickled at the edge of her mind, and a shiver ran over her.

"What are you?" Velestra narrowed her eyes on the girl. "Are you using your powers on me?"

"This is my… servant, Nyx."

"I'm a long story." Nyx pushed her long hair off her face. "Did you see what happened to this man?"

"No, you would do well to leave this place. This isn't your territory."

"You must have seen something." Nyx put her hands on her hips. "You were following me earlier. I saw you."

Velestra kept her composure. How could the girl have seen her? She had a glamour to blend in with her surroundings. Lightning had one, too. "I was busy watching you and that assassin." She scowled at the mention of the assassin. "I didn't see that man before you found him."

"Do you know anything about the assassin?" Nyx scanned her with her senses again.

"I know they'll die if they dare set foot here again." Velestra narrowed her eyes. "You are a mind whisperer."

Nyx furrowed her brow. "How do you know that?"

"I can sense your power. It's rude to read someone's thoughts without their permission."

"Sometimes it happens without me meaning it to."

Velestra turned her attention back to Darius. "Do what you need to do, then leave Varden territory." Once she retreated into the trees, she watched them awhile longer.

Nyx intrigued her more than anything. There was something familiar about her. A mind whisperer hadn't been heard of in over a century. What did this mean?

Maybe the village elder would know.

Velestra raced back to her village. Wooden huts spread out around her, covered in rich colours. Flags flew around each house.

Velestra dismounted and let a stableboy lead Lightning away. She hurried past the huts and several other riders who patrolled the forest.

The elder's hut stood on the edge of the village.

"My lady?" Velestra called out. "Are you here? I heard you had sent for me."

The chimes hanging from the ceiling jingled in the hut's front room. No one knew much about the elder. Just that she lived here for years. She appeared to not age and seemed to serve as a priestess to the goddess Ewa.

Velestra scanned the hut but didn't sense anyone.

"My lady?" she called again.

"What is it, Velestra?"

She almost jumped when she turned to find the elder behind her.

The elder looked as beautiful as ever with her pale skin, long raven hair, and piercing blue eyes.

"I… I—" she struggled to find the right words. Somehow, it felt like this woman saw through her very soul. Power clung to her like a second skin. "Someone was found dead in the forest close to the shield." Velestra finally found her voice. "He said something about her rising again… I think he meant our queen."

The elder's eyes narrowed. "What proof do you have?"

She hesitated. "Well, none but—but there's more." She went on to tell the elder about the assassin and the mind whisperer. "Surely this must be a sign?"

"Perhaps. We shall see."

CHAPTER 3

Velestra knew she had to track down that assassin. Others could be sure the assassin had killed that man. Either way, people were dying in her forest, and she couldn't allow that.

It could lead to the Archdruid's forces trying to burn the forest down again. It wouldn't take much for the Archdruid to do so. Velestra knew he still had his eye on Varden city and would kill anyone to get his hands on it at last.

Velestra rode through to the forest on her usual patrol route. Dismounting, she spread her wings and flew onto a huge oak tree the assassin had occupied the day before.

"Are you looking for the assassin, too?" Nyx hovered nearby.

Odd. Velestra hadn't sensed her approach. "Yes. People aren't permitted to carry weapons here." Velestra perched on one of the thick branches. "I will find her and make sure she does not set foot here again."

"What do you do here?" Nyx settled on the branch. "Do you have your own Forest Guard?"

Velestra snorted. "I'm one of the riders of Varden. We protect this forest and the old city. We are descendants of the Queen's Guard. The Archdruid tried to wipe us out when our queen saved the city with her dying breath."

"Who was the queen? I keep hearing whispers about her but..."

"She was the greatest queen Andovia ever had. She protected our realm and kept the peace for decades. Andovia was a crown jewel in the lower realm." Velestra smiled. "At least until the Archdruid destroyed my homeland. Someone betrayed our queen and helped him inside. They let down the shield so his Dragon Guard could lay waste on the city. Just like he's already scorched over half of Erthea."

"Isabella, the silvan queen, tried to find the queen spirit."

Velestra snorted again. "She could never find the queen."

"How can you be sure? I mean, no one knows what happened after the execution, do they?"

She hesitated. As much as the girl intrigued her, she still worked for a Valeran. For all she knew, he could have sent Nyx to press her for information.

No one knew what happened to the Andovian Queen after the execution. The Archdruid hadn't been able to claim her soul, at least. His forces were driven out and the queen's mate had taken away the bodies of the queen and her family. "Because even in death, our queen would have been too strong," Velestra said finally. "She would never fall under the control of the Archdruid or his false queen. I must go. I have to patrol today."

"I need to find out who sent that assassin after me." Nyx glanced around. "Maybe I can lure them out here."

"I want to find her too. She needs to know she's not welcome here."

"How about we work together then?" Nyx arched brow. "Then we'll both get what we want."

Velestra bit her lip. She knew the other riders would frown upon her working with a Valeran's servant. But using Nyx would be the best way to lure the assassin out.

"Very well. How do you think you'll draw her here?"

They both flew back to the ground.

Nyx sat down. "She's looking for me." Light flashed around her body. "You may want to stay back. My power might latch onto you with my shield down."

Velestra drew back as Nyx's energy grew stronger. It pulsed over her skin and seemed to strike like lightning. She already knew mind whisperers could not only read thoughts but compel people as well. If they unleashed their full power, someone could become a mindless slave to them.

Nyx took a deep breath and felt her power ebb as she slammed her shield back up. "I hope that was enough," she panted. "I can't open myself up to light like that for long. It's too... Overwhelming."

Aviva flew down. "What was that energy that just pulsed through the entire forest?"

"That would be me." Nyx pushed her hair off her face. "I didn't think it extended that far. Gods, I hope I didn't touch anyone with it."

"No, I felt it. You won't force anyone under your control." Velestra shook her head. "Aviva, go and fly around. Look for any sign of that assassin."

Aviva flew over to Nyx. "We haven't had a mind whisperer since the queen..." She perched on Nyx's nose. "You look like a true Andovian. Why do you work for that Valeran scum? Did he enslave you?"

"The druid—my druid—I mean, Darius isn't anything like his bastard father," Nyx replied, and her cheeks flushed. "He saved me from execution and treats me like an equal. You don't have to be afraid of him."

"The Archdruid destroyed all the soul readers."

Nyx frowned. "Soul reader?"

"It's the true name for a mind whisperer. A mind whisperer can see someone's soul," Velestra explained. "Someone is here." Velestra leapt to her feet.

How could she have been so careless? Chatting away when she should have been on her guard. A figure clad in black leapt from one tree to another.

"They're here. I'm going to—" Nyx's hand flared with light. Light flashed and knives hurtled towards both Velestra and Nyx.

Really? They were going to do this again?

Nyx shot into the air to avoid the blade. Velestra deflected hers with a wave of her hand.

The knives shot back into the air and came at them again. Aviva hit one with a tiny bolt of energy. The blade fell to the ground. Velestra took an opportunity and fired her staff at the assassin.

A scream broke out, and the assassin disappeared.

"Where did she go?"

They scoured the area, but found no sign of the assassin. But one thing was certain. The queen would return. All the signs were there.

CHAPTER 4

A few days later, Nyx returned to the forest. Velestra wasn't surprised. Another person had been found dead, this time a fae servant, so she had expected Nyx to return to ask her questions.

"Velestra, can I talk to you?" Nyx swooped down.

Velestra furrowed her brow, then nodded. "You've come to ask about the dead servant?"

"His name was Thyren. Do you know anything about Thyren and his servant?"

"They're dead. Both appeared in a flash of light, but the servant was already dead when he appeared."

"Why didn't you mention that the other day?" Nyx frowned.

"You didn't ask. And no, I didn't know either of the men." Velestra rolled her eyes. "Just because I used to live in the old city doesn't mean I knew everyone there."

"Wait, you lived there?" Nyx gaped at her. "Wouldn't that make you over a hundred years old? How are you still alive?"

Velestra chuckled, and it sounded like bells. "Don't look so shocked, girl. You know we can live for centuries. Much like the tyrant who now sits on the throne."

"Do you remember the queen? The Andovian Queen, I mean."

The other fae's expression darkened. "Of course. What the Archdruid did to her was unforgivable."

"What did he do?"

She shuddered. "You don't want to know."

141

"You must know something. Have you seen anyone coming and going through the forest?" Energy shimmered beneath her fingers. "The queen placed shields around the Varden Guard so they couldn't turn against her."

Velestra narrowed her eyes. "How do you know that?"

She shrugged. "I have no idea. Please tell me what you know."

Velestra sighed and climbed off her horse. "Come with me."

She pushed through the trees as Nyx trailed after her.

Velestra said nothing even though Nyx had asked a few questions on the way out, so she stopped trying after a while.

"Where are we going?" Nyx broke the silence between them.

"You'll see soon enough." Velestra pushed through the trees.

Nyx followed her. The great sandstone-coloured towers of the old city loomed ahead. Nature had reclaimed it over the last century. Tree branches and vines twisted around the towers.

"That is the old city and yes, I have seen someone lurking around the forest," Velestra admitted. "A figure clad in all black. But whenever me or the other riders got near, they fled."

"Do you know anything else about them?"

"They move with great speed and disappear into thin air."

"It's an assassin. They've tried to kill me several times already. We think Isabella sent them after me." Nyx ran a hand through her hair. "Because of that stupid prophecy."

"You don't remember who you are, do you?" Velestra frowned. "And you allied yourself with an enemy."

"Wait, do you know who I am?" Nyx didn't know how that was possible. "And Darius isn't my enemy. He's my closest friend. I trust him more than anyone."

Velestra gave a harsh laugh. "How can you call him a friend? He's the son of the Archdruid. And no, I don't know anything about you except you must be from the old city. One of the mind whisperers must have escaped or else you couldn't be here. You are far too young to be from that time period."

"The Archdruid swears he wiped them all out. I wish I could remember my parents—if I had any."

"You don't remember them?" Velestra frowned.

"I don't remember the first ten years of my life. Whenever I try to remember… bad things happen to me."

Velestra's frown deepened. "That can't be natural. No one erases memories unless there is something they wanted you to forget."

"I know the Archdruid burned the queen alive. I think there's more to it than that. What else did he do?"

Velestra paled. "The Archdruid destroyed her. He cut off her wings, ravaged her body, then burned her while she still lived. That's why they search for her soul. She was the most powerful of her kind. She had power to match the Archdruid's. He tried to bind her spirit, but she escaped. I hope she's at peace now."

Nyx shivered. "If no one can get in and out of the old city, why were both bodies dumped near there? I doubt Thyren got far with the injuries he had."

"Someone must have transported him from somewhere else." Velestra leaned on her staff. "But I found no trace of a circle."

"Thanks for your help. If you think of anything else, will you call for me?"

Velestra nodded. "I will, but you should leave. Living among the druids—being anywhere near the Archdruid puts you in even greater danger."

"Where would I go? I'm a former slave and falsely accused of murder. If I'm not the druid's servant, then I'd be sent to the slave islands, or worse. Besides, I won't leave him."

Velestra's eyes narrowed. "You have feelings for him, don't you?"

Nyx opened her mouth to protest, then closed it. "That's not your business. Like I said, he's my friend. Thanks for your help." Nyx spread her wings and took off in the opposite direction.

Velestra kept to her usual patrol routes over the next few days. She had seen Nyx a couple more times but hadn't had any luck tracking down the assassin.

A boom of energy radiated through the forest and light shot into the sky. She knew something was wrong. That had to have come from the shield. She urged Lightning onward and raced towards the old city.

She drew closer to the growing wall of energy. Two figures stood on the other side of the shield. Nyx and the assassin.

Good goddess, how had they got through? That was impossible. No one could get through, but many had tried.

She guessed the assassin must've attacked Nyx again and their combined magic somehow allowed them through. Mind whisperers had powerful energy. Perhaps strong enough to force their way through the shield. Nyx appeared to be injured, but she raised her hand and trapped the assassin in a web of energy.

She knew she had to do something. If she didn't help Nyx, the girl would die.

Velestra's senses prickled as she sensed someone else enter the forest. The Valeran. Maybe he could help.

She galloped off in the opposite direction and motioned for him to come and join her. His dragon swooped down towards her and Lightning.

"Velestra." Darius gave her nod.

"Valeran, we have a problem. Your servant has somehow infiltrated the shield. She is trapped in the old city with another fae."

Darius gaped at her. "How did she even get in there? No one can get through that shield."

Velestra grimaced. "I've no idea. No one has ever been through the shield. She and the other fae must have found a way through."

"How do you know she's in there? Do you know who she's with?"

"Another fae girl."

"Where Nyx and the other fae?"

"Follow me." Velestra guided her horse and trotted off in the opposite direction.

Darius and his dragon flew behind her.

Velestra glared up at him. "Must you bring that beast here?"

"She's not harming anyone."

Lightning stopped and pawed at the ground. "She makes my mount nervous. We all remember what the Dragon Guard has done to us over the years."

"I'm not Dragon Guard and not all dragons terrorise people. We need to move faster." He urged his dragon onward. They headed straight towards the old city.

Velestra and Lightning raced to keep up with them. When they reached the edge of the border between Varden Forest and the old city, Darius jumped from the dragon's back.

Nyx lay crumpled on the ground, unmoving. The assassin stood a few feet away from her.

Darius' eyes widened in surprise. "What have you done to her? Who are you?"

Her lip curled. "Why should I tell you anything? Your father killed my family and hunted my race to extinction."

Darius' jaw tightened. "How did you get through the shield?"

Velestra galloped over to him and dismounted her horse. "The girl looks like a true Andovian."

The assassin scowled. "This web won't hold me much longer. Once she's dead, I'll—"

"Do what?" Darius crossed his arms. "You're stuck in a city with no way out. Even if you get through the web, you'll most likely die in there."

"If I can get in here, I can find a way out." The assassin raised her chin. "I can leave this awful realm once and for all."

"If you had a way out, you would have left her there to die already." He turned his attention to Nyx. "Nyx, can you hear me?"

She didn't respond.

The assassin snorted. "She'll be dead within the hour."

Darius turned to Velestra. "There must be a way through. Think. You know the old city better than anyone."

Velestra shook her head. "There isn't. No one has gone through in the past century."

"Clearly there must be a way." He motioned to Nyx and the assassin. "How else could they have got through otherwise?"

Velestra opened and closed her mouth. "How did you get through?" she demanded of the assassin. "No one has been able to get through that shield. Yet you somehow managed it."

"I didn't do anything. It's her fault, she trapped us in here." She motioned towards Nyx.

Darius paced up and down.

A few moments later, a red-haired man appeared beside Darius in a whirl of light. "How did they—"

She recognised him as Ambrose, one of the elder druids.

Darius shrugged. "She won't say. Just help me get Nyx out of there."

"I—I can't. The shield's powers are too strong."

145

"We have to do something." He clenched his fists and hard power crackled between his fingers.

Ambrose turned his attention to the assassin. "You're from the Order of Blood, I see."

The assassin scowled. "How do you know that?"

"I recognise the emblem on your blades." Ambrose motioned to the fallen knives. "How did you get through the shield? I would give us some answers if I were you. You will be arrested for your crimes once we get you out of there."

The assassin snorted. "You don't scare me, old man."

"Ambrose, stop talking and get us through the shield." Darius held up a hand when Ambrose opened his mouth to protest. "Just try."

"Very well." Ambrose sighed. He raised his glowing staff and energy rippled towards the invisible shield. The shield flashed into existence. A glowing wall of bright blue light.

Ambrose raised his staff higher and pushed back against the energy.

A bolt of energy shot from the shield, struck Ambrose in the chest, and knocked him to the ground.

Darius knelt beside the other druid and energy sparked between his fingers. He rose and approached the shield.

"Using your power will weaken you further," Velestra warned. "Given your current state, it could kill you."

"Velestra, can you take Ambrose somewhere safe?" Darius asked. "And have a healer check on him?"

Velestra hesitated. "Isn't getting them out of the old city—"

"I'll figure it out. But I need him to be somewhere safe too."

"I'll have him checked." Velestra yanked Ambrose up and used magic to get him onto her horse.

EPILOGUE

Velestra dragged the old druid back to her village. She thought Ambrose would have known better than to attack the shield head-on. She knew the druid well enough, but she wouldn't call him a friend.

The village healer came to check on him and said he would recover soon enough.

She wanted to head back to the shield and see if Nyx and the assassin somehow found a way out. Would Darius call her to let her know what had happened?

With the aid of another rider, she helped Ambrose into her hut and onto her bed. The healer had told her to make sure he rested for a while. She would take him home later once he regained consciousness.

Velestra paced up and down and ran a hand through her long hair. Why were all these strange things happening? First the deaths, then the arrival of Nyx and the assassin. What did it all mean?

Perhaps the village elder would help. She ran off to the elder's hut and pushed through the front door.

"My lady, are you here? Please, I need your help." She glanced around but found no sign of anyone. "My lady!"

Goddess, where would the elder be? She didn't know how else to contact the woman. And who else would be able to help?

She searched the hut but couldn't find any sign of the elder. In the end, she headed back to check on Ambrose and gasped when she found the elder looming over him.

"My lady, can you help him? Two fae managed to get through the shield and one of them is injured. Ambrose came and tried to help get them out. The shield's magic struck him down." She put her hand to her face. "I don't understand how they could have got through."

"Simple, they are mind whisperers. Just like me." The elder grabbed her by the throat. "Now you're going to do everything I tell you."

DARK ASSASSIN

CHAPTER 1

Niamh Taliesin knelt in the Temple of Blood and bowed her head. This place had terrified her when she had first been brought here as a child. All hard stone and torture devices. Now it almost felt like home. Well, the closest thing she could remember to having a home, anyway. The Order Of Blood didn't just kill people, they were masters of torture and espionage as well. Although Niamh had no care for that stuff. She was a mind whisperer. Her gift allowed her to compel others with a single touch and hear their thoughts.

The circular room spread out around her with grey stone walls and an array of unoccupied seats for the other leaders. Torches flickered on the walls, casting dancing shadows around the draughty room.

Her long blonde hair fell over her face and the coldness from the flagstone floor seeped into her knees. She hated bowing before anyone. *I've been with the order since I was ten years old. You would think after eight years, I wouldn't have to kneel anymore.*

"We have a new mission for you," her mentor, Master Oswald, told her. "You're to travel to Andovia and track down the servant of Darius Valeran. Her name is Nyx Ashwood—she is a winged fae. You need to make this mission quick and clean. Once you've killed her, leave the realm. Her connection to a Valeran may cause problems."

Valeran… the name of the Archdruid's family. Everyone in the upper realm and beyond knew that name. Interesting. Why would anyone want to kill a servant?

She looked up and met his gaze. His grey hair and beard were short and trim. His washed-out blue eyes fixated on her. His weathered face and imposing demeanour had frightened her as a child. Now he looked old and frail. One day she would take his place in the Order and have the power and respect she craved.

Niamh didn't bother asking questions. She knew better than that. Why someone wanted another person dead wasn't her business. Besides, Master Oswald would lash her if she dared to question him again. She had learned that lesson the hard way after spending the last eight years training with him.

"I'll be in and out of the realm in a day or two." Niamh rose.

"Be careful on this one. Do not attack her when she is with the Valeran. From what I hear, the druid is quite attached to her. That is why you will need to be extra careful."

Niamh waved her hand in dismissal. "It's not my first mission. You taught me well." She flashed him a smile. "What kind of power does this girl have?"

"She's a former slave and her abilities are unknown, but I have heard she only has minimal power."

That meant an easy mission then. Good. She was tired of being cooped up in the temple all the time. She craved being able to travel again and see more islands around the lower realm.

Master Oswald held out a bundle of parchment. "These are the details of your mission. I don't need to tell you what will happen if you fail."

Niamh had to refrain from rolling her eyes. The price for failure would mean certain death. No one lasted in the Order for long if they failed to complete a mission. She never failed and she wasn't about to start now.

Niamh headed off to the chamber to gather the weapons and supplies she needed.

It would take a day or so to travel from the Elven lands of Ereden but first, she had to find a ship. She didn't understand why Oswald had been so anxious about this mission. She had gone after kings, lords, and anyone else that the Order viewed as a threat. Not always to kill them. Sometimes just to spy on them and get whatever information the Order needed. A servant would be child's play for her.

One thing did concern her, though. Why would a Valeran care about one servant? Servants would mean nothing to them.

She took out her best knives. Blades were always something she loved and she took pride in her collection. She included some throwing knives, daggers, and other weapons in her pack, along with some poison. Oswald wanted the job done clean and quick. Poison didn't leave traces the way weapons did. Not if you used the right poison anyway.

She eyed her crossbow. Another favourite of hers. This was a straightforward kill so she doubted she'd need it. Or maybe she would take it anyway. Perhaps she would find some time to do some hunting whilst there.

Niamh changed out of her leathers into a plain tunic and trousers. Dark travel clothes. She pulled a hood over her head and tucked her hair underneath it. She had a mask too and would put it on once she reached the dock. Keeping her appearance hidden was one of the first things she learnt from the Order.

It felt good to leave the temple and get back out into the real world. The Order had sent her on a mission almost a month ago and she didn't do well being cooped up with nothing to do.

She needed to be out and travelling. Working for the Order was just a means to an end. At only eighteen, she was the youngest in the Order. They liked to recruit people young and train them. Younglings were easier to mould into perfect killers.

Niamh made her way through the town of Eris. Wooden houses stood around the base of trees and smoke billowed through the air. Elves mingled everywhere. They didn't have much of a slave trade. That was one of the reasons she liked the elves. She detested slavery, but that was the way of the world.

Niamh had enough gold to barter passage, but she needed something inconspicuous. Passenger ships were always too crowded, and she needed to lie low. Besides, she hated being around too many people. It made her uncomfortable. She wanted something fast and low-key to travel on. Niamh moved along the dock past the crowded passenger vessels until she came to one of the smaller trading ships. Big trading vessels were good, too. Most captains never asked too many questions if you plied them with enough gold. One ship called *The Vanity* stood out. Large but swift. It didn't look fancy and had a trading flag on its red sails.

Niamh knew a pirate ship when she saw one. She had used pirate vessels before. Some were better than others. One or two captains had tried to stab her in the back but she'd stabbed them first.

This one seemed to have more on board than she expected. The buzz of thoughts echoed at the edge of her mind. A lot more people below deck. She scanned a little deeper and waited to see what her senses told her. Slaves. The captain of this ship had members of the resistance on board. As well as slaves they planned to help free.

That meant the ship would lie low and move fast. Just the thing she needed.

Niamh headed up the gangplank and approached a muscular, blonde man. Anxiety rolled off him in waves.

Not the captain. Aidan, a former Dragon guard turned bounty hunter.

"Where's the captain?" Niamh asked him.

"Right here." A young woman with long brown hair and crystal blue eyes came over to them.

"You headed to Andovia?" Niamh had covered her face with her usual mask so her voice sounded a little muffled. *Yasmine. Druid. There's a pretty big price on her head.* Niamh smiled underneath her mask.

"Maybe." Yasmine eyed her. "Why?"

"Good." Niamh pulled a bunch of gold coins from her purse under her cloak. "I need safe passage there."

"Does this look like a passenger vessel? We trade. We don't offer rides to masked strangers."

The mask made Yasmine nervous. That much Niamh sensed.

"I'll call out the Guard then. I'm sure they would be interested in you, pirate."

Yasmine's eyes narrowed and she pulled out her sword. "What did you call me?"

Aidan tensed, and his hand went to his sword.

"You heard me, Yasmine. There's a good price on your head. I'm sure the Guard would love to hear about those slaves that you have below deck."

A tall woman with long black hair jumped down from the crow's nest. "This one giving you trouble, Yasmine?"

"Will the Black." Niamh's grin widened. "There's a good price for you too."

"We don't take kindly to threats." Aidan drew his sword and aimed it right at her.

Niamh shoved the sword away and bit back a laugh. "I'm not here to cause trouble. I just need safe passage to Andovia." She tossed the coin purse to Yasmine. "Deal?"

Yasmine opened the purse and let out a low whistle. "Whoa, that's a lot of coin."

"We don't need it," Will insisted as she walked over to the captain. "This one is trouble. Never trust anyone who don't even show their real face."

Well, at least the pirate had some sense.

"You've got a long way to go to get those slaves to safety." Niamh crossed her arms. "So, what do you say, Captain?" She reached for her power. She'd compel the captain if she had to, but she wanted to save her energy for when she got to Andovia.

Yasmine sighed. "Fine, you better not give us any trouble." She pocketed the purse. "Weigh anchor and set the course for Andovia. And you, don't expect a—"

"You'll give me your first mate's cabin." Niamh's power pulsed through the air and reverberated around them like thunder without sound.

Niamh headed to the cabin. She wasn't about to bunk with refugees. Besides, she needed privacy. People seeing her weapons would only lead to unwanted questions. The cabin was little more than a messy wooden bunk and a small room with clothes strewn around the floor.

Argh, maybe I should have requested the captain's cabin. How does anyone sleep here?

She pulled out a folded piece of parchment. Oswald always gave her details to memorise for each mission.

Nyx Ashwood, servant of Darius Valeran, fae and suspected killer.

Good. Killing off the bad ones always pleased her.

Some might see being an assassin as a bad thing, but she liked to think of it as her way of getting rid of evil. A rough drawing of Nyx had been included. Once they got close enough to Andovia, it wouldn't take her long to find her target.

Maybe after that, it was time for a change. A chance to travel for her own pleasure for once. The Order owed her that much at least.

CHAPTER 2

Niamh quickly got bored of the cabin, so she headed back on deck for the evening meal. Darkness soon fell over them like a heavy cloak. Stars glittered like tiny lights.

A dark-haired woman came over and sat beside her. She wore a long black dress and had dark circles under her blue eyes.

Calena Reevus. Daughter of the former high lord of Doringa, one of the smaller islands in the lower realm. Now a rogue and a member of the resistance. That much Niamh could get from her mind.

"Hello, I'm Callie. What business do you have in Andovia?" Calena gave her a warm smile.

Niamh had taken her mask off to eat but kept her hood low over her face.

Gods below, why was this woman talking to her? Did Niamh have to compel her to go away?

Niamh preferred her own company most of the time. "My business is my own." She chewed on a piece of meat. *This woman needs to learn not to be so nosy.*

"Oh, of course. Aidan and I are travelling, too. We are going around the different realms."

"I'm sure our friend here would rather eat in peace." Aidan came over and put a protective arm around Callie.

"I thought she might appreciate some company." Callie squeezed his hand. "You must be lonely travelling by yourself."

"I'm used to it."

Callie's thoughts raced through her mind. She didn't seem so bad. There were few good people in this world.

Niamh pushed the thoughts away and quietened her mind.

"Are you visiting family?" Callie persisted.

"No, I don't have any." Niamh couldn't remember anything about her life before the age of ten. She had been found under a tree. Then she'd been passed around slave markets until she found her true home with the Order.

Callie's face softened. "I'm so sorry. I know what it's like to lose your family. That's what makes our work so rewarding. We help people."

Resistance work. Niamh didn't need to ask what.

"You shouldn't linger in Andovia long. The Guard there has been checking vessels more frequently. They'll kill resistance fighters like you." Niamh chewed on her meat some more.

Aidan and Callie exchanged a glance and both turned pale.

"Relax, your secret is safe with me." Niamh grabbed another piece of meat.

Aidan's hand went to his sword. "You know so much? Are you a seer?"

She snorted. "I'm a traveller. That's all you need to know." She raised her hand and her power pulsed through the air. Forget any suspicions you have about me. You will both forget meeting me once this is over.

"It will be good to see Nyx and Darius again when we get to Andovia." Callie smiled and relaxed.

"Nyx?" Niamh leaned forward. "Nyx Ashwood?"

She didn't know why that interested her. She never took the time to learn much about her targets other than basic things such as their powers as that could affect her mission. Targets rarely put up a fight. But it did happen on occasion.

Callie's smile widened. "Yes. You know her?"

"I've heard of her. Is—?"

"All hands on deck!" Will yelled from the crow's nest.

Niamh sensed the tension. "What's going on?" she asked Yasmine.

"We're getting close to the realm of the Undersea." The captain grimaced.

"You mean Merkind?" Niamh had heard tales of mermaids and the Undersea but thought it was just a myth. "They're not real."

156

Yasmine snorted. "Oh, they are real and they like to sink ships. We're headed straight into a storm. Damn, if only we had enough wind to fly."

"Wouldn't a storm create enough wind to fly?"

"Storms are too hard to fly in. Plus, we would be more likely to be struck by lightning." Yasmine grimaced again. "That's why we never fly during storms… Although I'd prefer that to being attacked by the Merkind. Your gold will come in handy now, traveller. Let's hope it will buy our way through."

Niamh frowned. "Buy our way through?"

Yasmine gripped the ship's wheel. "Merkind like gold and shiny objects. Sometimes they grant safe passage to people who give them stuff, but it depends on the mermaid. Some of them enjoy sinking ships."

The ship rocked from side to side. Aidan told Callie to stay below deck.

"You should go to your cabin," Yasmine told her.

"I never run from a fight." Niamh palmed one of her knives.

Yasmine's eyes widened. "Nice blade."

"I like weapons that look good and work well."

The ship turned to one side and Niamh almost fell. Waves crashed against them, and glowing silver forms darted beneath.

"Get us into the air!" Niamh slashed with her dagger as a hand grabbed onto the side of the ship.

Something screeched and the hand withdrew.

"I can't." Yasmine touched the runes that would activate the magic used to lift the ship and allow it to use the air currents. "It's not working. The runes don't have enough energy. Damn it."

Something leapt out of the waves. A half woman, half long tailed fish landed on deck. She slashed at Niamh with a long trident. Niamh dodged the blow and raised her hand to throw her dagger.

"Don't!" Yasmine let go of the wheel and raised her hands. "Don't kill her or we will all die. Aidan, take the helm." Yasmine approached the mermaid. "We have gold and other jewels. You can have them if you let us pass through."

The mermaid gave a harsh laugh. "You think gold can save you? You should know better than to enter our waters."

"In case you didn't know, this is the most direct route to Andovia." Niamh snorted and kicked the trident from the mermaid's grasp. "So, accept the gold or—"

The mermaid hissed and threw a bolt of energy.

Niamh backflipped out of the way, then rushed forward and grasped the mermaid's arm. Her power rose through her like a storm and shook the air around her. Like thunder without sound.

Yasmine yelped as the force knocked her backwards.

"Now you're going to leave and tell your other fishy friends we are allowed safe passage." Niamh glared at her.

The mermaid growled at her. "Your powers won't work on me, witch."

Niamh didn't let her surprise show. "No? This will." She pressed the blade against the mermaid's throat. "Now, you do as I say or I'll kill you." She pulled off her silver bracelet and tossed it onto the deck. "Take that as your bounty."

The mermaid grabbed it, then jumped over the side of the ship.

"What are you?" Yasmine wiped blood off her head from where she'd been struck. "What did you do to her?"

Niamh raised her hands and gasped as her power flowed free once more. Thunder shook the air again.

"Forget you saw me use magic. I saved you from the mermaid. That's all you need to know."

Niamh stalked back to her cabin. Exhaustion weighed her down. Using her power more than once drained her. Using it repeatedly in such a short time exhausted her.

She slumped onto the bed. The sooner she got to Andovia and completed her mission, the better. Being around people so much was too tiring.

A knock came at the door, and Yasmine walked in. "Thanks for what you did earlier."

Niamh looked up, stunned. Gods below, why hadn't she sensed the captain coming?

Damned exhaustion!

"You're welcome." She pulled the blanket over her head.

Damn, the captain had seen her true appearance. She didn't have the strength to use her power again yet.

"Do you have a name?"

"Call me Traveller. Now, if you don't mind, I'd like to sleep."

"Sleep well, Traveller. I owe you for saving me and my crew. I won't forget it." Yasmine turned and left.

Niamh lay there. She should have turned around and said she'd only done it to protect herself. But it felt good to have saved them and she fell asleep with a smile on her face.

CHAPTER 3

They finally reached Andovia the next morning.

Niamh had to admit she'd enjoyed being around the ragtag pirate crew and their passengers. But she had a mission to complete.

Yasmine changed her flag before they got into dock.

Niamh stood on deck as they headed towards the shore. Minds buzzed at the edge of her senses. Tiredness still plagued her, but she had enough energy to wipe the memory of herself from everyone's minds. But that made it harder for her to keep all the thoughts at bay.

Using her power on that mermaid had sapped her strength more than she realised. She had mastered her powers at a young age and rarely suffered fatigue from them. Compulsion took a lot more energy than hearing thoughts.

"We're finally here." Callie sounded excited. "Where are you headed to, Traveller?"

Niamh shrugged. "I need to find the person I'm looking for. Where are you headed?"

"To Eldara. To see our friends and get supplies."

Eldara. The druids' territory. That would be where she'd find Nyx Ashwood.

They drew into dock and moored the ship. A guard came on board. "Papers?"

Will came over and gave him a piece of parchment.

The guard frowned at it. "I need to inspect your cargo too."

"We have no cargo." Yasmine stepped over to Will's side. "We are here to buy supplies before we move on."

"We check all ships now." The guard handed Will the paper back. "Too many resistance workers have been slipping through recently.

160

No one can leave until I'm satisfied you're not smuggling refugees or stolen slaves."

Yasmine and Will shared a worried glance. Their thoughts pounded through Niamh's mind. She knew she had to do something, or everyone on the ship would die. It might not be part of her mission, but these were good people. They didn't deserve to die.

Yasmine, you can't stay here. Be ready to leave. Niamh touched the captain's mind.

Yasmine's eyes widened. *What? We can't leave. We came here for supplies—*

Forget that. You have enough gold to buy things at the next port.

But we can't leave. My ship can't fly unless it has more energy.

Will an Andovian crystal do? Because he has one on him. Niamh grabbed the man by the throat. Her power struck faster than he could blink.

His mental shield repelled her at first but she poured her energy into her touch.

After a few moments, she had a hold of him. "You're going to forget this ship was here. And forget seeing me. You're moving onto the next ship. Are we clear?"

The guard moved away in a daze.

"What was that? You're a mind—" Yasmine put a hand over her mouth.

Niamh swung her pack over her shoulder, donned her mask, and pulled up her hood. Her temples ached from using so much power.

Damned mental shields. This was why she usually avoided Andovia. A lot of the guards here all had shields to protect their minds.

"I am no one." Niamh knew she should wipe everyone's memories, but she didn't have the energy. After forcing her way through his shield, exhaustion weighed heavily on her. "You trusted me to keep your secret. Now I'm trusting you to keep mine. None of you will tell anyone about me ever being on the ship. Are we clear?"

"And if we do?" Will crossed her arms.

"Then it will be the last thing you ever do. If you know what I am, then you know what I am capable of."

"Your secret safe is with us. If you ever need a ship, you can call us again." Yasmine nodded.

"Yasmine—" Will protested.

"We owe her. She saved us more than once. The least we can do is protect her secret. Besides, not all mind whisperers are bad."

"I might take you up on that offer." Niamh made sure her pack stayed secure. "I had better leave before the other guard comes."

"Wait, what's your name?" Yasmine called after her.

Niamh ignored her, leapt onto the guard rail and over the dock.

The Vanity groaned as it rose into the air. Callie and Aidan both waved. She gave a wave back.

Oswald would have her hide if he knew she had let them live with the knowledge of what she was. Yasmine had told her the truth. She just hoped she wouldn't regret it. It didn't take her long to get a ride from the dock and into the heart of Eldara.

Visiting the nearby tavern confirmed Darius Valeran lived and worked nearby. If she found him, it would lead her straight to Nyx.

Hopefully, she wouldn't need to be here more than a day or two. After that? She deserved a break. Oswald would have to accept it. And with the growing unease in the realms, she wanted to travel before the Archdruid started another war.

Eldara had nothing but rolling forests. Minds bounced around her.

Niamh had always been wary of Druids. They were some of the most powerful magickind. Plus, the Archdruid would have her killed if he found out a mind whisperer still existed. She jumped off the cart and headed through the druid village. The air itself seemed alive with magic. Sprites danced around her head, but she ignored them.

After a couple of hours, she had learned Darius worked in the Forest Guard and often patrolled the woods with his servant. Niamh cursed when she learned that. How could she find anyone in such a vast expanse of forest?

She trekked through the forest and pulled out her list that Oswald had given her again. Just to check and see if she had missed anything. Something made her turn the page over this time and she saw a note scribbled on the back.

It read: *Use your senses. Trace her with your mind…*

Niamh furrowed her brow and read it again a couple of times. It made no sense to her. She couldn't track anyone unless she knew

162

them. She couldn't track a random person—her power didn't work that way.

What did Master Oswald mean? He knew how her abilities worked—he tested her enough over the years to see what she could do and pushed her powers to their limits.

She sighed and cast her senses out. A heavy green canopy hung overhead as trees filled with houses loomed above her. She carried on walking until she was away from the village. The forest remained dense but opened up a little so she could see the sky at least. Niamh figured she should keep her eyes open. If Nyx could fly, she might not be on the ground.

Something tugged at her senses and pulled her in a different direction. She never felt anything like it before and wondered what it meant. Had her power advanced? Could she sense her targets now just by thinking about them?

Niamh looked into the trees. She couldn't fly, but she could jump pretty far. She kept on moving in the direction her senses pulled her until she finally spotted someone sitting on a log below her.

Nyx Ashwood. Her long pink hair fell in a loose plait, and purple butterfly wings curled around her back. She wore a red tunic dress, dark hose, and boots.

Niamh grinned. If only finding all her targets was this easy. How had Master Oswald known she could track this girl? She would ask him the next time she saw him.

Good. She could be in and out of this realm within the day. Easy jobs were what she dreamt of.

Nyx sat and appeared to be meditating, completely unaware of Niamh's presence.

She pulled out one of her knives and traced Elven runes over it. The blade flared with light, then shot out of her grasp as it spun towards its intended target.

Nyx raised her hand. Waves of invisible energy rippled against Niamh, who flinched. Nyx pushed back against the oncoming blade with her energy.

Good Gods, Niamh hadn't expected the girl to be this powerful. Why had master Oswald not warned her about this? He had said she would have unknown power. How the heck did the servant get to be this powerful? Servants couldn't move things with their minds.

163

Nyx glanced around and called on her magic again. A tree branch broke off and flew towards her attacker.

Niamh leapt onto another branch before the branch had a chance to hit her. Curses. So much for this being an easy job. She palmed another knife and hurtled it towards the other fae.

Nyx waved her hand and sent the blade hurtling away from her. "Why are you trying to kill me?" she demanded. "Who sent you?" Energy prickled at the edge of Niamh's mind as Nyx scanned her with her senses.

The girl was far more than a servant. Fae in Andovia didn't possess such power. They were slaves and powerless.

Niamh scanned her with her senses again. Usually, her senses told her something. But not this time. Nothing. No thoughts came to her, nor did she sense anything else other than a strange tingling feeling.

She pulled out another blade.

Niamh knew if she couldn't hear the person's thoughts, she might not be able to use her touch either.

Nyx flapped her massive purple wings and took to the air. She rose high above the dense canopy of trees.

Niamh struggled to keep up with her as she leapt from branch to branch. Moving to the end of a thick branch, she finally spotted the fae again.

"Good luck catching me now." Nyx grinned and took off.

Argh, I should have brought my bow! She gritted her teeth. *I hate moving targets.* Pulling out two more knives, she spelled them and sent them after Nyx again.

"Holy spirits!" Nyx swore and dove out of the way.

The knives turned and spun back towards Nyx after she dodged them.

Come on, find her, Niamh willed the knives to find their target.

After a few moments, Nyx disappeared from view.

More knives whizzed around Nyx. Obviously, she had pulled a glamour spell around herself. Niamh narrowed her eyes and spotted the outline of the girl. Then Nyx turned and flew off in the opposite direction. Nyx dove through the thick canopy of trees and glanced behind her again. The blades were still following. The leaves and branches smacked against her. Nyx turned left, then right as she dodged different trees. She ducked around a large tree and scrambled onto a branch. The knives came straight at her. Nyx raised her hands and green light sparked between her palms. The blades hovered there.

Niamh felt the other fae pushing back against her magic. *Come on.* She pushed back, using the full strength of her powers. *Get her!*

More force repelled against her. Nyx used her free hand to trace runes in the air. Light exploded around the hovering blades. They fell away and dropped into the tree line.

A blast of magic shot up through the air.

Niamh had no idea what kind of magic Nyx might be using. Perhaps some type of fae magic. Wasn't that supposed to be illegal now? Especially in this realm.

She jumped onto another branch and realised her target had vanished. Niamh muttered a curse. One way or another, she would complete this job on time.

EPILOGUE

Niamh spent the next few days trying to kill her intended target. Every time, Nyx escaped from her and she was growing tired of this.

She headed out of the forest later that morning. It didn't take long to find Nyx again. Finding her was easy enough. Taking her out was a different matter.

Niamh had got her hands on a new crossbow in the local market and made some arrows so they wouldn't be traceable.

Tracing runes on the arrows, she fired and they shot towards their intended target.

"Avock!" Nyx threw a bolt of energy as power thrummed through her.

She liked this spell. The mind sharing hadn't been for nothing after all.

Niamh screamed as she lost her balance on the branch and plummeted down to where Nyx stood.

"Hello again." Nyx flashed her a smile. "You really have a bad habit of following me."

Niamh glowered at her from underneath her mask.

"So, who are you and why do you keep following me?"

Niamh thrashed against the web, hitting it with invisible blasts of energy.

Nyx traced some runes around the web to make sure it held.

"We can hang around here all day, but I want answers. Now." Nyx reached through the web and grasped her arm.

Enough was enough. Niamh might not use her powers to kill, but this time had to be an exception. She gripped Nyx's arm in return and let her power flow freely.

166

Energy shook the air between them like thunder without sound. It knocked them both to the ground.

Niamh gasped. *You are just like me. We have the same eyes. Good Gods, are we related?*

She needed to ask questions to learn the truth. Even if she didn't want to admit it herself. Oswald knew they were related to each other somehow. That was why he knew Niamh would be able to sense her.

What did that mean now? Could she really complete her mission now she knew there was another mind whisperer just like her? Had she found part of her long lost family?

Niamh couldn't answer any of those questions. One way or another, she knew she had to get answers.

DARK QUEEN

CHAPTER 1

Booms like thunder shook the air and rattled the walls around her. Fire lit up the sky with red and smoke as dragons swarmed around the capital city of Andovia.

This couldn't be happening. Queen Evony winced as the whitewashed walls of her temple trembled. A seven-pointed star glittered above the high altar and flashed with light as the temple's protections held in place.

"Mama, what's happening?" her eldest daughter asked. "What are those loud noises?"

Her triplet daughters huddled together in a corner.

Evony gritted her teeth. "The Archdruid is destroying our city. Why won't the shield go up? It's supposed to protect us." She paced up and down. "It should protect us." She ran a hand through her long hair that flashed with different colours. Her long, dark wings trailed on the floor behind her.

In the chaos fleeing from the palace, she hadn't had time to go to the shield and run the crystals that protected her entire realm. Someone should have activated it by now. If it hadn't activated as soon as the Archdruid and his forces set foot in her realm. She couldn't understand why. Why hadn't the shield turned on? It should have activated the moment her greatest enemy had dared come here. Her realm had been at peace for centuries. No one could conquer Andovia.

"I don't know, my queen." Lyra Duncan, her most loyal priestess, stood by the altar lighting candles, then recited a protection spell. Her long dark hair fell past her shoulders, her blue eyes had circles under them, making her pretty face appear hollow.

As if a protection spell would do any good now.

169

"Where are my guards?" Evony demanded. "Where's my damned husband? They should be here!" Something crashed against the temple's outer doors.

She couldn't understand why her husband, Ambrose, hadn't come looking for them. He had been acting strange last night, and she hadn't had a chance to confront him about his behaviour yet.

Something crashed against the doors again. No, they couldn't come in here. This place had protection. Wards, spells, and much more.

A guttural roar echoed around them. Good, the temples gargoyles had come to life.

Lyra shook her head. "I don't know. They must be fighting against the Archdruid's forces. My queen, we must flee." Lyra grabbed her arm. The priestess's whirling anxiety roiled through Evony like a storm. As a mind whisperer, she could sense emotions from most people. "The city has fallen. You must get to safety."

Flee from her own city? She almost laughed. "Never. I will not bow down to the Archdruid. My forces are just as strong. They will force him out."

Light flashed as an image of a woman appeared. Long, dark hair fell past her shoulders. Her eyes glittered like crystals. Evony's mouth fell open. She couldn't believe it. Her mother, the Great Guardian herself, and one of the oldest of immortals had actually come to see her.

"Mother." Evony blinked, half expecting it to be an illusion. "What are you doing here?"

She and her mother hadn't spoken to each other in decades. Even though they lived in the same realm. They had never gotten along very well.

"I have seen your demise. You need to leave this realm. Now."

"I will never leave my realm or my people." Her hands clenched into fists. "And since when do you hand out warnings? I thought you were determined to never interfere?"

"Andovia has already fallen. Most of your mind whisperers are dead, or they have chosen to align themselves with the Archdruid. I am just trying to keep you safe."

"I'm not leaving." Evony gritted her teeth.

Where would she even go? Nowhere was safe for her or her

children. Maybe she could get refuge in the upper realm but the Archdruid had followers all over Erthea. It wouldn't take him long to track her down.

"Please, daughter. Take sanctuary in the upper realm. Convince the elders to help you. Not all of them like the Archdruid."

"Nowhere is safe for me. Do you know what he's been doing to the other immortals? He traps them, paralyses them, and locks them away. He drains their power." Her fists clenched. "I won't let him possess me or mine."

"You cannot defeat him. Think of your children." Her mother motioned to the three girls huddled in the corner. "Think what he will do to them. He will either use them or kill them. You do not have the strength to defeat him. Not when he has the power of so many of us." Her mother's face drained of colour. "The Archdruid will be here soon. Please, leave while you still can."

The pounding on the door intensified.

"Mama, do something!" her eldest daughter implored.

Evony continued pacing up and down. "Where is my bloody husband?"

If Ambrose was there, they might stand a chance together.

"He's the one who let them in." Her mother grimaced. "That's why the shield never came up."

Her mouth fell open. "What? No. He wouldn't. He couldn't!" She swiped the candles off the altar and they crashed to the floor. "Damn him. I will kill him for this. How could he do this?"

"My queen." Lyra's voice grew more urgent. "Please, we must leave this place."

Evony rubbed her temples. She needed time to think, to decide the best course of action. But she didn't have any time.

Evony motioned to the guard with them. "Guard my girls. Get them out of here. Take them to the upper realm. They'll be safe there."

"No, Mama, we won't leave you." Her youngest daughter clung to her waist.

Evony shoved her away. "Stop acting like babies. All three of you need to go. Now."

The guard motioned for the children to follow, and they all vanished in a swirl of light as several rings rose from the floor.

"Be careful, daughter." Her mother vanished too.

She knew she couldn't fight off the Archdruid's forces all by herself. Even with her immortality, he would still capture her. The same way he had done with the rest of her kind. There would be no immortals left. Except for her mother, and she wouldn't do anything to save the others. Her children were too young to take up her quest. Besides, she couldn't be sure they would even be immortal since their father wasn't one.

Her senses prickled. The Archdruid was close. She didn't need magic to feel his terrible presence. Her power would be useless against him. It was too late to flee. But what could she do? If he captured her body, he could do whatever he wanted to her. But he needed her soul to get her true power. Her body was just a vessel. Maybe she just needed to find a new one.

"Lyra, if anything happens to me you must not let the Archdruid have my soul. I will need someone to host it for me." She gripped the priestess's shoulders. "You must be my new host. You're the only one strong enough to do it."

Besides, everyone else was already either dead or caught up in the chaos outside the temple. Lyra wouldn't be her first choice, but she would have to do.

"Me? But—"

The pounding on the temple doors grew louder.

"Say you will do it."

Lyra gulped. "I will do whatever I must to aid you, my queen."

Evony grinned. "Good. That will save me having to waste power." She grasped Lyra's throat. Her eyes turned black and lightning flashed between the two women.

Evony gasped as her soul passed into Lyra's body. Lyra's spirit passed into hers as lightning continued to surge between them. "Much better," Evony said in Lyra's voice.

"What have you done?" Lyra touched her new face. "My queen—"

"You said you would do whatever it takes to help me. That's just what you will do." Her smile widened. "I can't have the Archdruid capturing my true soul, can I? Besides, you took an oath to serve me in life and death. It's time to fulfil that oath."

The temple's outer doors burst open. Men and women clad in

black with red cloaks and black armour swarmed in like a tidal wave. They aimed their staff weapons at them.

Evony glowered at them, but refused to cower. She might be in a different body, but she'd never cower or bow to anyone.

One guard grabbed her arm and all of them surrounded Lyra.

"Careful, do not let her grasp you." Archdruid Fergus Valeran himself came in. His white robes were covered in dirt and scorch marks. His long blond hair fell past his shoulders and his piercing eyes fixated on Lyra. "Well, this is a sight I never thought I'd see. The Andovian Queen cowering away in the temple."

"I—we're not cowering. You have no right to be in this sacred space," Evony snapped and glared at Lyra. *Say something, you fool. I would not cower before the Archdruid. You are in a queen's body now. Act like it. I won't go down in history looking like a coward.*

"I… You're not welcome here." Lyra finally found her voice.

That was it? That was all she had to say?

Fergus laughed and raised his hand. Lyra screamed and sank to her knees as his power gripped her. White hot fire broke out over Evony's body, tearing through her long wings.

Two guards grabbed Evony's arms to hold her back. She watched as the Archdruid tortured her body and Lyra's screams rang in her ears.

The guards dragged Lyra out to a pyre. One of the guards dragged Evony outside and to the front of the crowd to make her watch.

Evony froze when she spotted her daughters lying slumped on the ground a few feet away. She covered her mouth to stifle her scream. No, they were supposed to be safe. The guard was supposed to have taken them away.

My poor girls…

They were children. They weren't a threat to anyone.

Ambrose, her husband, stood in the crowd, sobbing and held up by two guards.

Bastard. He betrayed her. Betrayed them all.

How could he have let the Archdruid into the city? Why would he do that to her? They had been together for decades. He was supposed to love her and their children.

Her pain quickly became replaced by anger as they burned her body. Lyra's screams echoed in her ears, but she didn't look away.

The Archdruid thought he could destroy her, and others like her. She had proven him wrong. He didn't know she had switched bodies. He hadn't even bothered to check.

Tears streamed down her face. She didn't take him much from the crowd of people gathered around.

"People of Andovia, your realm has fallen and so has your queen. Now watch her burn." Fergus turned and threw a fireball at her body.

Light exploded from her body as it burned. Evony gasped as her remaining power shot into Lyra's body.

The light grew brighter, taking everyone with it.

The Archdruid, the guards, all of her people faded.

It left her and Ambrose standing in the courtyard, surrounded by the dead.

So much death. Her fellow mind whisperers lay around her. People she had once called friends.

Evony went over to her children and gathered her eldest in her arms. She had always been the strongest. The one who had taken care of her younger sisters. Her middle daughter had been stubborn and headstrong. The younger shy and loving. She dragged them closer to her so she could hold all three of them.

"I will make this right. I won't let this go unpunished." She stroked her eldest daughter's pink hair. Then touched the other two. "You're too good for this world."

Ambrose came over. "What are you doing?"

She growled at him. "You did this. You brought him here and let him destroy everything we've built."

Ambrose shook his head. "I never meant... I just—I had to stop her. If Evony went to war..." Tears flowed down his cheeks. "I never meant for any of this to happen. My poor girls..."

When he reached for one of them, Evony bared her teeth. "Don't you touch them! You did this. You murdered them."

"No!" Ambrose sank to his knees, gasping with sobs.

Pathetic. He didn't even have the guts to admit what he'd done.

Evony let go of her children, rose, and grasped his throat. Thunder shook the air as she unleashed her power. "Command me, mistress." Ambrose looked up at her.

She growled at him again. So that proved it. His love for her had waned. Or else he would never have become enslaved to her will.

"Go to the Archdruid. Convince him you're a loyal ally. You will watch him. One way or another, I will have revenge. And I will find the others. No matter how long it takes."

CHAPTER 2

Evony swiped all the papers off her desk and let out a scream in frustration. A century had passed and she was still no closer to finding out what the Archdruid had done to the other immortals.

None of them had been seen over the past dozen years. Instead, they faded into legend and people worshipped them as gods. None of her searches had yielded any results. Being a priestess in the Order of the Blessed, an order who served the pantheon of gods in the lower realm, hadn't done any good either.

She had got as close to the Archdruid as she could. It didn't take much to turn his gaze her way.

A knock came at the door.

"Come," she snapped and bent to pick up her fallen papers.

Ambrose came in. "My lady, I have news."

She let the papers fall back to the floor and rose. "You have news on the others? Have you found where they are?"

Evony had done everything she could think of to find the others. Her brothers and sisters were the only family she had left. She had to find them and end the Archdruid once and for all.

"Tell me you found them." She gripped his tunic. After all this time, maybe she would finally have some good news.

"It's not about them. But something else."

Her face fell and she released him. "Another dead end." She sighed. "Tell me where you've hidden my body. Lyra's body grows weak and I need to find a way to restore my strength. This body is failing. That's why need to find the others!"

As one of the youngest immortals, she possessed some of the knowledge that the others did.

If she couldn't find a way to restore her soul to her true body soon and heal her body, she'd have to find a new host.

Being stuck in Lyra's body meant she couldn't access her full power either. Even using her touch drained her.

"It's not about an immortal. It's another mind whisperer. Her name is Nyx and she… She looks like our eldest daughter. Well, what I imagine she'd look like if…"

"If you hadn't let her die." Evony clenched her fists.

She wouldn't cry. Her girls were long dead and she had more pressing concerns. "Who is this girl? How old is she? I don't recognise her name."

"She's seventeen. Worked as a thief in Joriam. Much more powerful than I expected her to be," Ambrose said. "I don't see how she can be alive. Fergus killed all the mind whisperers.

"Not all. Some of them swore loyalty to him."

"They wouldn't have had children. You know that. No mind whisperer can have a child unless I used my power to make them fertile. That's the only way I can ensure people wouldn't use my people to breed other mind whisperers." Evony gathered up her papers.

"Seventeen? That's young. Who are her parents?"

"That's the thing. She doesn't remember her life before the age of ten. Mistress… What if our daughter came back?"

"How could she? The Archdruid killed her and her sisters. I saw that with my own eyes."

"But what if it is her? She's your flesh and blood. She—"

"Flesh and blood?" Evony let the papers fall from her hands and onto her desk. "Good gods, Ambrose, this may be what we need. Take me to the girl. I want to see her."

Maybe if she had a blood relative she could somehow restore her soul to her body. This might be the very thing she had been searching for.

"Take me to her then."

Evony and Ambrose reappeared near the Spirit Grove. Wonderful, they just had to come to her mother's domain.

"Why are we here?" Evony groaned.

"Look." Ambrose motioned to the tree line.

177

Out of the grove came Darius Valeran. Evony had known the Archdruid's son most of his life. She had made it a point to know him. He didn't seem like his father at least. Besides, he might prove useful to her one day.

A tall, young woman trailed behind him. Her long pink hair fell in a long plait and her large purple wings dragged behind her.

"Good gods." Evony covered her mouth with a gasp. "That—that can't be her… Can it?"

"I don't know. Perhaps you should speak to her."

A blast of lightning sent Evony crashing to the ground.

Her mother appeared as a projection and growled at her. "You're not welcome here, Daughter. Leave. Now."

Oh, how so much could change in a century. Instead of helping Evony restore her soul to her former self, her mother berated her.

"I'm not here for you, Mother." Evony glared back at her.

The Great Guardian's gaze flickered to Nyx. "Do not think about spilling innocent blood while you're here either. That girl is far more important than you can imagine."

Evony scrambled up. "Is that my child? Did you bring her back?"

"I never interfere with life or death. You know that full well." Her mother shook her head.

She'd gone to her mother many times over the last century and begged her for help. The Great Guardian always refused. She wouldn't even use her power to help her. Sometimes Evony wondered why she had even bothered coming to the temple to warn her that day.

Evony wished she had her mother's gift of foresight. Maybe then, she would have found a way to get her revenge and everything else she desired before now.

Instead, she remained trapped in this mortal husk.

"Who is the girl then?" Evony crossed arms. "Where is she from?"

"That's not your concern."

"Mother, if that's my child I have a right—"

"You are just as responsible for the death of those girls," her mother snapped. "I warned you to run. To not go against him."

"Your warning was useless. I'll find a way to save myself and the rest of The Twelve."

"Yes, and it will be your undoing." The Great Guardian vanished in a flash of light.

It left Evony wondering what she meant.

Several months passed, and Evony knew she was running out of time. She'd been researching more through ancient texts in the hopes of finding a solution on how to restore her soul to her body. Her mother refused to help, and her followers—though still loyal to her—insisted they had done everything they could.

Ambrose came by to give her regular reports and had been helping her read through the scrolls in the old palace.

When she rose, her hand trembled. Lyra's body grew weaker every day.

"Ambrose," she yelled. "Come to me!"

He would hear her call no matter where he was.

Ambrose appeared in a flash of light. "Yes, Mistress?"

She'd had him take people from the court. People who had been loyal to her had turned on her. Servants of former ambassadors had their uses. They gave her the chance to learn things about the Archdruid. Ambrose was only good for watching that girl next.

"Have you found anything that will help me restore my soul to my body?"

"Nothing, Mistress. Perhaps you should talk to your mother again."

"That won't do any good," she growled. "She won't help me. You know that. She refuses to interfere."

"I have brought you something else. Something I thought would please you." Ambrose kept his staff on the ground and a girl bound and gagged appeared. Pointed ears peaked through her long, green curly hair and her blue eyes were wide with fear. "I found another mind whisperer on my last visit to Glenfel Island. I heard rumours about a girl there running the prison. The Archdruid sent me to investigate when he didn't get regular reports from the warden of the prison there."

"Another mind whisperer? How is this possible? She looks too young to be one of the fae who swore allegiance to the Archdruid when my city fell."

"I did a test. Nyx is our daughter. So I went into the tomb where they were buried and there were no bodies there. Somehow, all three of our daughters must still be alive," Ambrose explained. "This is our youngest daughter."

Evony circled the girl. She didn't believe it. Her children had died. She'd seen it for herself and held their limp bodies in her arms. How could they have come back? What possible power on Erthea could have brought them back? She put a finger under the girl's chin and lifted her head up, forcing her to meet her gaze. "How? Who could have bought them back?"

Ambrose shook his head. "I have no idea. No magic can bring the dead back to life. It goes against nature itself. Even dark magic has its limits. I don't understand either. The Archdruid shot them with a staff weapon. That alone would have been enough to kill them."

"Why did you bring her to me?" She furrowed her brow. "You were supposed to be watching Nyx."

"I thought you might need her…? Nyx has some sort of link to Darius now. I'm not sure you could use her to restore your soul to your body. This girl's name is Novia. Like Nyx, she has no memory of her life before the age of ten. Our daughters somehow came back from the dead, perhaps they are the key to restoring you."

CHAPTER 3

Evony dragged the girl, Novia, into the old city. After a few days of testing with Ambrose, she concluded the girl wouldn't be much help her. As the youngest, she had always been the weakest of her daughters. Nor could they figure out how or why the girl had been brought back to life.

Nyx had always been the strongest of her daughters and she decided it was time to introduce herself to her properly. Other than seeing the girl sneaking around the temple with Darius last night, and them talking about an assassin being after Nyx, she hadn't had much of a chance to interact with her.

So, she convinced Ambrose to talk Nyx into letting Evony take over as her mentor.

Nyx came to the great temple that morning. Lyra found her in front of the high altar, staring at the symbol of the twelve gods.

She hesitated as she took a step towards the girl. How could this girl be her daughter? Nyx might look like her eldest—or at least what Evony imagined she would look like—but she didn't possess the same name as her daughter.

"Pretty, isn't it?" Lyra's voice made her jump.

"I guess, but it doesn't give me a good feeling." Nyx put a hand over her mouth.

"As well, it shouldn't. Now it's just a reminder they are gone from this world."

"What? Gods are real?" Nyx's frown deepened.

"The Twelve are more than gods. They have been here since Erthea began."

"Where are they now?"

"Gone or forced into hiding by the Archdruid."

"He killed them?"

"No, they can't be killed. I don't know what he did to them. He destroys everything."

Nyx glanced back at the star. "Ambrose said you were going to train me. How do you plan on doing so?"

"Indeed. I know you've been struggling with your powers."

"My powers are... more controllable than they used to be."

She was glad she had forced Ambrose to give her daily reports about the girl. "You don't have complete control, do you? You're afraid of what you are."

"I never said that." Nyx scowled.

Evony's skin prickled. Nyx had scanned her with her senses. Her eyes widened. "Do you do that around the Archdruid?"

"Do what?" Her frown deepened.

"Read someone. You're strong but your technique is sloppy."

She had forced her daughters to practice controlling their gifts from a young age. Without her guidance, they must have lost that control as they had grown older.

"What are you?" Nyx narrowed her eyes.

"I'm a priestess. I serve the old gods. I served the Andovian Queen herself before he... before he destroyed her." Her fists clenched. "I can help you master your gifts, but you have to be willing to learn."

"If you're not a mind whisperer, I doubt you can help me."

"Come. We need to practice somewhere more open than this oppressive place." Evony grabbed her arm and light flashed around them.

Nyx gasped when they reappeared in the forest. Trees spread out all around them, a mix of green, gold, and brown.

Evony nodded. "Much better." She needed somewhere to practice with the girl without being in the confines of the great temple.

"Where are we?"

"In Varden Forest."

"Won't the Varden mind us being here?"

Evony snorted. "The Varden are my friends. They won't mind a bit." She smiled. "Come, sit." She sat down in the centre of the circle and put her hands on her knees.

"If you aren't a mind whisperer, can you really help me?" She slumped to the ground.

"I grew up around them. I was a priestess to the queen herself." Evony pushed her long, dark hair off her face. "I'm probably one of few people left alive who remembers them. Other than Ambrose."

"Ambrose? What do you mean?"

"Well, he was mated to one of them, of course. Didn't you know?"

Nyx gaped at her. "No, I didn't."

"Let's begin. Show me your power."

"Alright then." She reached for Evony's arm.

"No, no, no. I meant let your power flow free. I want to see how well you control it."

Nyx grabbed Evony's arm and unleashed her power. Energy surged from her into Evony. It shook the air around them and sent leaves flying.

"Your touch won't work on me. Or your own kind either." Evony flinched and slapped her hand away. "Show me your power. Lower your shield and let it flow free."

"Are you mad? I've spent months learning to hide my power. I can't let it free."

"You are in a protective circle. No one will sense you in here."

"You don't trust me. Good, you shouldn't trust anyone but yourself. It will keep you alive." Evony nodded. "Don't let your feelings for that Valeran cloud your judgement either."

Nyx sighed and let her power flow free. Orbs of light sparkled around her fingers.

"You're holding back." Evony frowned.

"I am not!"

"Yes, you are. I can see it. You're afraid of what you are." Evony sneered. "Afraid you won't be able help the people around you."

Nyx gritted her teeth. "I am not."

"Yes, you are. You've lost control of your power before. And you'll do it again."

Evony knew she had to set the girl off to make her relinquish control of her power. It was the only way to see how strong she was. "You will lose control. It's inevitable. Perhaps you'll even enslave the Valeran you care so much about."

"No!" Nyx screamed.

Power burst out of her. Thunder shook the air without sound. Leaves whirled around like a tornado. The stones trembled under the force of her power.

Evony grinned. "That's much better."

Good, she had the kind of power Evony needed. Maybe she was strong enough to help her.

Nyx clenched her fists and squeezed her eyes shut. She grappled to get control over her magic again. Ambrose was mad to think this woman could help her. All Evony did was infuriate her.

"Stop!" Evony grabbed her wrist. "To control your powers, you need to control your emotions. Panicking and forcing them into submission isn't wise."

"But Ambrose—"

"Ambrose isn't a mind whisperer—despite being bound to one. Concentrate on your breathing and calm yourself."

Nyx took a deep breath. More leaves whirled around them.

"I sense druid magic inside you. Have you been sleeping with the Valeran?"

"That's not your business." Nyx was breathing hard. After a few moments, the leaves finally settled.

"There. You see. Control will come if you let it."

"I can't afford to be reckless. If anyone finds out how powerful I really am—"

"You are powerful, and you need to embrace it if you want to survive in this world."

She blew out a breath. "Why can't I remember where I come from? I need to know if there are others out there like me."

"That knowledge is deep inside you. You just have to reach deep enough to find it."

"How do I reach it? Because nothing else I have tried so far has worked." Nyx pushed her long hair off her face.

"You just have to focus and learn to truly embrace your power. The answers will come to you in time."

Nyx rose to her feet. "I should go. Darius is expecting me back."

Evony rose too. "We'll meet again tomorrow. The only way you will learn is if you practice."

Nyx unfurled her wings and flew off. Evony watched her go. She'd found a solution for getting back into her body. Now, the question was, how could she use Nyx to do that?

CHAPTER 4

Evony spent the next few days working in the old city, doing research in the library and training Nyx whenever she could. She was running out of time. Lyra's body was falling apart, and if she didn't find a way to restore her soul to her true body within the next day or so, she would have to find a new host. She had managed to find a scroll that talked about using the ancient art of blood magic.

Now all she could do was hope it would be enough. So she sent Ambrose to collect her true body.

Evony left the safety of her old palace when she sensed the feel of her daughter nearby. Novia was still locked up in the temple in Alaris, so it had to be Nyx. Ambrose had been taking care of Novia. Evony had no use for her. The girl had always been weak.

How had Nyx gotten into the city? The shield should have kept anyone out. Including her.

She rounded a corner and spotted Nyx along with a blond-haired girl. Evony bit back a gasp. That had to be her other daughter. So all three of her girls had survived after all.

The two girls stood holding Ambrose's staff and watching an image of her execution—or rather Lyra's execution—playing out before their eyes.

"The queen's soul escaped," Nyx remarked.

"Very good, Nyx. I wondered when you would figure it out." Evony stepped out from behind a tree. She held out her hand, and Ambrose's staff flew into her grasp. "But it's good you are here. It saves me having to come and take you myself."

"Take us where?" Niamh growled.

"Oh, not you, Niamh dear, you're not the one I need. Nyx is."

186

"Need for what?" Nyx scrambled up. "Why are you doing all this?"

"You'll find out soon enough." Evony laughed.

"You are not doing anything to my sister." Niamh threw one of her knives at the priestess.

Evony waved the blade away as if it were an annoying insect. She tapped the staff on the ground. Niamh vanished in a bright flash of light.

"What did you do to her?" Nyx cried.

"I got rid of her."

Nyx raised her hand. "Stay back."

Lyra laughed again. "You know your powers won't work on me."

Yes, she did know that. She might not be able to use her touch against Evony, but maybe the force of her magic would be enough to keep her away. Or she could move something and use it as a weapon.

Staff! Nyx willed it to come to her. If she could get hold of it, she could go back through the shield.

Green orbs sparkled around the staff, but it didn't move as Evony gripped it tighter.

"Stupid girl, you really think your power can match mine?" She raised the staff.

A blast of energy sent Nyx crashing into the remains of the burned-out pyre.

Nyx winced from the force of the blow. "I won't help you."

"You won't have much choice." Evony raised her free hand. An invisible pulse of energy dragged Nyx into the air. "I'm the first mind whisperer. I have lived for thousands of years. My power allows me to control my own kind."

An invisible noose tightened around Nyx's throat as Evony gripped her in her power.

Nyx reached for her magic, and let go of all the control she had over it. It crashed around her, and shook the air like thunder. But it did nothing to free her from Evony's grasp.

Evony walked over to her. "I could end you with a single thought, little girl."

Tears sprang to Nyx's eyes as she choked for breath.

"I need a mind whisperer's blood to help restore me to my former self. You're going to help me return to my true body and bring about the rising."

Evony dragged Nyx into a spell circle where she had placed a stone coffin. She had put a cuff on Nyx's wrist that rendered her powerless. "What's that?" Nyx frowned at the coffin.

"My original body lies in there. It took me years to finally find it. That's why I had Ambrose kill those people, since they were the ones who helped him dispose of my corpse." She laughed. "It took longer to break him than I expected, but he will be dead soon enough. Once I'm back to full power, I'll finally get my revenge on the Archdruid."

"What do you need me for?"

"The Archdruid destroyed my body. I need the blood of another mind whisperer to restore me." Evony took her hand. "Finally, after being stuck in this weak vessel, I will be free. I'll be my true self again."

Nyx pulled back, but Evony gripped her tighter.

Evony began chanting in the old language of the ancients.

Then she cried out as something burned through her skin when she reached for Nyx. "I should have known that no-good husband of mine would cast a protection spell on you."

Nyx grabbed Ambrose's staff that Evony had placed on the ground beside them. "Stay away from me." She aimed the glowing staff at her.

Evony laughed. "You can't use that against me. I control this city." She raised her hand. An invisible noose wrapped around Nyx's throat again. "Pity. I did enjoy the time we spent together. You're the first mind whisperer I've been around since my demise. But your time has come to an end now."

Nyx aimed the staff at Evony. A blast of energy shot out and pinned Evony in place. Evony screamed. How could that girl have overpowered her?

The staff stood erect, and flew from Nyx's grasp. The crystal grew brighter as a projection of Ambrose appeared.

He smiled at Evony. "Hello, wife. If you're seeing this, I've no doubt you've done something to dispose of me. Did you really think I wouldn't recognise you in Lyra's body?"

188

Evony's face twisted with anger. "You couldn't see anything that's right in front of you, you fool."

"Don't think you've won. I know you want your true body back, but that will never happen. Not whilst I'm still alive."

The light grew brighter and Evony screamed in agony.

She wouldn't be overpowered by one girl. Even if that girl was her daughter. Why couldn't Nyx understand she needed to be restored to her body? Calling up her power, she pushed back against Ambrose and his magic, and finally broke free. Then she hurled a blast of energy at the girl.

Nyx flapped her wings and dodged the blasts to keep out of the way. She dove lower and screamed as a blast struck her back. She lost momentum and fell. Grabbing the fallen staff, she raised it and sent a blast of energy to strike Evony.

Evony screamed as the blast knocked her backwards and into an old well shaft. She reached for her magic to slow her descent but it wouldn't come. Fire blazed above her as Nyx, Niamh, and Darius stared down at her.

"We have her. She won't be getting out of this," Nyx remarked.

Don't be so sure of that. One way or another, she would get back her freedom, her power, and revenge on those who had wronged her.

189

DRUID'S FATE

CHAPTER 1

Ambrose Brethian knelt before the Archdruid and kept his gaze on the floor to hide his shame. He couldn't believe it had come to this. Having to turn against his own wife. But what choice did he have?

Evony wouldn't stop her campaign to find the other immortals. Her quest had already led to numerous deaths. She wasn't the voice of justice that she claimed to be anymore. Instead, she turned her people into killers. Mind whisperers were supposed to be a voice of justice and reasoning. Protect the innocent and punish the guilty. That was their way — it had been that way for centuries.

"Why have you come?" Fergus Valeran asked the Archdruid, perched on his throne that twined with branches.

"To ask for your help." Ambrose met his piercing blue gaze.

Lady Mercury, the Archdruid's sorceress wife, snorted on the throne beside him. "Why would we help you? You are our enemy."

Ambrose rose, which earned him a look of disdain from Mercury. "Because our interests are aligned. My wife is waging war around the lower realm. All in her quest to find others like her."

The other immortals had left Erthea. What reason did they have to stay here? The world was falling into chaos, and there was little hope.

The Archdruid claimed to want peace, but Ambrose didn't trust him. He just needed someone to stop his wife. No one had the power to do that but the Archdruid.

"You expect me to believe you would turn against your wife? Aren't you bound to her?" Fergus arched an eyebrow.

"My soul isn't hers. I still have free will. Or else I wouldn't have come here." Ambrose missed the familiar weight of his staff in his hand. But he couldn't bring it here or the guards would have taken it away. He couldn't risk that.

"Can you help or not?" Ambrose couldn't stay away long. He had to make preparations. Getting his three daughters somewhere safe was his first priority. The girls wouldn't want to leave their mother, but he would have to convince them. Somehow.

"What do you expect me to do?" Fergus demanded. "Your realm is protected by a shield. No one can enter without permission. Not even my forces."

"I can let you in and make sure you can step into the city. You can take the queen into custody, but you will not harm her or my family. I want her to live out her days in peace." Ambrose knew he had to ensure the Archdruid agreed to his requirements. "And no one in the city's to be harmed."

Mercury laughed. "You expect us to let your queen go?"

"If she's removed from power, she won't be a threat to you anymore. Let her live in exile."

"Exile?" Fergus snorted. "Why would I let her do that? She'd remain a threat and retaliate against us."

"You can have her realm for all I care. I want immunity for myself and my children. Give Evony amnesty."

"What guarantee would we have she wouldn't retaliate? Your wife is a dangerous woman." Fergus' hands tightened on the armrests of his throne. "Do you think I would let her go? I vanquish my enemies. I don't show them mercy."

"Strip her of her powers then," he snapped. "If she has no power, she is no threat to anyone." Ambrose knew stopping Evony would come at a heavy price, but she would never listen to reason. If he couldn't stop her, it would lead to inevitable war.

"You would do that?" Mercury furrowed her brow. "Destroy your own wife?"

"I have to do this. It's the only way I can stop her. You're the only one with the power to end her reign of terror." He turned to Fergus. "Grant me everything I asked for and I will ensure the shield will be down."

"What of your queen's army?" Fergus demanded. "And the other mind whisperers?"

"I can arrange for them to give a peaceful surrender. Will you agree to my terms or not?"

Fergus and Mercury shared a glance.

"If you ensure the shield is down and Evony will not fight, then you have my word. I accept your terms."

Ambrose headed home back to the city of Varden. Darkness had already fallen. He had to make sure everything was ready. The shield would be easy enough to turn off, but he had to get the girls to safety first.

He hurried up to their room and spotted Velestra, one of their guards on duty.

"Are the girls in bed?"

She nodded. "The queen is looking for you."

Curse it. He hadn't meant to be gone so long, but he'd been putting everything in place.

A boat waited for him and his daughters on the river. He had to get them ready and out of the realm within the hour.

Ambrose opened the door and headed in.

Light flared around them, and his wife's face appeared from the shadows. "What are you doing? Where have you been?" she hissed.

"I… I had something to do." No one could deceive a mind whisperer, so he had to be careful what he said.

"What?" Evony demanded. "You've been gone for hours. And you didn't answer any of my calls."

She had called for him with her mind several times, but he had ignored her. If he had answered her calls, she would have sensed what he had been doing.

"I'm sorry." He kissed her forehead. "I didn't mean to worry you. It's late, you should get some rest."

She sighed. "Fine. Come to bed then." She headed towards the door.

Ambrose hesitated. He should have known she would suspect something. Why hadn't he got back sooner? Why hadn't he sensed her presence here?

He took her hand and led her away, then slipped a note to Velestra on his way out. Telling her to take the girls to safety. He knew Evony wouldn't let him out of her sight again and he wouldn't be able to slip away as he had intended.

Ambrose couldn't leave his wife again until early next morning. He found the girls in their room. All three triplets were awake and playing.

Holy spirits, why were they here?

Velestra wasn't on guard duty, but he couldn't ask her why she hadn't taken them as he had asked her to.

"Girls, gather your things. We need to go somewhere." He grabbed a pack for each of them.

His eldest daughter, Aerin, frowned. Her long pink hair fell over her face and flashed with different colours. "Where are we going, Papa?"

"Somewhere safe. Hurry, all of you." He waved his hand. So their toys, books, and other possessions went inside the packs. "We're going on an adventure."

His middle daughter, Anisa, didn't look convinced. She'd always been too clever for her own good. "We have lessons. Mama gets angry if we don't learn anything."

Yes, he knew his wife's temper well enough.

"Where are we going, Papa? To see the floating islands again?" His youngest daughter, Ava, with her long, curly green hair, grinned.

He'd already ensured that the shield would stay down, but he needed the girls somewhere safe before the Archdruid arrived.

"Perhaps. Come along." Ambrose led them outside.

"My lord, where are you going?" Velestra blocked their way.

"That's not your concern. Why didn't you carry out my orders last night?" He narrowed his eyes at her.

"Because —"

A dark shadow filled the sky and grew in size. Ambrose froze. Dragons. He would know them anywhere. The Archdruid's Dragon Guard had come.

Holy spirits, this wasn't supposed to happen.

Damn the Archdruid, Ambrose should have known he wouldn't keep his word.

"Take them to the temple," he told Velestra. There was no time to get them out of the city now.

"Papa, where are you going?" one of his daughters called after him.

Ambrose ignored their cries and hurried off to the control room where the controls for the city's shield stood. When he got there, two of the Dragon guard grabbed him.

They dragged him away, and he wondered how he could remedy this.

They beat him outside the control room and dragged him in front of the crowd at the palace.

Evony lay in a crumpled heap, broken and bloody, on a dais. They dragged Evony over to a pyre.

Ambrose's heart lurched, and he yelled at them to stop. What had he done? This wasn't supposed to turn out like this. He'd wanted to stop his wife, but now everything was falling apart.

"Death will never hold me. I will return and you will pay," Evony vowed. Tears streamed down her face.

Ambrose frowned. Evony couldn't feel pain. She could turn off her feelings if she chose to. She never cried. Not even during childbirth. Light exploded from her body as she screamed. The light expanded, enveloping everything in its wake. People screamed and something yanked away the guards holding him.

Ambrose sank to his knees and clenched his eyes shut until silence fell.

When he opened them again, everyone was gone. The Archdruid, his guards, the dragons, the bodies of the people the guards had killed. Everyone.

No one remained except for Lyra, his fallen daughters and Evony's burned corpse lying on the dais.

The bodies of his daughters lay a few feet away.

"My girls..." someone gasped.

He turned. Lyra Duncan, the chief priestess, came over and fell to her knees beside the fallen bodies.

Evony had switched bodies with Lyra. He could feel it. Lyra's mortal body couldn't conceal the queen's power.

"I never meant for this to happen." Tears streamed down his face.

"Do you hate me that much?" she screamed. "Enough to murder our own children?"

"They were supposed to be safe. I just lowered the shield to stop…"

"To stop *me*." Evony slapped him hard. "I should have known you'd do something foolish. Now you've destroyed everything."

She grasped his throat, and her power shook the air like thunder without sound. "Don't think you will escape me so easily, husband. I'm not going anywhere and neither are you. You will remain mine for eternity."

CHAPTER 2

"Ambrose!" He looked up from his desk as Darius Valeran ran in.

Odd. He hadn't expected the boy to arrive for their daily lessons together for at least a couple of hours. Nor had he ever expected to become a mentor to the Archdruid's son, but the boy needed proper guidance. Darius would never get that from his parents.

"What is it, boy?"

Darius bit his lip and a strand of long blond hair flopped over his face. At thirteen, he already looked a lot like his father. "I — I —"

"Well, spit it out."

"I did something bad." Darius winced. "I didn't mean to, but Lyra came and asked me to help her."

Ambrose tensed at the mention of 'Lyra'. What was Evony up to now? She still thought she had him locked in her power, but he'd broken her hold over him. "What did she make you do?"

Darius had a mental shield. One of the few good things the Archdruid had given him. Ambrose had been afraid Evony would use her touch on the boy, too. Now she will never get a chance to.

"She used my blood for something. Some kind of ritual, but I didn't understand the words she used in the spell."

Ambrose gritted his teeth. Blood magic. Holy spirits, what had Evony done now?

She had never stopped trying to restore her soul to her true body. The Archdruid had destroyed it and nothing she tried so far could restore it. It amazed him how long she managed to survive in Lyra's body. But it was growing weaker. A mortal body couldn't hold an immortal spirit indefinitely.

"What happened after that?"

"Nothing. She seemed disappointed, but I sensed someone within the earth. You need to come and check." Darius tugged at his arm.

Ambrose grabbed his staff and tapped on the ground. Light flashed around them as they reappeared near the shield that protected the old city.

"Where did she take you?" Ambrose held up his glowing staff, and the shield parted for them.

"This way." Darius ran on ahead.

Ambrose scanned the area with his senses. No Evony or any of the Varden guards around, either.

The shield closed behind him as he hurried after the boy.

Darius ran deeper into the woods. Ambrose wondered where Evony would have performed the magic. People still dwelled within the old city. It wasn't empty, as most people believed.

Why hadn't Evony performed her magic in the old palace? It seemed odd for her to be out here in the middle of the forest.

"This way." Darius pushed through the trees and climbed up a steep embankment that gave way to the river below.

Holy spirits, why did they have to be here, of all places?

Evony, what have you been doing?

"Here. I can sense someone. They're calling for help."

Ambrose froze.

How could anyone be alive? This was where he buried his daughters. No one lived near here. Those who remained within the city's limits were scattered around the forest. He had chosen this place because he'd wanted his daughter's to be laid to rest somewhere peaceful.

"Ambrose?" Darius stared at him.

He remained frozen, fixated on the burial mound.

"Ambrose!" Darius scrambled down the hill and shook his arm. "Please, we need to help."

He shook his head clear. "There's no one here. You must be mistaken."

"I'm not. Lyra was here with a large box — like a coffin. She used my blood for something."

Evony had used his blood to restore her body.

Thank the spirits it hadn't worked.

"What happened after that? What did she do? Tell me everything — it's very important."

"She seemed upset. She made the box disappear, and she left. Lyra said the shield would allow me out but not to go anywhere else," Darius explained. "I ran back to the shield then came to get you."

Something tingled at the edge of his senses. Recognition.

"Holy spirits," he muttered, and rushed over to the side of the mound. *"Scailte."* Light flashed, and an opening appeared in the side of the hill.

Ambrose raced through the winding passage until he reached the burial chamber. Darius ran to keep up with him.

"There's no one here." Ambrose furrowed his brow.

Something small sat huddled in the corner, whimpering.

"Blessed spirits. Are you alright?" Ambrose moved closer and froze as the girl with a dirty, tear-streaked face stared up at him. "Aerin?" Despite being covered in dirt, he recognised his eldest daughter.

"It's a girl." Darius's eyes widened. "How do you know who she is?"

"She is… mine. My daughter. Aerin." He reached for her and she flinched away. "How is this possible? You were… gone."

"She's afraid. It's alright, we won't hurt you." Darius stepped forward. "Let's get you out of here."

Aerin didn't respond.

"Aerin, it's your papa." Ambrose crouched to her level. "You're safe now." He still couldn't believe Evony had resurrected her, with Darius's blood, no less.

"You never told me you have a daughter," Darius murmured.

"She — my daughters died a long time ago. They were buried here." He rose and stepped over to the crypt where Aerin had climbed out.

Had his other daughters come back as well?

This shouldn't be possible. The Archdruid killed them. No magic could reverse death. Not even the Archdruid had found a way to do that.

Ambrose went over to the open crypt. The lid had been moved and scratch marks covered the side.

Holy spirits, he dreaded to think how traumatising it must've been for her to be buried alive. But if Aerin was awake, why hadn't her sisters awoken too?

As triplets, they were connected by their magic, and they died together. In theory, Evony's spell should have brought them all back.

"Hey, it's alright. You're safe." Darius raised his hand and light sparkled over the girl.

The dirt and grime faded. Her bright pink hair and large purple wings curled around her like a cloak.

A hand reached through the dirt as someone scrambled up. Anisa, his second daughter and her sister, Ava's, heads rose through the dirt as they gasped for breath.

Holy spirits. They were all alive. "Ava. Anisa." Ambrose caught hold of one girl and yanked her out of the dirt. He set her down and then grabbed the other girl.

"There are three of them?" Darius frowned. "But how —?"

"That's a long story, boy. *Glan.*" He raised his hand so the other two became calm. "Come, we need to get them somewhere safe."

The sisters all cried and clung to each other.

Ambrose stood there, still staring.

What would he do with them now they were back?

One thing was certain. He couldn't let their mother find out they were alive. There was no telling what she would do if she did.

CHAPTER 3

Ambrose transported them all back to his house. The three girls clung to each other, still inconsolable.

Ada, the house brownie, who had moved in with along with Darius, gave them some tea and food. None of the girls seemed interested in eating.

Ambrose held back, unsure what to say or do. What could he say to them? Yes, he might be their father, but he didn't know how to act around them anymore. They had been gone so long.

Ava and Anisa fell asleep after a while. Only Aerin stayed alert.

"Master Ambrose, what should we do?" Darius wanted to know. "The girls are weak and tired. Spirits, they must be terrified."

That was what Ambrose wanted to know. The girls couldn't stay with him or in Andovia. Not with the Archdruid's forces everywhere. Andovia wasn't safe for mind whisperers.

"I — I don't know." He rubbed the back of his neck. But he knew he had to do something.

"Maybe you should try talking to them. You're their father. They will listen to you."

Would they? What would he even say? He wanted to weep and tell them how sorry he was. Their deaths were as much his fault as the Archdruid's.

Ambrose took a deep breath and tapped his staff on the floor. He chanted words of power and the staff's crystal flared with light.

The other girls perked back up.

"Girls, what do you remember?" He knew he had to be careful, he didn't want to traumatise them any further. In truth, he would have been glad if they remembered nothing.

"Papa," Aerin said. "Is that you? You look so different."

He ran a hand through his dark blond hair. He changed his colour over the years to try and blend in with the other druids in Andovia. And, in an attempt to make people forget who he really was and how he had once been married to the queen.

"Yes, Aerin. It's me. It's… been a long time… since the Archdruid attacked our city."

"But the Archdruid shot us," Anisa said and her tiny hands clenched fists. She'd always been the most stubborn and strong-willed of the three. "Men came and dragged us out of the temple. They took Mama away too."

"Where's Mama?" Ava asked in a small voice. She'd always been quiet and withdrawn.

"Why were we buried?" Anisa demanded. "Were we dead?"

"I don't think we were dead. I think we went to sleep. Velestra gave us something to drink before the men broke into the temple," Aerin spoke up.

Ambrose's eyes widened. "She did?"

Why had she never mentioned anything about that? He had met with Velestra after the massacre and she had been distraught over what happened. But she had been the one who had helped him carry away the girls' bodies. She knew where they had been buried, but Evony hadn't. The queen had been too consumed by anger to pay any attention to where he had buried their children.

Ava drew back and started crying again.

"You were —" Ambrose struggled to find the right words. "I — I don't know," he admitted. "You were gone for a long time. That's why I buried you. But in truth, I don't really know what happened, but I promise you I will find out. All that matters is you three are safe now."

He had to find out if this magic was permanent or not.

"Girls, listen to me. I know you're afraid, but what happened to you has long since passed. We should go and see your grandmother. She will be glad to see you."

If anyone could help him fix this, he hoped the Great Guardian could.

They reappeared in the Spirit Grove. Light danced around the towering trees and voices echoed in the wind. This place existed outside of time and space — a place where the veil between the worlds grew thin.

Ambrose, the girls, and Darius and wandered deeper into the growth.

The boy and Aerin seemed to have struck up a conversation.

"My lady?" Ambrose called, as he pushed his way through the glowing trees.

After a few moments, he passed through the growth. Up ahead, a glowing white tree glittered like moonlight.

"My lady?" He kept his voice low.

It felt almost wrong to speak here.

The trees sparkled and voices echoed in the wind.

Light flashed as the Great Guardian appeared. "What have you done?"

She would already know why he had come to see her.

"I didn't do anything. Evony did."

"Yes, now she can learn there is a way to restore her to her former self." She sighed.

"Grandma." Anisa threw herself at the Great Guardian.

The Guardian clung to her and wrapped an arm around Ava as well.

Aerin held back, uncertain. "It's so good to see you all." The Guardian smiled. "Aerin, come here."

Aerin hesitated, then walked into the Guardian's embrace.

"Sombre." The Guardian raised her hand and all three girls fell to the ground, unconscious. Even Darius fell asleep, too.

"There's a link between the boy and Aerin now. They're bound to each other. Just as the other girls are linked to her life."

"What should we do? They can't stay here."

"No, they cannot. I'll send them to trusted followers. They can't remember who they are."

"You want to split them up? But they've never been apart from each other," Ambrose protested.

"It's too dangerous to keep them together. If they're separate, they will be less likely to attract unwanted attention."

"What about Aerin and Darius?"

"It's safer if they are apart. They can't come together until they're meant to. You should say your goodbyes to them." The Guardian raised her hand, so Darius disappeared, and the girls reawakened.

"Papa, what's going on? Can we see Mama now?" Aerin asked. "Did something bad happen to her?"

Ambrose knelt in front of the girls and wrapped his arms around them. He held them close for several moments without saying anything. "All of you are going to be safe. I am sorry for what happened. I hope you can all remember that."

Ambrose hoped his daughters could find peace in some semblance of a normal life now. One day, he hoped they would forgive him for what he had done.

SPELL OF LIGHT

CHAPTER 1

Novia Lancaster knew her day was going to be hard the moment the alarm sounded through the halls of Glenfel Prison. She groaned as she got up from her kitchen table. She hoped the other guards were already handling the situation.

"So much for breakfast," Novia grumbled as she shovelled a couple of rolls into her waist pouch. She pushed her long curly green hair off her face and checked her belt to make sure her weapon and ring of keys were in place.

Novia glanced around the kitchen with its bare stone walls table, stove and washing area. She would have to clean up later. As the acting warden she had to find out what was going on.

Heading out the door, she blurred away from her chambers and raced outside towards the prison.

What is the alarm for? Her white owl, Archimedes, asked and flew along beside her.

"It's probably just birds again. So I head and see what you can find out." Novia hurried across the courtyard into the massive fortress that served as the prison.

Worse still she had a ship of the prisoners coming in that morning. Among them would also be refugees headed for the resistance sanctuary underneath Mount Glenn. Novia would have to make sure no one got mixed up.

Once inside the prison, she headed through the long winding hallway until she reached the main guard room.

Edessa, one of her fellow guards came out. Her long black hair fell in long wisps down her neck and her pale face beaded with sweat. "Thank the gods you're finally here. I was just about to call you."

"What have we got?" she asked.

"No idea. It's coming from level four. I think the druidon guards are already up there. One came and asked for the warden again."

It was getting harder to explain the warden's absence. Yet if she told them the truth — that the real warden had died months ago — word would get back to the Archdruid. Then someone else would be sent to take over. A new warden would no doubt find out about the resistance settlement on the island and expose all of them. Too many lives depended on her and she couldn't let that happen.

She and Edessa headed up to the fourth level. One of the druidon guards stood by the door of an open cell. "What's going on?" Novia asked him. "Why is the cell door open?"

The druidon guards were golems — creatures created out of magic. They resembled living beings and looked like muscular men. Runic tattoos covered their faces and the rest of their skin visible beneath their armour. An Archdruid had created them centuries ago to guard the prison and protect the island. At one time they had run everything. Until the warden had been assigned. The Archdruid didn't want guards who could be bribed or influenced in any way.

Glenfel housed some of the worst prisoners on Erthea. No one escaped from it. Not even in death since the island's magic to keep people alive no matter what ailed them.

"There's a dead prisoner," the druidon told her. "Another guard alerted us during their rounds."

"What?" Novia pushed past him. The legend about people not doing dying on the island was true enough. But those cells were under the fortress. Deep within the island.

A man lay on his back, his glassy eyes wide open. Novia flinched. She seen a lot after eight years of living on the island but death never got any easier. She recognised him as Cyrus Allen. One of the prison's most notorious killers. He had once been an assassin and worked for the Archdruid himself.

"Has the warden been called?"

"I will tell her what's happened." Novia knelt by the body. "What is he doing up here? This isn't his cell." Light flashed between her fingers as her as a list of different prisoner names and their corresponding cell numbers appeared. "This cell was unoccupied. There's no way he could be up here."

There didn't appear to be any signs of trauma. Something didn't feel right to her. She always listened to her instincts.

"We will have to move the body to one of the empty storage rooms," she told Edessa. *Archie, call the healer up here. I want to know how this man died.*

The owl hooted and flew off. She and Edessa had to drag the body out themselves. The druidon guard was impervious to their plight and headed off when Novia gave him another order.

"He could have helped us," Edessa puffed. "What do you think killed him?"

Novia shrugged. "I don't know but something doesn't feel right. How could Allen even got up here?"

"What do you mean?" Edessa furrowed her brow. "Perhaps one of the other guards moved him."

She shook her head. "It feels wrong somehow. Don't ask me to explain."

Edessa's doubts rang through her mind. As a mind whisperer, she could hear people's thoughts.

"You're the boss."

"Shush, don't say that," she hissed. "The druidons need to believe Ophelia is still alive or you know what will happen."

Edessa sighed. "Novia, it's been six months. How long do you think you can keep up this ruse?"

"Forever if I have to. As long as I make reports to the general in Andovia and keeps the druidons occupied then I can keep up the facade." She pushed her hair out of her eyes. "Now we have a boat arriving with new prisoners. Can you handle things here for a while? The healer is coming to examine the body. Be careful, don't let the druidons see her."

Novia touched the body and searched for any lingering traces of thoughts. Her power didn't work on the dead but he hadn't been gone long so something might linger. Nothing came to her.

Another alarm broke her out of her thoughts. She knew what this one was. That alarm always rang if a prisoner had got out of their cell.

Good gods, would the trouble never end today?

She was used to keeping the peace. Most oof the prisoners behaved and if they did fight she usually used her powers on them to keep them in line.

How had anyone managed to get out of their cell? All cells were

208

locked and spelled.

Archie, are you back yet? Novia called to him as she ran and used her speed to reach the prison's lower levels where the more dangerous inmates were kept.

"Now what?" she asked the druidon already there. "Please tell me there's not another dead prisoner." Novia didn't know what she'd do if another prisoner wound up dead. That would lead to paperwork and unwanted questions from the other guards. Even the druidon ones.

She didn't want to use her touch on people unless she had to. Novia hated the feel of it. And how it sapped her energy.

"A prisoner has escaped. A man named Syrus Allen. A murderer and dark sorcerer."

"I know who he is." Novia gritted her teeth. "We already found him dead earlier."

Syrus was a sadistic killer. She had to use her touch on him more than once to keep him under control. He often attacked guards and prisoners alike. Only she and the druidons could be around him. The druidons never got intimidated by his anger or tendency towards violence.

"It appears someone opened his cell," the druidon told her.

"How? I'm the only one — the warden is the only one with the keys to these cells. And I have them." She took the small ring of keys from her belt. "No one could have taken these. They remain with me — or the warden at all times."

The druidon remained expressionless and silent. No doubt waiting for his next command.

"Make sure all of the prisoners are in their cells and accounted for. In the meantime I'll send out other guards to scour the entire island. We have to find him."

Novia couldn't believe what a nightmare her day had already turned into. It made her long for Ophelia. If she were here, she would have everything in order. Novia felt like she was being pulled in too many directions all at once.

On one hand she needed to stay here and keep the prison in order. On the other someone needed to search for Syrus' possible killer, too.

People lived and worked under the mountain. Those people

depended on her as much as the prison did.

Archie flew down the corridor towards her.

"Archie, go back to The Underlight and warn Derek there's a dangerous prisoner on the loose look around and have everyone on the lookout for him." She ran a hand through her hair and sighed. "I'll be there as soon as I can. Gods, I wish we had someone here to help us."

But I thought he was found dead earlier? The owl settled on her shoulder and stared at her with his huge golden eyes.

"He was but something doesn't feel right. Warn them anyway. People aren't supposed to die on the island. And if he is dead, we need to find out who and what killed him."

CHAPTER 2

Niamh Taliesin looked at the chains shackled to her wrists and wondered why on Erthea she thought this was a good idea. She felt almost naked and exposed in the loose shift dress and her long blond hair flowing around her shoulders. But if she wanted to get on Glenfel Island she couldn't go there dressed in her usual tunic and hose or armed to the teeth with dozens of weapons.

The Vanity rocked back and forth against the churning waves. "Are you really sure you want to enter Glenfel as a prisoner?" Captain Yasmine asked her. Her low brown hair blew across her face and her blue eyes creased in a frown.

She shouldn't have been surprised the pirate brought refugees and prisoners to Glenfel Island. Since leaving Andovia she'd spent the last two months travelling around with the pirates and trying to stay one step ahead of the Order of Blood.

"Agreed. Why not just go in with the refugees?" Callie asked.

"Because I need somewhere to lay low for a while. Plus, I need to find someone who used to be part of my Order. I need to talk to them and find out how they got free."

Niamh still found it hard to believe she had left the Order of Blood. She'd been working with them as an assassin and spy since the age of ten. But she wouldn't kill her sister. For her betrayal, the Order would send assassins after her and her newfound sister Nyx.

Niamh needed to lay low for a while and figure out what her place in the world was. Being an assassin hadn't felt fulfilling for her for a while. She wanted something more. But what? What could a former assassin even do? She only killed people out of necessity and didn't want to become a hired blade.

Working with resistance worked for Nyx so Niamh decided to try that for a while and she'd enjoyed seeing Yasmine and the crew again. They had helped her get to Andovia and leave undetected. And they'd all become good friends.

"You'd be safer if you went in as a refugee." Yasmine turned the ship's wheel. "Prisoners lose their magic for one thing. You might not be able to rely on your powers for help."

Niamh waved a hand in dismissal. "I can take care of myself. Besides, a refugee wouldn't be able to access the prison like a criminal would."

She wouldn't stay in the prison for long. Just long enough to find her man, get answers and get out. Maybe Glenfel would be safe to stay on for a while. Hopefully the Order wouldn't be able to track her here. It had been hard staying one step ahead of them over the last month. Still, she wished she could have spent longer with Nyx. They had a connection. Niamh hoped Nyx forgave her for trying to kill her. But she hadn't known they were sisters at the time.

They should be together so they could figure out their forgotten past. Like why neither of them could remember anything up until the age of ten or why they had both been found under trees in different places in the lower realm. Niamh had always wondered about her past but hadn't found any answers. Not until she found Nyx.

"What happens if you into trouble on the island?" Callie, one of the resistance members, persisted. "You won't have anyone there to help you. And you won't be able to call anyone for help either."

Niamh bit back a laugh. She wasn't used to anyone being worried about her. It felt odd.

"Tell Novia you're not really a prisoner. At least you'll have an ally, then." Yasmine swung the ship to the west.

"Who's Novia?" Niamh frowned.

"She's the warden — well, in all but name. She runs the prison and The Underlight. That's what they call the resistance who live underground underneath Mount Glenn. A lot of former slaves and refugees go to stay here. It's one of the few places in the lower realm that's safe for them."

"I can take care of myself. I can't afford to have the Order finding out where I am."

"You're not invincible, Niamh." Yasmine turned the wheel and fought against the churning tide. "If you don't have your powers or weapons, how will you be able to escape if something goes wrong? Callie is right. You won't be able to call us to come and get you."

Niamh opened her mouth and closed it again. She had never been to a place where she might lose her powers or smuggle in any weapons. She could fight but she doubted she'd be able to escape from a cloaked island on her own.

She sighed. "Entrusting my identity to a stranger is hard for me. I just want to find a way to get the Order off my back so I can be with my sister again."

"Novia can be trusted, believe me. I've known her for years. And she has secrets of her own."

Niamh let her senses wander and got a glimpse of Novia from Yasmine's thoughts. Along with information. Fae. Talked to animals. Possible seer. Yasmine didn't know her true power.

"You're doing it again, aren't you?" Yasmine scowled at her.

Niamh blanched. "Doing what?"

"You're reading my mind again. Spirits, your sister does that. It's rude."

"Sorry. I can't help it. It's something I do without thinking." She shrugged.

She would have to be more careful from now on. Most people never noticed when she read their thoughts.

"If you want to know something, just ask. It's disturbing to think what you might find in my mind." Yasmine turned the wheel again. "We've almost reached Glenfel. We should be passing through the island's barrier any moment now."

Niamh closed her eyes, called on her power and thought of her sister. *Nyx? Are you there?*

I'm here. Finally! I haven't heard from you in weeks. Where have you been? Are you alright?

Just the feel of Nyx's presence in her mind felt somehow comforting. I'm fine and I'm sorry for not contacting you soon enough. Things have been hectic since I left Andovia. I've had to stay one step ahead of the Order. I'm almost a Glenfel. I don't know if I'll be able to call you whilst I'm there.

That's… Annoying. But you still have the crystal I gave you so we should be able to communicate with each other through that.

Niamh clutched the small black crystal in her pocket. *I hope so.*

I'm working on a new spell with the druid to help us remember our past. One way or another we will go missing memories back. Nyx sounded confident.

Good, are you still having nightmares? Niamh had no idea why neither she nor Nyx could remember their past. Other than a vague memory Nyx had seen of them playing in the garden. Niamh couldn't remember anything.

Nyx attempted to get her memories back during a mind sharing with Darius Valeran, a friend of hers. She remembered being buried alive too.

Sometimes but I haven't remembered any more. My other memories are still out of my reach. Be careful while you're there.

I will. You be careful to. I still say should be with me. Andovia is too dangerous for us.

You know I can't leave. I belong here.

Niamh scoffed. She knew Nyx wouldn't leave because of the druid. How Nyx could call the Archdruid's son her friend was beyond her. But, she knew Darius was in love with Nyx so she hoped he would keep her safe.

There's something else I need to tell you. Nyx paused. After you left, we explored the old city further and found someone locked up in one of the buildings. Her name is Novia and she's our other sister. She left not long after you did to return to Glenfel.

What? Niamh gasped. Gods below, how many of us are there? Why didn't you tell me this sooner?

Because I haven't been able to reach you. And it's just her, I think. She looked like us and we're all the same age. Maybe we're triplets instead of twins.

What's she like? Does she know why we can't remember anything? Does she know who our parents are? Niamh rapid-fired questions at her sister.

No, she couldn't remember anything either. I didn't get the chance to know her very well. She seemed shaken up after her ordeal. All she did was ask me a few questions, then demanded to go home.

Nyx sighed. Novia got a lift on a prisoner ship that was back to the island. Maybe you should talk to her.

She almost laughed at the suggestion. Talking and saying the right thing wasn't something she was good at. *Fine. I'll try. I might need the help once I get the prison anyway.*

Just be careful. We have no idea what the queen might have done to her or how traumatised she really is.

You, too. I will contact you again as soon as I can.

Energy reverberated through the air as *the Vanity* passed through an invisible wall of energy. The small island of Glenfel loomed into view. Most of it taken up by a mountain and a stone fortress. Neither looked very welcoming.

Niamh didn't know what to feel over the possibility of another sister. She was so used to being alone. When she found Nyx she had felt like she found the missing part of herself. Part she hadn't known was missing.

How would Novia react to meeting her?

Two guards covered in runic tattoos stood waiting on the dock. Both had long dark hair and wore black guard uniforms.

Niamh hated having shackles on. She knew she had to keep up appearances but couldn't Yasmine have picked some lighter shackles?

Light blurred and another girl with pointed ears appeared. Long green curls cascaded past her shoulders and she had piercing blue eyes. How had moved so fast? No magickind should move like that. Except perhaps a lykae. She had met one in Andovia.

"Prisoners are to be taken to keep at once."

This must be Novia, she realised. She looked around eighteen. The same age as her and Nyx. How could someone so young run this entire island?

Druidon guards. Niamh had heard of them. Damn, she couldn't use her powers in them. Only the Archdruid could control them.

The guards traced runes on each of the prisoners' hands. She knew what they meant. Runes to dispel magic. But she would not let anyone bind her powers. Her plan had failed already.

Niamh backed away. *Yasmine, help me.*

"Wait, this one isn't a prisoner." Yasmine jumped down off the ship.

"Then why is she shackled?" Novia furrowed her brow.

"She's —" Yasmine hesitated. Don't let them mark her. She is not prisoner; she is a friend. She needs to go inside prison. You have to help her.

Niamh reached out to touch Novia's mind and then nothing. A wall of silence greeted her along with a tingle of recognition.

Novia didn't look surprised, just confused. "Who are you?"

"Someone who needs your help. Can you help me or not?"

CHAPTER 3

"Head back to the keep at once," Novia told the druidon guards. "Take the prisoners to their cells. Then get back to searching."

"What about her?" The first druidon pointed towards the only female prisoner.

"Bring her in. She is accused of theft. So she's not a security risk."

"She needs to be marked. The rules state —"

"I will her. Just go!" She waved her arm and sighed. Novia had no idea why anyone would want to sneak into the prison. And couldn't believe Yasmine would suggest such a thing.

She didn't need this and already had enough to deal with.

Worse still she couldn't get anything from the girl either. That surprised her. She could read almost everyone. At least a little. Even if she couldn't hear more than a few surface thoughts.

The girl had long blond that hair fell past her shoulders. Blue eyes, pointed ears. She looked more fae than Elvin.

"Yasmine, what are you playing at?" Novia demanded once the druidons were gone. "Are you trying to expose me? Now is not the time to sneak anyone into the prison. Why is she here?"

"She has a name. I'm Niamh. I need to get into your prison to speak to another prisoner." The girl raised her chin. "It's a matter of life and death."

"Niamh's a friend. Her sister is an ally of the resistance," Yasmine said. "She saved me and my crew more than once. Just let her into the prison to talk to someone. She's not here to cause any harm."

Novia sighed and ran her hand through her long hair. What had she done to deserve all this trouble? All she wanted was things to go back to normal after being the queen's prisoner. Would it take to make that happen?

"I don't have time to argue." Novia grabbed hold of the shackles. "Leave your supplies here then leave at once. We have a security breach."

"Is anything we can do to help?" Yasmine asked. "Given how much you helped us over the years it's the least we could do. And you know I wouldn't ask for such a huge favour unless I needed it."

She shook her head. "Leave as fast as possible. I don't want there to be any way off this island."

Novia had to wait for Derek and Irene, two of her friends from The Underlight, to appear to unload all the refugees. All the while she felt Niamh's eyes on her.

Novia had to touch each new refugee to compel them not to leave the island, not come near the prison and to remain on the island. It left her feeling exhausted. She went to use her power Niamh.

"You're wasting your time. Your touch won't work on me. Even if you hadn't drained all of your strength," Niamh told her.

Novia narrowed her eyes and grasped the girl's throat.

"You can't hear anything from my mind, can you?" Niamh arched an eyebrow.

"How do you know?"

"Because I'm mind whisperer like you. Our touch doesn't work on each other. Believe me, I used to my sister and it drained my strength for no good reason."

Novia lowered her hand and yanked at the chains.

"I'm taking you to your cell. I have marked you with a rune. It won't bind you but you will need it to —" she froze. "If you're like me I can't let you loose in my prison. Why have you come here?"

She hated not being able to read someone. And to not be sure of someone's motives. Ophelia always told her not to rely on her gift. That it wasn't infallible.

"Because I need to know how to stop someone evil."

She dragged Niamh along with her. Curse it, she needed to get the keep. Novia hated moving so slow. "If you're going to kill someone —" Novia gritted her teeth.

"I'm not. I just need to know how to stop someone. If killing them was the answer I would have done it already."

Novia couldn't believe she was anything like this girl. Under normal circumstances she would have been thrilled to meet another mind whisperer. Other than Nyx who she had met in Andovia and the queen who had kidnapped her she never met anyone else like her.

"There's a lot of fear on this island. What's your security threat?"

Novia hesitated. She didn't know this girl. She shouldn't tell her anything. "That's not your concern."

Niamh yanked back on the shackles. "You can't lock me up."

"I can't let you roam free either. It's not safe."

"For me for others?"

"Both. Now move or I will call the druidons down here to fetch you. Your powers are useless against them."

Niamh smirked. "We'll see. I could probably find a way to shift their allegiance away from the Archdruid."

Novia shook her head. "It won't work. Believe me, I've tried."

"Who escaped?"

She yanked the girl's shackles. "I'm not sure if anyone did escape will not. The missing prisoner is called Cyrus Allen but he was found dead earlier this morning. He's a killer — a dangerous one."

Niamh arched an eyebrow. "Then how can he be missing?"

She hesitated. "He might not be."

"I know Cyrus Allen. He is a legend where I come from and I doubt anyone could have killed him. Can I see his body?"

"No. I can't just let you go wandering around doing whatever you like. It will raise a lot of unwanted questions."

"Judging by how you are pretending to be the warden and getting keeping secrets is pretty natural for you. If I can help you figure out who killed Cyrus, isn't that worth the risk?" Niamh rubbed at her shackled wrists. "I have powers like yours. Let me help."

"Why should I trust you?" Novia put her hand on her hip. "Who are you really? How do you know Cyrus?"

"I work with resistance. Now can you take the shackles off?"

"No. I have keep up appearances or the druidons will ask questions. Let's go."

"Wait, given the reputation Glenfel has, how did Cyrus get out of his cell?"

Her mouth open. "How do you know he escaped?"

Niamh rolled her eyes. "I'm a mind whisperer like you. I can hear the other guards' thoughts."

Novia hesitated.

"Showing me his cell won't cause any harm. Will it? I'm guessing you don't know how he got out."

She sighed. "You're playing a dangerous game that could get everyone on this island killed."

"Do you want to find out what happened to him or not?"

Novia used her speed to get Niamh back to the keep. She booked her in and made a show of taking her to a cell. Then they headed down to Allen's cell.

"How are you going to track him?" Novia crossed her arms and wondered if she'd gone mad. But she was desperate.

"I can track people's mind. It's part my gift. Years of training helped me hone it."

"You trained with someone?" She sighed. "No one ever taught me to control my gift. I had to learn for myself."

Niamh ran her hands over the door. "Were you found under a tree when you were ten?"

Novia's mouth fell open. "How — I mean, why would you ask that?"

"No reason. How did you end up here?"

"The warden found me and raised me. She was like a mother. She was the only one who understood me." Novia looked away.

Was she telling that to a complete stranger?

Nor did she know if she could trust her. But she hadn't received any warning.

"Sorry to hear that. So you don't remember anything about your life before that?"

Novia hesitated. Ophelia always told her to be careful with her secrets. She never shared her secret with anyone, not with her friends at the prison or anyone in The Underlight. If anyone asked, she told them she was a seer.

"Wait, are you my sister? Nyx said I had another sister but I don't know if I believe her. I thought I only had one."

"That would be me. I'm Niamh. Somehow you, me and Nyx are all related to each other." Niamh smiled and grimaced as she touched the door again. "Someone did help Cyrus to escape. From the looks of it he's been coming and going for a while now."

"What do you mean someone helped him escape?" Novia put her hands on her hips. "How could they have? Only me and one of the druidons have keys to that cellblock."

"I'm not sure if it was a guard. Someone used magic. There's faint traces in runes here on the door." She touched the door again. "I recognise this magic. The Andovian queen has been here. She must have let him out."

Novia looked closer. "How do you do that?"

"I told you. I studied a lot of magic and I've had dealings with the queen before. Please, let me see his body. We need to make sure he is really dead."

Novia shook her head. "The queen couldn't have helped him escape today. Nyx told me she was trapped in Andovia back in the old city where she held me prisoner."

"These runes don't look recent. She probably allowed him to escape around the time she took you."

Novia shuddered. "I still don't know how she got on the island. People can't transport in and out. And Yasmine had the only ship that comes here aside from the prison ships."

"It wouldn't have taken much of the queen to get on the prison ship. Didn't anyone notice you were missing? I'm surprised they didn't raise the alarm."

"The other guards covered up my absence. They searched for me but couldn't find any trace of me. I still don't know why she took me."

"Probably because your mind whisperer like me and Nyx. She seemed interested in Nyx the most though. But she needed the power of the mind whisperer to help her get back into her true body. As when she tried to kill Nyx." Niamh clenched her fists. "She brought you and me along in case that didn't work."

"I'll take you to see the body. We had better find out if he escaped or not."

CHAPTER 4

Niamh and Novia hurried down to one of the store rooms where Novia had ordered one of the other guards to keep watch over the body.

Niamh was eager to see the body for herself. If she knew Cyrus Allen, he wouldn't let anyone stab him to death. The stabbing and using daggers had been his trademark as an assassin. She preferred using knives herself back in her old life.

"Has the healer come to examine the body?" Novia asked the guard.

He nodded. "She came earlier and said a single stab wound to the chest is what killed him."

The guard is telling the truth, Novia told her in salt.

Niamh pushed them and pulled the sheet off the body. It appeared to be a dark-haired man with a weathered face, tanned skin and rippling muscles.

She traced some runes over the body.

"What are you doing?" Novia furrowed her brow as she walked into the room.

"Just wait." Light flared over the body and transformed it into the corpse of an older dwarf woman.

Novia gasped and looked away. "Gods above, that's the healer works in The Underlight. Her name is Marigold. Why is she here? What has he done to her?"

"Cyrus has the power of dark sorcery. Some people said he could bring his victims back to life. It wouldn't have taken much for him to transform another body to look like himself." Niamh threw the sheet back over the dead woman.

"My guards searched the entire prison and guard houses for any intruders."

"Where do refugees live?" Niamh arched an eyebrow.

"Under the mountain. We call it The Underlight since everything is so secret and hidden down here."

"Then that's where we should be headed. Sounds like it's the perfect place to hide out."

"Let's go."

Niamh couldn't believe they had to walk everywhere on the island. No one could transport anywhere due to the magic that cloaked the place and prevented people from leaving. And the island was too small to have any kind of transport or animals for transportation.

Novia hadn't said anything else about them being sisters — much to Niamh's surprise. Didn't she have questions? Niamh had certainly had some when she had first met Nyx.

But they had find Allen. Allen used to work for the Order and had been the only one who'd left years before his arrest. She had to find him and find out what he'd done to achieve freedom. Niamh didn't want to fight off assassins for the rest of her life. She needed to get the Order away from her. Short of killing them all she didn't see how she would do that.

They arrived at the edge of the mountain. It looked smaller than she'd expected. Nothing like the mountains around Ereden.

"People live under here?" She furrowed her brow. "How is that possible?"

Novia pressed part of the rock and the wall moved aside. "There are tunnels beneath the mountain and caverns. My adoptive mother turned this place into a sanctuary years ago."

They headed through the tunnels. The crystal walls shimmered in an eerie glow and dripping stalactites hung overhead.

Now she could see why they called it The Underlight.

"Do you know why you don't remember your past?" Niamh broke the silence between them.

"You ask a lot of questions." Novia narrowed her eyes. "No, I don't remember. What do you want with Allen?"

She hesitated. "To find out how to stop the Order of Blood from coming after me and Nyx. I just found her again and I'm not going to lose her." Her fists clenched and she hesitated. "Before I met Nyx I was an assassin who worked for the Order of Blood. They sent me to kill her. We were both abandoned as kids. I never knew about her until a few months ago months ago." She stopped when an owl flew around the corner and landed on Novia's shoulder.

"Archie, fly on. We'll right behind you." Novia turned to her. "How fast can you run?"

"Not as fast as you." She held out her hand.

Novia grabbed her and yanked her along the she used her speed. Niamh bit back a scream as they blurred.

They reappeared in a much larger cavern. Dazzling light shimmered overhead. "Please don't do that again." She gasped for breath.

People mingled about carrying food and other items.

"This way." Novia blurred off again.

And she thought Nyx being able to fly was bad.

She ran to keep up and followed her senses down the tunnel.

The owl flew along beside her, unable to keep up with Novia either. Niamh's senses prickled. Allen's presence was nearby.

She finally caught up with Novia in an empty cavern.

"Archie said he was here." Novia glanced around in confusion. "So where is he?"

Niamh stopped to catch her breath. "He must be here somewhere. I sensed him. But keep looking."

They trudged further along the tunnel. Stalactites and glittering light hung overhead. Niamh would have found the place fascinating but she didn't like being on the ground. It made her uneasy.

What if the mountain gave way and buried them alive? She'd never liked enclosed spaces.

"Nyx said you didn't stay in Andovia very long." She broke the silence between them. "I stayed there for as long as I could after I found out she was my sister. It's a shame I could have stayed longer but it's not safe there for mind whisperers."

Novia shook her head. "I couldn't stay. I'm needed here. Besides, why would I want to stay in such an awful place? I spent the gods only know how long trapped in the old city."

She hesitated. How could she say something comforting? She barely knew this other girl and she'd never been someone that was good at talking. "It's alright if you want to talk about it."

Novia stared at her, incredulous. "I don't. Let's focus on the task at hand, shall we?"

"Did the queen hurt you?"

Novia blew out a breath. "Niamh, I'm glad I met you you but I have more important things to deal with."

"Right, Allen is —" She span around see Allen in the doorway. "Here."

Cyrus looked just as he remembered from when she'd met him as a child. Not long after she'd been taken to the Order.

He flashed her a smile. "Niamh." Then he raised his hand and black smoke curled from his fingers.

Niamh shoved Novia out of the way and hit him with a blast of light.

Cyrus dodged the blast and more smoke filled the chamber. She'd know his dark sorcery anywhere. He'd never been shy about showing off his magic either.

Her mind raced. What had her mentor Master Oswald always told her about Cyrus?

"Remember to use the light against his darkness…" he'd one said when she'd mentioned she felt afraid of Allen.

Let's go. Niamh motioned for her to follow.

Novia, can you throw light from your hands? Niamh hurried down the tunnel after her with Cyrus close behind them. Gods she wished she had her sister's speed.

Yes. Why?

Good, is that cavern you ahead a dead end?

Novia nodded. You think we can trap him?

She smirked. I like the way you think, sister. If we're lucky. But we need to join powers. Take my hand. She reached out for her.

Novia grabbed her hand as they stood near the cave entrance. Light exploded around them.

Oh no. She pulled Novia with her as rocks rained down around them.

The cavern entrance disappeared under the rocks and she knew there was no way out.

SPELL OF SHADOW

CHAPTER 1

Novia winced as she woke. She coughed as dust flew around her from the cave-in. It took her a moment to remember what happened.

She and Niamh had been searching for Cyrus Allen, an escaped prisoner. Niamh was a mind whisperer, pretending to be a prisoner so she could talk to Allen, and apparently, her long-lost sister. They had managed to track Allen down to The Underlight. A series of caverns underneath Mount Glenn. The mountain served as a sanctuary for refugees and members of the resistance.

Novia scrambled up and coughed as more dust assaulted her. Her head throbbed from where a rock had struck her.

She groaned. How could she be stupid enough to walk right into a trap? She should have known better and been more careful.

But no, she'd been so desperate to protect her secret and get Allen back into prison.

Why had she agreed to work with Niamh? Novia didn't know her or anything about her. Worse still, her mind reading wouldn't work on her either, so she didn't know if the other girl could be trusted. She still didn't know how to feel about finding her other long-lost sister.

"Archie?" She scanned around but found nothing but a pile of fallen rocks that reached to the ceiling. No sign of her owl anywhere.

Had he been hit, or was he on the other side of the cave-in?

Niamh lay a few feet away, unmoving and covered in rocks.

"Niamh?" Novia winced as she crawled over to her. "Niamh, are you hurt?" Her head throbbed and her fingers came away bloody when she touched her forehead. She wiped the blood on her dress.

Niamh remained motionless. She reached out and touched Niamh. Sometimes people's minds were more accessible when they were unconscious because they were less aware than in their waking states. She scanned Niamh with her senses. Nothing. Her mind remained closed.

She touched the back of Niamh's head and spotted a huge gash there. Much worse than the scrape she had on her own forehead.

Novia scrambled up and stared at the fallen rocks. She couldn't move them on her own, and even if she did, they would be buried alive. "Niamh, please wake up."

Nothing.

She ripped off a piece of her dress and wrapped it around her head. Hopefully that would stop the bleeding. Then she ripped another piece off to try and stem the blood leaking from Niamh's head.

Archie? she called for her owl.

No reply came.

Edessa? She tried calling several guards, but silence greeted her.

Why wouldn't any of them answer? Couldn't they hear her?

Novia cast her senses out and a wall of energy greeted her. Someone had put a ward up outside the cave-in to make sure they couldn't get out.

Curse Allen!

Novia should have brought a couple of guards with her. Trusted ones, who already knew about The Underlight. But no, she had been so determined to handle things on her own. She should have refused to let Niamh even come onto the island and concentrated on dealing with Allen herself. At least then Niamh would have been safe. But she couldn't deny Niamh had been helpful. Without her, she wouldn't have realised Allen was still alive until it was too late to do anything about it.

"Niamh, you need to wake up," Novia said. "Please."

Niamh didn't respond.

Novia knelt and dug her way through the rocks. She had to do something to get them out of there.

Gods, what if Niamh didn't wake up? Novia had to find a way out. Her speed would do no good.

She dragged Niamh over to a clear side of the cavern and checked the head wound again. Novia didn't know much about healing beyond aiding basic injuries.

How could she help her?

She fumbled through Niamh's pockets. She didn't know what she expected find. Perhaps something to help them escape. She found two knives, a small coin pouch full of Elven gold, and a small black crystal.

What was that? She clutched the stone in her fingers. Energy jolted between her fingers and her eyes snapped shut.

Novia blinked and found herself standing in a dense forest. A leafy canopy hung overhead. *Where am I?*

A branch snapped and another girl came into view. Her long pink hair a plait down her shoulder. She had blue eyes and large purple wings that trailed behind her. "Novia?" Nyx gasped.

Her eyes widened when she caught sight of her other sister. "Nyx—where am I? I don't know how I got here."

"You're in Andovia. You must be using a crystal like this." Nyx fumbled in her pocket and held up a black crystal.

"That's like the one I found on Niamh."

Nyx's mouth fell open. "You've met each other?"

Novia nodded. "She is here on Glenfel. She was helping me track down an escaped prisoner but now we are trapped underneath Mount Glenn."

"Why do you have her crystal?" Nyx furrowed her brow. "Are you both alright?"

Novia hesitated then shook her head. "No. Niamh is injured, and I can't get us out of this cave. I found the crystal on her—I hoped she might have some way of getting us out. There's too many rocks for me to move on my own." Novia doubted Nyx could do much good from where she was, but she had to tell someone.

"How bad is she hurt? Are you injured?"

"I have a few scrapes, but I'll be fine. She… She has a head injury, and I don't know how to get out of here." Novia glanced around, hopeless.

"Can you call someone to help?"

"No, the escaped prisoner put a ward up outside the cavern. I can't call anyone. Except you."

Nyx gripped her own crystal. "Can you move things with your mind?"

"No, why? I have speed and I can talk to animals. You know that. As well as hearing thoughts and influencing others. But I can't even call my owl for help."

"I'd better come and help."

"But you're over two days journey away. No ship can get to the island without—"

"I won't need one. I have something better. I'll be there soon as I can."

"But how—?"

"Don't worry about that. I'll get there. Just keep Niamh warm if you can. Is she conscious?"

"No, I couldn't wake her."

Nyx flinched. "Hang tight. I'll get you and Niamh out of this. I'm not about to lose either of you."

CHAPTER 2

Nyx raced back to Darius' Castle to find the druid. She knew she needed him to get to Glenfel. Fast. "Druid?" she called out. She knew Darius would be here before he went out to do his usual patrols around the forest.

His patrol didn't start until later that morning. She didn't stop until she reached the castle grounds. Darius Valeran stood still in the garden with his dragon, Sirin.

"Thank the gods you're here." Nyx stopped to catch her breath.

"We were waiting for you." Darius stood a head taller than her with long blonde hair, a chiselled face, and piercing blue eyes.

"Never mind that, I need you to take me to Glenfel. Right now."

"Why would you—?" Darius furrowed his brow.

"I need to save my sisters. Niamh's hurt, and she and Novia are trapped." Nyx held out her hand and her pack appeared. She checked inside it to make sure she had some healing supplies.

He shook his head. "You can't go to Glenfel. Portals don't open there, and people can't transport onto the island either."

"Well, let me borrow Sirin and I'll open a portal near—"

The white dragon was all rippling muscle and narrowed her golden eyes. *I can't fly to Glenfel.*

"You can't open a portal anywhere near the island. The entire area is shielded by magic."

"Niamh got there. The resistance go there all the time. I have to go." She hooked her pack over her shoulder. "So either you're going to take me, or I'll get there myself."

"How? No one can fly there either. My ancestors did a good job of making the island impenetrable."

"Then how did Niamh and the *Vanity's* crew get there?" Nyx put her hands on her hips. "There must be a way."

"The only way to get onto the island is by using a crystal enchanted by the Archdruid. That's the only thing that will allow entrance."

"Get me one then."

Darius shook his head. "It's not that simple. The crystals are only given out when ships are due to transport prisoners there."

"Druid, I have already lost my foster sisters. Please don't make me lose these sisters, too." She winced at the mention of her foster sisters. She still looked for them every chance she got. Niamh and Novia were her sisters as well. She might not know them very well yet, but they were still part of her.

He sighed. "I have one crystal, but it will only work once. Going to Glenfel is a huge risk. Which is why you're not going alone."

Nyx put her arms around him. Yes, she might be his servant, officially, at least. But he was her dearest friend, and nothing would change that.

Darius returned her embrace. "We need to go. The spirits only know how we'll pull this off." He pulled away from her. "Let's go." He held out his hand and his palm flashed with light. A black oblong crystal etched with runes appeared.

He and Nyx scrambled onto Sirin's back.

"Travel there won't be instantaneous," Darius warned. "I just hope this works or we could end up being thrown into the sea."

"We'll make it. No barrier is going to stop me from reaching them." She wrapped her arms around him. "Thanks."

"For what?"

"For being there when I needed someone."

Sirin took off and Darius opened a portal by tracing runes in the air.

Nyx braced herself and held onto him tighter. Sirin roared and shot into the portal.

Her head spun as dizzying lights whizzed past them. A few moments, she felt like she floated through nothingness. Nyx gasped as they re-emerged on the other side. Blue sea stretched out, meeting the cloudy grey horizon. There was no land in sight.

"Where are we? How far away are we from the island?" Nyx furrowed her brow.

"I'm not sure. Travelling between realms takes a lot of power. Plus, Glenfel is shielded and repels people from entering. Why did Niamh want to go there?"

"To find a prisoner. Someone she thinks can help her defeat the Order of Blood." Nyx cast her senses out but heard no minds nearby.

She explained about the crystal and seeing Novia. "I still can't believe I have another sister. I wish she would have stayed in Andovia longer so I could have gotten to know her better." Nyx had been disappointed when Novia had insisted on returning to Glenfel a few days after they had rescued her from the old city.

"Do you know which prisoner Niamh was trying to find?"

"Someone named Cyrus Allen."

Darius grimaced. "Allen is a notorious killer, he used to work for the Order of Blood. If someone helped him out of the prison, then we won't be able to keep it a secret for long. My father—"

"We'll find a way to deal with this like we always do. Together."

"It may not be enough. I have limited authority. Novia might be able to pass herself off as the warden, but we still have the other guards to deal with. I'm not sure how they will react to my presence."

"I could use my touch on them."

"Your touch won't work on the druidons."

"Druidons? What are they?" The name sounded familiar but she couldn't place it.

"They are golems. Beings created out of high magic and they only answer to one person. Only an Archdruid can control them. My ancestors created them to guard the prison. The worst of the worst are sent to Glenfel. Some people who commit terrible crimes. But some of them are just the Archdruid's enemies." Darius guided Sirin in a different direction. "I suppose it makes the island an ideal place for the resistance to hide."

They flew on as more ocean stretched out before them.

"I can't sense the island." Nyx cast her senses again.

"It's still a long way."

"I can't wait that long." Nyx fumbled in her pack and pulled out a dagger and stylus. She pricked her finger.

"Wait, what are you doing?" Darius turned as best he could. "You can't use blood magic."

"I need to find my sisters, and this is taking way too long." She traced runes on Sirin's back and leaned over Darius to trace some in the dragon's long neck.

"What do those runes mean?"

"No idea." She often remembered different runes and had no idea what they meant. The knowledge of what they were was hidden away somewhere in her mind. She lost access to those memories when she was a child.

Nothing she had tried so far had helped her retrieve the memories. She still only had one memory of herself with Niamh around the age of ten.

A glowing portal appeared around them and swallowed them up. They re-emerged a few moments later and Sirin slammed into a barrier of energy.

Dragon, druid, and fae all screamed as they plummeted towards the sea.

Darius raised his arm and all three of them stopped mid-fall. "I think we're here."

Nyx breathed a sigh of relief and unfurled her wings so she could hover without falling.

Sirin huffed. Don't mark me with runes again.

"I'm sorry, Sirin. Druid, how do we get through?"

Darius fumbled for the crystal.

Sirin pulled free of his magic and flew underneath him so he could climb back on.

Nyx flew over and grabbed onto his waist. "I hope this works."

Darius held out the crystal and an island appeared below them. Most of it taken up by a towering mountain of jagged rocks and a fortress built into the mountain.

Sirin edged forward. Am I going to be hit again?

Darius shook his head. "I hope not. But we'll be careful."

"I thought you said those things had to be used in a limited time?" Nyx rested her chin on his shoulder.

"I guess we'll find out."

Sirin craned her neck and they held their breaths.

The crystal shimmered between Darius' fingers. "Hold tight."

Nyx closed her eyes and the wind roared past them as they went through the island's protections.

"Sirin, head straight to the prison. No one can land on the island without the druidons knowing. We'll have to let them know we're here first."

Nyx gritted her teeth. Every second they wasted, was another second her sisters remained trapped. "You do that. I have to find them." She unfurled her wings.

Darius grabbed her arm. "Nyx, we can't expose ourselves. Think of all the innocent lives you'll be putting at risk."

She gritted her teeth. "Fine, but we need to hurry."

They descended and headed towards the fortress. The moment they landed outside; the fortress guards came running towards them. Men with runes etched on their faces aimed staff weapons at them.

"Stand down." Darius dismounted and his eyes flashed with power. "I'm the Archdruid's son."

The guards hesitated then lowered their weapons and bowed their heads in respect.

"I'm here because you have an escaped prisoner. Do you have any leads on Allen?"

Nyx slid off Sirin. It surprised her how easily he slipped into the role of the Archdruid's son. Despite insisting he had no power or authority, she begged to differ.

Druid. My sister could be dying.

"Why isn't the Archdruid here?" one guard asked. "He has not come for many years."

"Because my father is a busy man. Now tell me about Allen. When did he escape?"

Nyx couldn't wait any longer. She flew off and headed straight for the mountain. She swooped lower. How the heck could she get inside?

One way or another, she would find her sisters before it was too late.

CHAPTER 3

Novia brushed her long hair off her face. She sat close to Niamh—her sister. She still didn't know how she felt about that.

How long had they been trapped here now? Hours, at least. Perhaps longer. She'd tried hitting the rocks with her light and moving them, but that only caused more rocks to fall.

Novia huddled closer to Niamh. "Please, you have to wake up." She cradled Niamh's head in her lap. "I don't want to lose you. I have so many questions. Where do you come from? Where do *we* come from?" She rested her head against the cave wall. "Why don't we remember our past?"

She wanted to use the crystal again and call Nyx. It would take her at least a day or more to get to the island. Maybe longer. What if they ran out of air before then?

This reminded her of being trapped in the tiny cell back in the old city in Andovia. The queen had her locked in there for days, and she still had nightmares about it. Novia pushed those thoughts away.

If she died, who would take care of everyone on the island? People here depended on her and needed her to look out for them.

A tear dripped down her cheek. She hated feeling so helpless. Just like she had been when the Andovian Queen kidnapped her. Her powers had been useless against the Queen.

She clung to her unconscious sister tighter. "Nyx will be here. I always knew I had a sister—I didn't realise I had two. It was… a feeling. Like part of myself was missing. Now I know what it was." She gave a sad smile. "Please don't die. Not before I have a chance to know you." Her senses tingled.

Gods, Nyx was here. Somehow, she just knew. Something pulled her towards her sister.

"Nyx?" Novia scrambled up. "Nyx, are you there?"

Yes. Now you and Niamh need to keep well back, Nyx told her in thought. We'll get you out.

Alright. Novia grabbed Niamh and pulled her back as far as they could go to the cave wall. *We are ready. Hurry. I still can't wake Niamh.*

Try to shield yourselves as best you can.

Novia pulled Niamh against her and covered her head with her arm. Rock exploded as something blew it apart.

Novia? Nyx called out.

Her ears rang from the force of the explosion. "I'm here." She let go of Niamh and scrambled up.

Nyx herself rushed in, followed by a blond-haired young man. "Thank the spirits we got here in time." Nyx threw her arms around Novia.

For a moment, Novia clung to her. Just to make sure she was real. "Quick. Niamh needs help." She gasped when she got a better look at the man who had arrived with her sister. "You're the—"

"The Archdruid's son." Nyx nodded. "He's a friend. We work together. How long has she been unconscious?"

Novia's eyes widened as she took in the sight of Darius Valeran. With one word he could end everything she had been working for. She shook her head to clear it. "Since Allen trapped us in here."

They hurried over to Niamh and Darius touched her head. "Her breathing is shallow." His hand glowed with bright light as he said something she couldn't understand. The wound closed over but didn't fully heal.

"Let's take her back to my chambers at the cave." Novia motioned for them to follow. "We have a healer here in The Underlight. I'll call for her."

Darius lifted Niamh into his arms. "Good, we need to get her checked over."

Niamh groaned as her eyes opened. "Nyx?"

"I'm here." Nyx took hold of her hand.

Niamh gave her a sad smile. "I remember us being in the garden together. Where's Novia?"

She stepped forward. "I'm here."

Niamh rested her head against Nyx's lap. "We need to get our memories back."

"We will, but we have to make sure you're both alright first." Novia squeezed her sister's hand.

She wasn't alone anymore.

But the question remained, where was Allen and who had helped him to escape?

Novia breathed a sigh of relief when they got back to the keep.

Niamh had wanted to go looking for Allen but the healer had told them she needed to rest and recover from her head injury. "I still can't believe I have two sisters or that you're both here." She laid out a tray of tea as she and Nyx sat around her tiny kitchen table.

Niamh lay on the other side of the room on the divan. "You said you always thought you had a sister," Niamh murmured. "I don't see why I need to rest. I'm fine."

"Because I will put a web around you if you don't rest," Nyx warned her. "And yeah, Novia, I know this is a lot to deal with. But at least we're all together now."

Novia shook her head. "It… Just makes no sense. Why were we abandoned?" Novia sipped her tea. "Why don't we remember anything?"

Nyx shrugged. "I can't be sure. When I came close to death, I remembered us playing together in a garden," she said. "But I keep having a nightmare of being buried alive."

Niamh scrambled up. "I remember that. Not just what you showed me—I saw Novia there, too. Something bad must've happened. Someone erased our memories for some reason."

"I don't remember anything. But I wonder why we don't look alike." Novia shook her head. "I don't have wings. And Nyx doesn't have pointed ears like us."

"My ears were cut off by the man who took me in. Not all fae children are born with wings from what I have learnt." Nyx gripped her cup. "I was found in Joriam. Niamh in Ereden. Where were you found?"

Novia hesitated. She hadn't told Nyx very much when they had first met. It felt odd to be sharing her story with these two strangers. Yet at same time, it felt natural to be around them. Like a missing part of herself had been returned. "The slave islands. If Ophelia, the

239

warden of this island, hadn't found me and took me in I'd be dead by now. Or sold to someone awful." She shuddered.

"I wonder why we weren't found together." Niamh stumbled over to the table.

"Stubbornness must be a family trait." Nyx got up and helped her onto the third empty seat. "You're supposed to rest."

Niamh scowled. "Don't fuss over me."

"That bump could have killed you," Nyx said. "It's strange what different paths we've taken. I was a thief, Niamh was an assassin, and you run one of the worst prisons on Erthea."

"You killed people like Cyrus did then?" Novia furrowed her brow.

"I only kill bad people. Besides, I don't work for the Order of Blood anymore. Not after they sent me to kill Nyx."

Novia's eyes widened. "She tried to kill you?"

"She came pretty close but then we realised we were sisters. Don't judge her for what she was. We all make mistakes."

Novia didn't know how to feel about that, but who was she to judge? If she had ended up in Ereden, she might have followed the same path as Niamh.

"At least we are together and we can figure out what happened to us." Nyx reached across the table and took hold of both of her sisters' hands.

Light flared between their joint hands and energy swirled between them.

"That was… Odd." Novia's frown deepened. "I thought I was the only mind whisperer left."

"We had to have come from somewhere." Niamh said. "The Archdruid couldn't have wiped all of them out."

"Speaking of the Archdruid, how can be sure we can trust his son?"

"I have asked her that too." Niamh stirred her tea. "The druid works with the resistance. And she's in love with him." She motioned towards Nyx.

Nyx scowled at her. "I never said that. And he's just a good friend."

"I doubt a friend would risk everything to come here and help us. Besides, it's obvious he loves you."

240

Novia held up her hands. "Wait. I still don't understand how Cyrus got out of his cell, let alone learnt how to access his magic again. He was marked with runes which rendered him powerless."

"Someone must have helped Allen escape from his cell."

"Only me and one of the druidons have the keys. I didn't let him out and the druidon wouldn't either."

"Would one of the other druidons have let him out?" Nyx arched an eyebrow. "Maybe someone used magic and managed to sway one of them."

Novia shook her head. "The druidons are designed to be infallible. That's why the Archdruid created them. They wouldn't allow non-druidon guards until a few years ago. Now they take orders from the warden. Well, me to an extent. My mother, Ophelia, died six months ago. I haven't told the druidons because when a warden dies they're supposed to report it. I can't risk someone coming here and finding out about The Underlight." She gripped the edge of the table. "It's getting harder. I can't keep up the ruse forever. Which means I have to find somewhere else to take The Underlight."

Niamh snorted and clutched her head. "I doubt you can get anywhere safer than this island. Don't go to Andovia, that is one of the most dangerous places in the lower realm."

"The queen could have swayed one of them," Nyx pointed out.

Novia shook her head again. "I don't think so. How could she?"

"Because she is the first mind whisperer and the most powerful of us all." Niamh rested her head against the table. "If you could compel someone as powerful as Ambrose, then she could bend most people to her will."

"Darius said the Archdruid hasn't been here in decades and the magic used on the druidons is growing weaker. Let's concentrate on finding Allen. What are his powers and his crimes?" Nyx made a parchment and quill appear.

"He used to be an assassin for the Order of Blood and he killed for pleasure too. I heard he worked for the Archdruid…" Niamh held a block of ice Darius had conjured for her to her head. "He can use dark sorcery."

Novia nodded. "That's right. The Archdruid locked him up when Allen tried to kill him. We have orders to never release him from his cell. But some of the guards grant him favours."

"Who would help him?" Nyx scribbled down some notes. "Did he work with anyone?"

"No, we have records of every prisoner from when they're sent here. Ophelia kept a detailed archive." Novia sipped her tea.

"Allen never worked with anyone. Only alone. Like everyone within the Order of Blood does," Niamh remarked. "The queen must need him for something."

Niamh shuddered. "Are you sure she can't get out? She didn't have much trouble coming to the island and grabbing me before."

"It's okay if you want to talk about what happened to you." Nyx squeezed her hand.

Novia shook her head again. "I don't. I'd rather forget about it."

"You'll have to talk about it sooner or later, or it will eat you up inside," Niamh said.

"There's nothing to talk about. She took me and used me for my power. As long as she stays locked up, the matter is done with." Novia looked away. She didn't want to remember her time being stuck with the queen, or how she had nightmares about being trapped every night. Novia's senses tingled. "The druidons are here."

Her door burst open and three druidon guards came in and started firing their staff weapons. Bolts of energy zipped through the air.

All three sisters screamed and ducked beneath the table.

"What are they doing?" Niamh hissed and pulled out her daggers.

"Blades don't work on them. And they're immune to magic," Novia warned.

Nyx waved her arm when one druidon advance towards them. Her power rippled against him, useless.

"Told you." Novia rose. "What are you doing here? I gave you orders to search for Allen. You—"

He grabbed Nyx by the throat and yanked her off her feet.

"Stop!" Novia yelled. "She's not a prisoner."

Niamh threw one of her knives. It embedded in the druidons throat. He didn't even flinch.

"Stop," Novia repeated. "You're not supposed to be here. Go back to work and—" she ducked as a second druidon fired at her head.

The first druidon continued to choke Nyx as she thrashed and kicked at him.

Darius burst in and fired a bolt of lightning at the druidon holding Nyx and flung him against the wall.

Darius raised his hands, and the other druidons stopped fighting. "This is not good."

CHAPTER 4

Nyx coughed and gasped for breath as the druidon finally let go of her.

"Are you alright?" Darius cupped her face.

She nodded and gave him a quick hug. "I'll be fine."

Novia and Niamh scrambled up. "Why are they attacking us?" Niamh ran a hand through her long blond hair. "It makes no sense. What did you do to them?" Niamh picked up her knives and frowned. "They don't bleed."

"Of course not, they're not living beings. I used magic to stop them. Someone has tampered with them." Darius glanced between them. "The magic that designed them isn't linked to the Archdruid the way it once was."

"That's impossible. Even I couldn't change that." Novia ran a hand through her hair. "No one can change them."

"The magic used to create them is growing weaker. My father hasn't set foot here in decades. Magic like this has to be renewed. Have you noticed anything odd about them? Have they been failing?"

Novia furrowed her brow. "No, but they don't always seem to follow orders anymore. Even Ophelia had trouble getting them to cooperate with her." She tapped her chin. "They act... Confused sometimes. They ask for the warden. Like they need to be told what to do. They never used to do that."

"That would be a sign of the magic failing." Darius nodded.

Nyx rubbed her throat. "What are we going to do with them?"

"Well, we can't let them loose." Darius crossed his arms. "We may have to contain them."

244

"Contain them?" Novia gasped. "I can't leave the prison unmanned. We don't have enough guards to keep the place secure without them."

"Put the prison on lockdown," Darius suggested. "At least until we can figure out what to do with them."

"How would someone even know how to control them?" Nyx glanced between the frozen guards and Darius. "Aren't they made from ancient magic?" She slumped back onto a chair.

"Yes, but few people would know how to use it. My father taught them to me but it's complicated high magic."

"You can do that."

Nyx and Darius had done mind sharing together and shared each other's knowledge. She had a good idea of how the magic used to create the druidons worked.

"I doubt it. Even if I knew how, you need to be skilled to use the ancient magics."

"Here's a question," Niamh said. "Why would they try to kill us?"

"They probably view us as a threat." Novia set her table back up. "Although, I can't imagine why anyone would want to attack us."

"Maybe it's someone from the Order of Blood," Niamh mused. "They want me dead at all costs. Or maybe Nyx, since I didn't complete the job."

"Yes, but why do they want me dead? I don't have any enemies." Novia grabbed a broom and swept broken shards into a corner.

"You're a mind whisperer," Darius pointed out. "That makes you a danger in the eyes of other magickind. You're lucky you've been hidden away here all these years."

"Let's go and find Allen. Then we can find whoever is helping him." Nyx put her hands on her hips. "He must be on the island somewhere."

"The Underlight would be the best place to hide." Novia turned when her owl came in. "Archie, did you find Allen? I've been worried about you."

She talks to animals, Niamh explained. Odd gift.

Nyx shrugged. Sounds useful to me. We all have different gifts.

"Archie said Allen is still under the mountain. Let's go."

The four of them headed back to The Underlight but there was too much ground to cover so they split up.

Nyx went off with Darius. "Do you think Lyra—the queen could have somehow used her power here?" she murmured.

"How could she? She's trapped at the bottom of the well."

"Yeah, but she is the most powerful of all mind whisperers. I wouldn't put anything past her." Nyx shook her head. "Who else could have changed the druidons programming? We know she's been here once already when she took Novia. What's to stop her from putting some kind of failsafe in place?" Nyx stopped and stared at him. "She could have used her powers on the druidons before we even came here. Maybe this was part of her plan in case something happened to her."

"What good would that do?" Darius frowned.

"I don't know yet. She must have known we would come here once we found Novia. She probably knew Niamh would come looking for Allen as well. Maybe this is her way of trying to stop us."

"I still can't believe a place like this exists. It reminds me of the tunnels in Andovia. But the crystals here have so much energy." Darius grinned. "Must be how my ancestors hid the island away. It's the perfect place to keep a prison."

"Nothing is perfect, druid. Someone clearly found a way on this island and—"

"Looking for me?" A dark-haired man appeared further up the tunnel.

"You must be Allen." Darius' hand went to his sword.

"I never expected a Valeran to come here." Allen smirked.

"Who helped you get out?" Nyx put her hands on her hips.

Allen's smile widened and he threw a bolt of energy towards them.

They ducked and Nyx waved her arm. Alan stumbled from the force of her power but didn't hit the wall like she'd intended.

Damn it!

Two robed figures appeared beside Allen and hit Nyx and Darius with bursts of light.

Nyx cried out as her body slammed into the cavern wall.

Where had those two come from? She didn't sense anyone approach.

Allen advanced towards her.

Nyx raised her hand and let her power flow free. Energy shook the air like thunder without sound. Allen and the two robed figures froze for a moment then continued to blast them with energy.

So much for that working. Nyx gritted her teeth.

Why wouldn't her power work? Did they have mental shields?

Darius struck the two figures with bolts of lightning. But it wasn't enough to kill them. He grabbed Nyx's arm and threw a shield between them and their attackers.

"Time for us to go, my friends." Allen spoke again then smoke billowed around them as all three men vanished.

SPELL OF DARKNESS

CHAPTER 1

A black-robed man swung the sword at Novia. Not the way she had expected her morning walk around Glenfel Island to start before she attended her duties at the prison.

Novia didn't have any weapons of her own, aside from her magic. She used her speed and blurred out of the way as the man came at her again.

She grabbed a sword from one of the men and pointed the tip of the blade at his throat. "Who are you and why are you here?"

Another man crept up behind her and grabbed her arm. Novia yelped and moved out of his reach.

Novia hit him with her magic, too.

The first man threw a bolt of energy at Nyx. She winced as it struck her shoulder.

Enough was enough.

She raised her hands and let her power flow free. As a mind whisperer, she could not only hear his thoughts, but influence them as well. Power impacted the air like thunder without sound and sent leaves blasting through the air.

"Who are you?" she asked the stunned men.

Both men stood dazed as her power took hold of them. She reached into their minds and found a wall of resistance.

Oh no.

"We are immune to your parlour tricks, girl."

Parlour tricks? Ha.

"You can't kill me either." She kept out of their range.

The second man threw a crystal on the ground. Both he and his companion retreated behind a tree. That couldn't be good.

Novia didn't have time to wonder what it might be. Energy exploded from the crystal and sent her crashing back to the ground. She clutched her head. Her skull throbbed and an intense ringing sound tore through her ears.

Good gods, what was that?

The two men advanced towards her, blades drawn.

She knew she should use her magic again, but she couldn't focus as the ringing sound grew more intense.

A white owl flew over and thrashed against the first man's head.

Two knives flew through the air and embedded in each man's throat. Her sisters, Niamh and Nyx, ran over to her.

"Are you hurt?" Nyx bent to check on her. "Gods, what is that awful sound?"

Both sisters covered their ears.

"Crystal." Novia motioned to it with her hand.

Both her sisters helped her up, then dragged her away from the bodies. Having some distance from the crystal lessened the pain a little.

"Niamh, you didn't have to kill them." Novia rubbed her aching temples. "We need to find out who they are."

Niamh, with her long blond hair and pointed ears looked very different to Novia. But all three of them had found each other and knew they were sisters linked by blood and magic.

Nyx had long, braided pink hair, large purple wings and the same blue eyes. Novia shared their eyes and Niamh's pointed ears. Her hair was long, green, and curly.

Niamh scowled. "Forgive me for trying to save your life."

"It's not that. I just need to know where they came from." Nyx flicked her plait over her shoulder.

"What was that crystal?" Novia furrowed her brow. "It sounded awful."

"Reminds me of an amulet the druid and I found once, when we helped Yasmine get her ship back." Nyx shuddered. "Are they from the Order of Blood?"

Niamh shook her head. "I doubt it. People from the Order don't attack out in the open like this. They don't look like assassins either. They are not well armed enough."

She headed back over to the bodies. Novia knelt and examined the first man. "There's no marks on him."

"The Order of Blood don't have visible marks. We try to work in the shadows. Not draw attention to ourselves." Niamh crossed her arms. "The Order wouldn't dress like that either. They look more like priests than assassins."

Nyx came over and knelt beside her. "You weren't always in the shadows when you tried to kill me." Nyx made her pack appear and grabbed a healing balm to use on her shoulder.

Niamh flinched. Novia knew her sister didn't like to mention how she and Nyx had met. Niamh had worked for the Order of Blood and had been sent to kill her. She might have succeeded if they hadn't found out they were sisters. The Order had brought them together.

"I'll see if I can sense anything from them." Novia held out her hand.

"How? They're dead." Niamh bent and yanked out her daggers.

"There might still be energy left inside them." Nyx took Novia's hand and held her free hand out to Niamh. "Come on, it's worth a try, isn't it?"

Niamh took her hand and energy jolted between the three of them. Their minds and senses merged as one. They scanned the bodies but found no trace of thoughts.

Niamh pulled away and grabbed one of the swords. "These are marked. Has someone sent them after Nyx, or us? How would they know where to find us? Glenfel is hidden."

"How did they even get onto the island?" Novia wanted to know. "I thought your druid reinforced the island's protections?"

Nyx nodded. "He did and he's not my druid. Darius is just a friend. Perhaps the queen sent these men."

"How could she have? She's still trapped in Andovia." Niamh shook her head. "They must be the same men who helped Cyrus Alan escape."

Recently, a prisoner and assassin named Cyrus Alan had escaped from the prison and tried to kill the sisters in their attempts to capture him. So far, they hadn't been able to find him again.

"Maybe she can still use her powers from a distance. We all know the queen got on to the island before when she kidnapped me." Novia shuddered.

"She is not coming back. Nyx's druid helped us trap her in Andovia," Niamh added.

Nyx sighed. "Please don't call him my druid. He's — never mind. We still don't know where those men came from."

"But why?" Novia held out her arm. Archie, her owl, flew over to perch on it. "We haven't done anything wrong."

"We are mind whisperers. If the Archdruid doesn't know about us, the queen could have told someone else about our existence. Especially me. People think I'm part of an ancient prophecy." Nyx rolled her eyes.

"That could apply to any of us," Niamh pointed out.

"They only tried to kill Nyx, though." Novia stroked Archie's feathers. "If they don't work for the Order of Blood and they weren't sent by the Archdruid, why kill us?"

"Everyone will want us dead, Sister. Just for being what we are." Niamh dropped the sword. "We should burn them or dump them in the sea."

Light flashed around the bodies and they disintegrated.

Nyx gasped. "What was that? I didn't do anything."

"That was odd." Niamh stepped back. "Could it be the island's protections?"

Novia shook her head. "The protections shield the island, they don't that. Besides, they somehow got through."

"We can't stay here any longer. It's not safe for us."

Nyx glanced around as if she expected someone else to be there.

"I can't leave," Novia protested. "I'm the warden. Well, not officially, but I oversee everything at the prison."

Glenfel prison held prisoners from all over Erthea and was said to house some of the worst criminals. Novia had worked there for most of her life.

"You can't stay here, and we need to figure out who is after us." Niamh sheathed her daggers. "We should leave. You don't want to put the Underlight at risk, do you?"

Novia scowled. "Of course not. But I can't leave the prison without supervision."

"We'll figure something out. I'd say our safest bet is going to Andovia," Nyx suggested.

One way or another, they had to find out who was after them or none of them would be free again.

CHAPTER 2

"We can't go back to Andovia. We'll be walking into the Archdruid's hands. He could be the one who sent those men after us." Niamh couldn't believe Nyx wanted to walk right back into a trap.

"Andovia is where we come from, there could be answers there about who we are."

Niamh rolled her eyes and stood in front of Novia's window. Novia's chambers looked out into the rocky outcrop of the island. "Are you sure you're not just desperate to see your druid?"

Nyx scowled. "No, I'm—yes, I want to see him. But I want to know about where we come from. Don't you?"

Novia brought out a tray of tea. "I still don't feel comfortable leaving. Who will watch over the prison and the Underlight whilst we're gone?"

Niamh hated tea but drank it out of politeness. She never stayed with people like she had with the sisters the last few weeks. She'd always been alone. Having sisters still felt odd, but she wouldn't change it.

They might disagree at times but they were hers. Her family. She never had a family before. The Order had taught her to kill, to survive in this world. They didn't teach her how to love people or to feel part of something.

Nyx had two sisters from what she heard and her foster father had been abusive but at least she had known what it was like to have a home.

Novia had a mother. Or someone close to it.

"Why can't the druidons handle the prison?" Nyx poured out her tea. "Didn't they used to run things before a warden came here?"

Novia nodded. "Yes, but we know the druidons aren't as infallible as they were designed to be. What if someone came here and changed them the way the queen did?"

"We have to leave." Niamh crossed her arms. "It's not safe for any of us here."

"Then where will we go?" Novia ran a hand through her long, curly hair. "I'm glad we got to spend the past months together, but I'm not giving up my life here."

"You may not have a choice. You've been safe on this island for the last eight years. But you're a mind whisperer. That makes all of us targets."

Novia sighed. "But why now? You weren't hunted before, were you?"

"I wasn't either until a year ago." Nyx sipped her tea. "But people know about us now. That means we're not safe. Plus, that man said he came because we are her daughters. That must mean something."

Niamh paced up and down. "We should keep moving until we can track down whoever is after us."

Novia's eyes widened. "Is that to be our lives now? Running until they catch us?"

"We are not running. We will go to Andovia, figure out who is after us, and stop them once and for all."

"I can't leave." Novia slammed her hands down on the table. "You may not have ties anywhere, but I do. Now I have to get back to work." She stormed off.

Niamh glared after her. "What's wrong with her? Does she want to die?" She couldn't understand Novia's resistance to leaving. They were all in danger. If one sister stayed, she died.

"This place is her home. It's all she's ever known. It's hard for her to leave her life here."

"We're her sisters, shouldn't that mean something?" Niamh sighed. "I've never had a home. Not one I can remember. Why can't we be home for each other?" She slumped onto a chair. "Do you think she doesn't like me? Because of what I was?"

"We all have a past. I can't say we wouldn't have followed your path if we ended up in Ereden instead of you."

"How can we convince her to leave?"

"We need to call Yasmine and ask her to come get us. Then we'll decide where we're going from there." Nyx gulped down her tea. "My friends can help us figure this out."

"And what if we have to run?" Niamh leaned back in her chair. "Can you do that? Can you walk away from the druid?"

Nyx flinched. "No, because we're going to stop whoever is after us. I've left everything behind before, but Andovia is my home, and I won't give it up."

Niamh blew out a breath. *There's that home word again.*

"You sound as bad as Novia."

"Just call Yasmine. Tell her to get here as fast as she can."

To Niamh's surprise, Yasmine and her ship, *The Vanity*, arrived a few hours later.

Now they had to face the next challenge; convincing Novia to leave. But Niamh had a good idea about that. She went off and found one of the druidons. Druidons were beings created from magic to serve the Archdruid. They had been assigned to watch over the prison centuries ago.

Darius Valeran, the current Archdruid's son, had attuned their magic to him.

Niamh called the druid, who confirmed the prison would be safe if Novia left.

The druidons would call him if anything went wrong. She and Nyx packed up their things just as Novia came in from her guard shift. "What's going on?" Novia glanced between them and furrowed her brow.

"Yasmine is here. We're leaving," Niamh said. "It's up to you if you come with us."

"Niamh." Nyx sighed. "Novia, she's right. We can't stay here. So we are headed to Ereden to see if we can find out anything from her contacts. We are going to see if we can find the spot where she was found."

"Were you going to leave without telling me?" Novia put her hands on her hips.

"No, we did tell you. It's up to you if you want to come with us." Niamh swung her pack over her shoulder.

256

Novia ran a hand through her hair. "I'm coming. I'm not about to let you get yourself killed."

The ship arrived in Ereden a few hours later.

It felt good to Niamh being back in Elven lands. She hadn't set foot here in months. Not since she left to go to Andovia to kill Nyx. She hadn't planned to come back here since. Not until she took care of the Order, at least.

"I've been here with Ophelia before. She used to come here to commit prisoners," Novia remarked.

"The spot where they found me isn't far from here." Niamh pulled a mask over her face and pulled her hood down. "I can't risk anyone seeing me here."

"We will find out what we can, then get back to *The Vanity*." Nyx pulled her cloak tighter to cover her wings. Her long hair turned dark brown.

"Nov, you need to do something about your hair." Niamh motioned to her sister.

Novia furrowed her brow. "Like what?"

"Change its colour like Nyx did. Too much colour will stand out here."

"I don't know how to," Novia protested.

"Just concentrate and use your magic." Nyx squeezed her shoulder. "My hair used to change colour all the time."

Novia closed her eyes and her curly locks turned black. "What an awful colour."

"It doesn't matter. At least you'll blend in now."

They headed up the road until they reached a small patch of trees.

"This is it." Niamh stared at the ash tree. "I remember waking up here."

Nyx frowned. "We're not far from the road. Whoever left you here must have wanted you to be found. Who found you?"

"A merchant. Goes by the name Liam. I think he might still live nearby."

"Let's go."

CHAPTER 3

Novia hated having to leave Archie on the ship. It still felt odd to be away from Glenfel. She should be doing her rounds at the prison now. She wasn't about to let anything happen to her sisters, though. Plus, she wanted to know where they'd come from as much as they did. Novia had to see this through. Once they found out who was after them, she could return home. Or at least she hoped she could.

Glenfel would always be home. She couldn't imagine living anywhere else. Nor would she spend her life on the run either. That was no way to live.

She followed her sisters as they passed through the bustling Elven village.

Wooden houses stretched out before them. It made Novia wonder how they didn't get blown away during a bad storm.

"Are you sure the merchant will be able to tell us anything?" Novia glanced around, uneasy. She feared someone might attack them again and wanted to be ready for anything.

"I talked to him a couple of years ago. He claimed he didn't remember much, but maybe we can use our combined powers to find out more." Niamh pulled her mask down and knocked on the door. They waited a few moments until a man finally opened the door.

The Elf stood a head taller than them. His long, dark blond hair fell past his shoulders and pointed ears stuck out. "You." He gasped when he caught sight of Niamh.

"Hello again. I'm here to ask—"

"You need to leave. There are men looking for you."

Nyx narrowed her eyes. "What men?"

"Dangerous men. You girls had best leave." He pushed the door to close it.

258

Niamh stuck her foot out to block him. "Wait, who were they? I need you to tell me everything you know." She grabbed his arm and her power burst through the air.

Novia winced as the force of her sister's magic rattled her bones.

"Who is after me?" Niamh demanded.

"Bad men. They wore dark robes." The man's expression grew dazed as her magic took hold.

"Tell me what you remember about the day you found me eight years ago."

Novia spotted someone in the shadows. Two cloaked figures.

Nyx, look. Novia's hand went to the dagger in her cloak.

Nyx cursed under her breath. "Niamh, we need to leave."

"You were under the tree. You were filthy and covered in dirt. There was no one else around. You couldn't remember anything about where you'd come from," the Elf said.

"Niamh," Nyx hissed and grabbed her arm.

Niamh turned around and yanked one of her daggers out.

"We need to go." Novia's panic grew. She wasn't a warrior like her sisters. She had rarely fought anyone. Not even at the prison. "We should run."

Niamh scoffed. "I never run from a fight."

"She's right. If we use our powers out in the open, we'll draw even more unwanted attention." Nyx grabbed Novia and Niamh's hands. "To protect us from evil again, send us back from whence we came."

Novia gasped as orbs of light sparkled around them. A few moments later they reappeared under the tree where Niamh had searched earlier.

"This wasn't the place I meant," Nyx grumbled.

"You should let me kill them," Niamh complained.

"We're supposed to be lying low. Let's get back to the ship." Nyx headed back to the road.

"Going somewhere, Niamh?" An old man appeared and held a dagger to the Elf's throat.

Niamh growled at him. "Master Oswald. I should have known you'd make an appearance."

Oswald. Novia remembered Niamh had mentioned him before. He had trained her to be an assassin. Part of her wanted to kill him for taking away Niamh's childhood. For turning her into a killer.

"You shouldn't have come back here." Oswald smirked. "You were foolish to betray your order."

Robed men came up behind them. Swords drawn. "So you're the one who sent these men."

"Oh no, they're from the Order of the Blessed. It seems they want you dead as much as I do." Oswald pressed the blade against the Elf's throat harder.

Niamh raised her hand to release her power but Nyx grabbed hold of it. *Don't. He's wearing an amulet that blocks our magic. I can sense it.*

"Let him go, Oswald," Niamh growled. "Your quarrel is with me, not him."

Niamh!

I'm not running away this time. Niamh slid out a dagger from underneath her cloak and threw it at Oswald. The old man dodged it.

The two men advanced towards Nyx and Novia.

Novia blurred out of the way when the man slashed at her. Using her speed, she blurred and punched him in the face.

Nyx spun and kicked her assailant in the head.

Niamh knocked the Elf aside and lunged for Oswald. The old man dodged her blow and grabbed her by the throat.

Niamh screamed as the amulet's power tore through her.

Oswald pulled a dagger, about to strike Niamh down.

"No!" Novia shot towards him and slammed the old man against the wall.

Niamh doubled over, clutching her head.

Nyx hurried over and yanked the amulet off. She smashed it on the ground, then grasped his throat.

Novia gripped him too. Both mind whisperers let their power loose. Energy reverberated through the air and blasted through the wooden walls.

Novia didn't care. This man wanted to kill their sister and she wouldn't let that happen.

"Listen to me, you're going to tell the rest of the Order Niamh and I are dead. We were killed by the Order of the Blessed. You will order them to stop looking for us. You will forget we escaped and will never harm any mind whisperers again." Nyx drew back. "We need to get out of here."

Novia wrapped an arm around Niamh. "Come on, Sister. We need to get moving."

Nyx led the way back towards the dock.

As they passed the market, Novia sensed someone's fear.

It surprised her. She didn't get overwhelmed by her powers. She had learnt to accept them. Nyx was the strongest and Niamh had disciplined herself so much she kept a tight handle on her gifts.

I can't believe they're going to kill us, someone thought. *Gods help us.* The voice sounded familiar to her somehow.

Niamh pulled away from her when they reached the town square that led to the docks. "I'm fine," she grumbled. "You should have let me kill Oswald. I doubt you compelled him to think I'm dead. He is known for getting his targets."

"Nyx and I both used our powers. It would take a lot to break through that. You've seen how strong Nyx is." Novia rubbed her temples. "I don't know how she recovers so fast." Using her touch always left her feeling drained.

Nyx turned further ahead of them.

"I know. I envy that about her." Niamh sighed.

"You recover faster than I do," Novia pointed out.

"Yeah, but she's so strong. She can—"

Novia froze when she spotted a green-skinned woman with fangs in a cage. A halfling. "That's Desmia." She covered her mouth with her hand.

The nargol's dark gaze locked on hers. "Novia?"

"Niamh, I need you to help me get that nargol out." She gripped her sister's arm.

"What? You've got to be joking."

She spotted Olaf, an ogre, and Sid, a goblin, near the cage.

"I know them. They've worked with the resistance and at the prison before. Please, you have to help me save them."

"But — but they're demons."

Novia scowled. "I don't judge you for being what you are. Please, they're good people."

"We can't just break them out. Not in front of these witnesses." Niamh shook her head.

261

Nyx? she called out.

Nyx ran back over. "I heard. Niamh is right. We can't—"

"You help people all the time. Help me save them. I heard their thoughts. A slave master captured them." She crossed her arms. "I thought we were fighting for a better future?"

Her sisters shared a glance.

Nyx hesitated. "I have never used my power on this many people. If someone sees us—"

"We can join powers. We're stronger together." She held out a hand. "Why can't we compel them all?"

"I thought you weren't recovered yet?" Niamh arched an eyebrow.

"We can do this. Together."

Nyx and Niamh grasped her hands.

Novia took a deep breath and prayed it would work.

"I hope you know what you're doing, sister," Niamh muttered. "We could end up killing everyone here."

"We just have to let our power flow free. Together. Ready?" Nyx gripped her hand tight.

Novia nodded. "I'm ready." Power and energy surged from deep inside her.

White light flared around the three sisters and shook the air around them. The world seemed to fall silent.

Everyone stood there, dazed.

Novia and her sisters all gasped for breath. She had never felt power like that before. It shook her to her core.

She and Niamh struggled to stay upright. She felt beyond exhausted now.

"Come on." Nyx hurried over to the cage.

Novia forced her body to comply.

"Novia, what's going on?" Desmia frowned at her. "Who are these girls?"

"They're my sisters. We are going to get you out."

Nyx raised her hand and blasted the lock apart. "Let's go."

CHAPTER 4

Nyx breathed a sigh of relief once they were back on the ship. Fatigue weighed on her, but she pushed it away.

Niamh and Novia both stumbled onto the bed in the captain's cabin.

She didn't know what to make of the newcomers. An orc, a goblin and an ogre. The three made an unlikely trio.

"What happened back at the square?" the nargol asked. Novia mentioned her name was Desmia.

"We rescued you." She rubbed her temples.

"But what are you?"

Nyx tossed her cloak away and breathed a sigh of relief as she unfurled her wings. Her hair shimmered and turned back to its usual shade of pink. "I'm fae. In case it isn't obvious." She stretched out her wings.

"That's not what I meant. What power did you use? What you did in the square — it was unnatural."

"I'm like my sister Novia."

"I know Novia is a seer. But that was… different."

"What I am isn't important." She tossed her plait over her shoulder. "My sister said you didn't deserve to be killed, so we saved you. End of story."

"But you did something to all those people. What? We trust Novia because we know her."

Nyx gritted her teeth. "We're powerful, that's all you need to know."

She didn't want word spreading all over the lower realm about her and her sisters, or compelling Oswald would mean nothing. She wanted to reach Andovia, reunite with her friends, and plan their next move.

She headed to the helm. "How long until we reach Andovia?"

Yasmine pushed her hair off her face. "A few hours, but we should reach there before nightfall. Bet you'll be glad to see your druid again." The pirate smirked.

"He's not my druid. I just work with him." Nyx rolled her eyes.

Yasmine snorted. "Right. I've never seen Darius look at anyone the way he looks at you."

"You know we can't be together." She scowled. "Not just because of who and what he is."

Her sisters might envy the strength of her powers — she'd seen as much — but being a mind whisperer came at a heavy price. Mind whisperers couldn't just fall in love and be with someone the way other women could.

She pushed those thoughts away.

Don't tell Desmia and her men about me being a mind whisperer. The less people who know about us, the better, she told Yasmine.

"Did you find what you were looking for in Ereden?" Yasmine tapped some runes and stepped away from the helm.

"No, we were attacked by the Order of the Blessed, again."

Yasmine arched a brow. "The servants of the gods? What did you do to piss them off?"

"I don't know. They came after us on the island and again in Ereden. The sooner I get home the better. Maybe the druid will know something." At least she hoped he would. Or their friends would. She longed to see all of them again after spending the last few weeks on Glenfel.

Novia and Niamh came back on deck a while later.

"I thought you were asleep?" Nyx frowned.

"No, just resting. Why do ships have to sway so much?" Niamh's face turned almost as green as Novia's hair.

"Drink this." Yasmine tossed a jar at her. "No vomiting on my ship. It takes forever to get rid of the smell."

"Drink something. It will make you feel better," Nyx told her sisters.

Niamh grabbed a canteen and gulped down some water. "I've been thinking. We should cast a spell again."

Nyx flew up onto the mast and perched there. "Which spell?"

"The one we cast to take us back from where we came. Maybe we need to reword it."

"Alright, how about something like powers of the sisters rise, course across the skies, unlock the door to our past, bring back our memories at last?"

Energy reverberated through the air and orbs of light sparkled around them.

Nyx gasped as she and her sisters appeared somewhere surrounded by trees.

"What just happened?" Novia furrowed her brow.

"Nyx transported us somewhere." Niamh pulled out her knives. "Where did the ship go?"

"I didn't mean to." Nyx shook her head.

Someone groaned behind them. Desmia, Olaf, and the goblin lay sprawled on the ground where they had fallen.

"What just happened?" Desmia scrambled up. "Where are we?"

"That's a good question. Nyx?" Niamh arched an eyebrow at her.

"I don't know. I didn't mean to transport us anywhere." She pushed loose strands of hair off her face. "I just meant to change the spell."

"It's probably because you chanted it." Niamh gave her a shove. "We need to figure out where we are."

"I—we're in Andovia." She breathed a sigh of relief. "Look, there's the old guard tower. We're outside the old city."

"Which city?" Desmia came over to them.

"Varden city."

"Varden? That's where the Archdruid massacred dozens of fae." Desmia shuddered. "Why do you want to bring us here? It's a place of death and spirits."

"I told you, I don't know!" Nyx threw up her hands in exasperation. "If we are in Andovia, we're all safe. You can leave now."

"No, we can't. We owe you a debt for saving our lives." Desmia shook her head. "We'll stay until that is paid."

Nyx's mouth fell open. "You can't stay here—you're right in the middle of the Archdruid's territory. There are guards everywhere."

Niamh shook her head. "Only the Varden are here. They won't allow many people to enter their forest."

"She's right. The Varden might not like you being here," Nyx agreed.

"But they are friends. Why can't they stay with us?" Novia put her hands on her hips. "The gods know we might need help if more of the Order of the Blessed show up."

"Fine, they can stay." Nyx reached out to Yasmine with her mind. *Sorry we disappeared. We're in Andovia now. In Varden forest.*

Good, I wondered where you disappeared to. Do you need me to come and get those rogues for you?

Nyx glanced over at Desmia and her companions. *No, they're staying with us. For now.*

Alright. Stay safe, my friend.

"We must have come here for a reason," Novia mused. "Nyx said to reveal our past. Maybe that's why we're here. Weren't mind whisperers killed here?"

"Mind whisperers. That's what you are, aren't you?" Desmia gasped. "I thought you were extinct."

"We are trying to find out where we came from," Novia replied. "We were all found abandoned when—"

"Novia!" Nyx and Niamh said in unison.

"What? I trust them." Novia crossed her arms.

Nyx blew out a breath and moved forward. She flinched when she hit an invisible wall of energy. The shield hadn't disappeared then.

"Maybe we should go into the old city," Niamh suggested.

"We can't get through."

"We did before." Niamh raised her hand against the shield and yelped as she got a jolt of static.

"It's light. We'll come here tomorrow. Let's head out and get some rest. We'll come back."

Nyx didn't know if Darius would allow their new companions to stay at his castle.

She opened a portal to get there. She was too weary to travel on foot or fly.

"Finally — somewhere with a warm bed." Niamh sighed.

266

"This is Darius' estate. He owns all the lands around it and most of Eldara," Nyx explained. To her surprise, she found a guard outside.

Odd. Darius didn't have his own household servants or guards. He hadn't even used the castle until a couple of months ago.

Nyx approached the guard and he smiled at her. "I'm Nyx Ashwood."

"Aye, my lady. He'll be glad to see you've returned." The guard bowed his head.

"Lady?" Niamh scoffed. "Guess you're more than a servant now, Sister."

Nyx glared at her and hurried through the courtyard.

"This place is beautiful," Novia breathed.

"Of course it is. What do you expect from the Archdruid's son?" Niamh rolled her eyes.

"Archdruid's son?" Desmia froze. "You've got to be joking."

"No, Darius is the second-born son. I work with him and the resistance. He won't do anything to harm you." Nyx hurried up the steps and into the small hall.

Lucien and Ranelle sat around a table covered with books.

"Nyx!" Ranelle leapt to her feet and threw her arms around her. "You're back. I missed you so much."

Nyx returned her embrace. "I missed you too. These are my sisters. Niamh, you've already met, and Novia. Oh, and Desmia — she's Novia's friend."

Lucien came over and hugged Nyx as well. "Good to have you back. He's missed you."

A small woman with bark-like skin came in. "Blessed spirits, you're home at last." Ada beamed. "Where you been, my girl?"

Nyx bent to wrap her arms around the brownie. "Long story."

"Well, I'll 'ave a feast for you in no time."

"Really?" Niamh's eyebrows rose.

"Of course. I'll show you to your rooms." Ada motioned for them to follow. "Give you all a chance to clean up before dinner."

Nyx spoke to the others a little longer then a warm familiar presence washed over her.

Darius. She hurried out of the room and threw herself into his arms, almost knocking him over. "Miss me?" She leaned and drank in the sight of him.

"Maybe a little." Darius smiled. "I don't have anyone to nag me."

She gave him a shove then pulled him in for a kiss. "Bet you were lost without me."

Darius laughed and held her close for a while longer. "I thought you were on Glenfel."

She sighed. "I was. I have a lot to tell you."

CHAPTER 4

Niamh moaned as she leaned back in the wooden bathtub. She couldn't remember the last time she had a bath, let alone a room to herself. It had been so cramped staying in Novia's chambers at Glenfel prison. As much as she enjoyed being with her sisters, she missed simple luxuries. They didn't have running water at the prison.

How Nyx had left this place she couldn't fathom.

Novia had opted to have a bath in her room. Nyx had been too ecstatic to see her druid and told them she'd see them at dinner. Niamh wanted to get into the old city and find out why the spell brought them there.

The city held answers they all needed.

The door creaked open and Desmia came in.

"What are you doing here?" Niamh glared at her. "Ever hear of knocking?"

Desmia only stared at her.

She grabbed one of her knives. "What are you staring at?"

"You are different from your sisters," the nargol remarked.

"Yeah, and? We're all different."

"Not like you. You embrace your darkness and make it part of you."

"I — would you please leave?"

"You intrigue me." Desmia flashed her a smile that showed her fangs. "You shouldn't be ashamed of what you are."

"What's that? A mind whisperer?"

"No, an assassin. I heard you were the best."

"I don't do that anymore."

"You can't change what you are."

"What I am is annoyed." Niamh threw her knife at the nargol's head.

Desmia ducked and chuckled. "Not afraid of me, are you?"

"Of course not. Get out!"

"What's going on?" Novia, now in a clean dress, peered around the door.

"Nothing, the orc was just leaving." Niamh flushed.

"Indeed." Desmia flashed her another smile and left.

"Niamh, she's not an orc. Calling her one is insulting." Novia furrowed her brow.

"Tell your friend not to come in uninvited then." Niamh scowled. "I thought you were in the bath?"

"I already bathed. Nyx has the lady's chambers. Right next to Darius."

She rolled her eyes. "What a shock. They're in love with each other, if you haven't noticed."

"But he's—"

"I know. Love is blind as they say. He loves her. I've seen it."

"I thought a mind whisperer couldn't fall in love. Because of our powers."

Ah, yes, that stupid matter of anyone becoming enslaved by a mind whisperer who slept with them. Niamh hadn't believed that until she experienced it first-hand.

"That doesn't stop us from falling in love. But I've never seen it as a problem. I only slept with people who deserved it."

"Niamh!"

"I'm joking." Niamh leaned back in the bath. "All power comes with a price."

"What if we want to marry and have a family someday?" Novia sat on the edge of the bed.

"I have a family. But I will never be tied down by anyone. Romantic love is a waste of time anyway."

"I'd like to find love. Without anyone being enslaved to me. Taking a mate sounds awful."

Niamh slumped back. She wouldn't be enjoying her bath after all. "It doesn't work that way. Now, can I please enjoy my bath?"

Novia didn't take the hint. "It's so romantic how she and Darius stay together even—"

"My bath is getting cold."

"What? Does it really take you that long to bathe? You'll get all wrinkly."

"I like to relax. Especially when we have hot water for once."

"Alright. See you at dinner. Ranelle is showing me around the castle. I guess you don't want to come?"

"Maybe later."

Novia scampered off and finally left her in peace.

Niamh found a wardrobe full of dresses. Fancy dresses. Under normal circumstances, she might have liked them, but she preferred tunics and trousers. They were easier to move in.

But she picked out a simple blue dress and headed downstairs.

The rich smell of meat made her mouth water. Gods below, she never had to eat prison gruel again.

Nyx came out. Her pink hair fell in waves around her shoulders. With only part of it plaited. She wore a violet dress with flowing sleeves. "You look... different." She smiled.

"So do you. Now you look like the lady of the castle. I guess that's what you are, Lady Nyx."

"Niamh." Nyx scowled.

"What?" Niamh chuckled.

"I'm not a lady. I'm a servant."

"Servants don't wear gowns like that."

She and her sister headed into the dining hall.

Novia came in wearing a low-cut green gown. She squealed. "You both look so beautiful."

"I hate gowns." Nyx fidgeted. "But Ada insisted I change into something formal."

Darius came in with Ranelle and Lucien.

Together, they enjoyed an evening of chatting and telling stories.

Niamh realised for the first time she had a family now.

Niamh woke early the next morning. She headed into Novia's room and dragged her out of bed to go to the old city.

Once Nyx was up, they headed out.

"If we use our powers, we should get through the shield." Niamh raised her hand and static rippled over the wall of energy.

"We need to use our powers together."

Novia bit her lip. "What if we get trapped in there?"

"We got out before." She crossed her arms.

"Barely." Nyx shook her head.

"Your spell led us here. We need to go through. Call your druid if you're that worried."

"I already told him where we're going."

"Good, let's go." She grabbed her sister's hands. Nyx and Novia placed their free hands against the shield.

Niamh took a deep breath and released her power.

Thunder shook the air as their combined magic flowed free.

A blast of energy sent all three sisters flying.

They hit the ground hard.

"Did it work?" Niamh groaned. "We got through before."

"Ow!" Novia moaned. "I don't think it will let us through. How did you do it last time?"

"We were fighting. Somehow we passed through." Nyx stood up. "Maybe we need to be in a different spot." She unfurled her wings and hovered.

"We can't fly though." Niamh shook her head. "We were over the city before. It wasn't this spot."

A cackle came from somewhere behind them.

Niamh's hand went to her dagger as she scanned with her senses. "Who's there?"

Nyx landed beside her sisters as they headed towards a large oak tree.

A woman emerged from the bark.

Is that a dryad? Niamh asked.

No, she's something else. Old and powerful, Nyx replied.

"Who are you?" Niamh palmed one of her knives.

"You won't find the answers in the city," the woman said.

"Who are you?" Novia frowned.

"They call me the Norn. Been here since Eartha began. Will be here long after it's gone."

Niamh narrowed her eyes. "Why should we believe you?"

She turned to her sisters. *I can't read her.*

Neither can I. Novia shook her head. *Nyx?*

No, but Norns are real. Nyx stepped forward. "Why are you here?"

"To tell you you'll only find answers in death."

***

"In death? What does that mean?" Novia furrowed her brow. "Does that mean one of us has to die?"

"It makes sense. I was close to death when I had the memory of Niamh and I in the garden together." Nyx paced up and down.

"I was close to death when I saw Novia." Niamh leaned back against the tree. "The answers are in death. One of us needs to be close to death or dead to remember."

"That sounds dangerous. What if one of us stayed dead?" Novia held her hand to her chest.

"We could take something that makes us dead for only a few moments. Poisons could do that." Nyx stopped pacing.

"Wouldn't we need more than a few moments?" Niamh arched an eyebrow. "We won't be able to remember much in that short time."

"We can't stay dead long," Novia insisted.

"Only one of us should do it," Nyx suggested. "It would be safer. I should do it. I'll call Lucien to bring me something."

"That's a bad idea. You've already been poisoned. I should do it. I'm immune to a lot of poisons." Niamh crossed her arms.

"It may not work on you then," Novia pointed out.

"Let's toss a coin." Nyx pulled out a silver coin. "Heads, I do it. Tails, Novia does it."

Niamh scowled. "But — oh fine."

"No using your powers." Novia shook a finger at her.

Nyx tossed the coin into the air and caught it. It landed on the side with a dragon's tail.

Lucien arrived a few moments later and gave Novia the poison.

She stared at the black liquid, and her stomach churned. Couldn't he have at least made it look like it tasted good?

"You don't have to do this," Nyx added. "Let me do it."

Lucien gaped at her. "Do you want Darius to rip my head off?"

Novia shook her head and gulped down the poison. "No, I'm doing this. Just be ready to bring me back." She slumped to the ground. Darkness dragged her under.

After a few moments, she found herself in a garden. Flowers spread out before her and filled the air with sweetness. She was on the grass, surrounded by two other girls. One with blond hair, the other girl's kept changing colour. Niamh and Nyx.

273

She wanted to scream with joy.

A woman came running towards them. Lyra, the priestess the queen had possessed.

"Girls, get up. We have to flee. Come on!" She grabbed Novia's hand. "Come. We must leave. I can't let him find you. If he knows you're the Morrigan's daughters, he will kill you."

Novia gasped as she woke. "Why am I back? I need to see more."

"You can't. If we had left you any longer, your death would be permanent," Lucien warned.

"What did you see?" Nyx sat down beside her.

"Did you remember anything?" Niamh sat down on her other side.

"I saw a woman. We were all in the garden together. It was Lyra. Or, at least I think it was her before she became possessed. When we were children… I think she tried to save us."

"So you didn't remember anything useful?" Niamh's shoulders slumped. "I hope she wasn't our mother."

"No, she said we were Morrigan's daughters."

"Who's that?" Niamh frowned.

"At least we have a name. Now we can find out who we really are." Nyx squeezed her hand.

Novia smiled and grasped both her sisters' hands.

All that mattered was they stayed together.

The past couldn't stay hidden forever.

If you enjoyed reading this collection be sure to leave a review on Amazon or another book site.

ALSO BY TIFFANY SHAND

ANDOVIA CHRONICLES

Dark Deeds Prequel

The Calling

The Rising

ROGUES OF MAGIC SERIES

Bound By Blood

Archdruid

Bound By Fire

Old Magic

Dark Deception

Sins Of The Past

Reign Of Darkness

Rogues Of Magic Complete Box Set Books 1-7

EVERLIGHT ACADEMY TRILOGY

Everlight Academy, Book 1: Faeling

Everlight Academy Book 2: Fae Born

Hunted Guardian – An Everlight Academy Story

EXCALIBAR INVESTIGATIONS SERIES

Touched By Darkness

Bound To Darkness

Rising Darkness

Excalibar Investigations Complete Box Set

SHADOW WALKER SERIES

Shadow Walker

Shadow Spy

Shadow Guardian

Shadow Walker Complete Box Set

THE AMARANTHINE CHRONICLES BOOK 1

Betrayed By Blood

Dark Revenge

The Final Battle

SHIFTER CLANS SERIES

The Alpha's Daughter

Alpha Ascending

The Alpha's Curse

The Shifter Clans Complete Box Set

TALES OF THE ITHEREAL

Fey Spy

Outcast Fey

Rogue Fey

Hunted Fey

Tales of the Ithereal Complete Box Set

THE FEY GUARDIAN SERIES

Memories Lost

Memories Awakened

Memories Found

The Fey Guardian Complete Series Box Set

THE ARKADIA SAGA

Chosen Avatar

Captive Avatar

Fallen Avatar

The Arkadia Saga Complete Series

ABOUT THE AUTHOR

Tiffany Shand is a writing mentor, professionally trained copy editor and copy writer who has been writing stories for as long as she can remember. Born in East Anglia, Tiffany still lives in the area, constantly guarding her work space from the two cats which she shares her home with.

She began using her pets as a writing inspiration when she was a child, before moving on to write her first novel after successful completion of a creative writing course. Nowadays, Tiffany writes urban fantasy and paranormal romance, as well as nonfiction books for other writers, all available through eBook stores and on her own website.

Tiffany's favourite quote is *'writing is an exploration. You start from nothing and learn as you go'* and it is armed with this that she hopes to be able to help, inspire and mentor many more aspiring authors.

When she has time to unwind, Tiffany enjoys photography, reading, and watching endless box sets. She also loves to get out and visit the vast number of castles and historic houses that England has to offer.

Printed in Poland
by Amazon Fulfillment
Poland Sp. z o.o., Wrocław
12 April 2022

01804b22-9a93-4d71-a03f-73b0ab255cdbR01